HONEYMOON IN HELL

A piercing scream brought Judith vaulting around the sofa and across the floor. Renie stood frozen, the kindling clutched in her arms like a newborn baby. At her feet was Mrs. Hoke, long arms and legs at awkward angles. At her side was the bright pink kite the cousins had tried to fly in vain that afternoon.

And around her neck was the long, strong string. Her face was a ghastly shade of purple and the gray eyes bulged up at the cousins.

Judith and Renie knew she was dead.

Other Avon Books by
Mary Daheim

FOWL PREY
HOLY TERRORS
JUST DESSERTS

DUNE TO DEATH

MARY DAHEIM

AVON BOOKS ◆ NEW YORK

DUNE TO DEATH is an original publication of Avon Books. This work has never before appeared in book form. This work is a novel. Any similarity to actual persons or events is purely coincidental.

AVON BOOKS
A division of
The Hearst Corporation
1350 Avenue of the Americas
New York, New York 10019

Copyright © 1993 by Mary Daheim
Published by arrangement with the author
Library of Congress Catalog Card Number: 92-97292
ISBN: 0-380-76933-6

First Avon Books Printing: May 1993

AVON TRADEMARK REG. U.S. PAT. OFF. AND IN OTHER COUNTRIES, MARCA REGISTRADA, HECHO EN U.S.A.

Printed in the U.S.A.

RA 10 9 8 7 6 5 4 3 2 1

To my husband and our children,
in memory of those sand-filled, charcoal-scorched suppers
I make them on the beach.
My intentions are often better than my cooking.

ONE

JUDITH GROVER MCMONIGLE rolled over, stretched, and felt something warm and furry next to her in the bed. *Sweetums.* The wretched cat had dared to crawl under the covers. Barely awake, she nudged with her elbow. There was no response. The aggravating animal obviously was playing possum. Judith jackknifed her knees, then gave a mighty heave.

The growl that met her ear sounded more like a dog than a cat, but it was neither: Joe Flynn clung to the edge of the king-sized bed, fighting for leverage. His usually imperturbable round face was blurred with sleep, his red hair stood on end, and the green eyes with their flecks of gold were murky slits.

"What the hell are you doing, Jude-girl? I practically fell on my backside!"

Horrified, Judith stared with round black eyes at her husband. *Her husband.* That was it, she and Joe were married. He wasn't Sweetums, and she wasn't home, at the bed-and-breakfast. Judith was on her honeymoon. She fell back against the pillows and began to laugh.

"Mrs. Joseph Flynn! I can't believe it! Happy day!"

Joe as not as amused. Clambering back into bed, he punched one of his pillows and gave Judith a sidelong look. "I'd hate to see you when you're *not* happy," he grumbled. "I'd have landed out there on the beach in somebody's picnic lunch."

Shifting her body under the covers, Judith turned to Joe, brushing his faintly receding disheveled red hair from his forehead. At just a shade under six feet, Joe was still muscular, with only a slight paunch to remind Judith that he had passed the fifty-year mark a couple of summers ago. "I dreamed you were Sweetums," she said with a grin that was almost penitent. "Being married is going to take a bit of getting used to."

Joe grinned back and kissed the tip of Judith's nose. "At least you didn't dream I was your mother." He shuddered, not entirely facetiously. "I could have killed her at the wedding."

Judith rolled her eyes. She had not been pleased with Gertrude Grover, either. Judith's mother had almost as little fondness for Joe Flynn as she had had for her daughter's first husband, the late and seldom lamented Dan McMonigle. Still, Judith felt it had been going too far when Gertrude tied a black ribbon around her walker. And told the other guests she was wearing crepe pants. When Father Francis Xavier Hoyle had asked if anyone present knew why the pair should not be joined together, Gertrude had whipped out a list. Fortunately, Auntie Vance and Aunt Deb had shushed her.

Actually, Auntie Vance had pulled Gertrude's maroon felt hat over her ears, but Judith hoped no one except Uncle Corky noticed. Gertrude had let out a squawk, which had fortunately been drowned out by the howls of the youngest Dooley baby who was—according to Aunt Ellen—under siege from the Rankers's grandchildren. No one had actually mentioned the word "hotfoot," but the votive candles weren't the only thing burning on the side aisles, or so said Cousin Marty.

Still, the wedding had gone off well, Judith reflected. Or, maybe it had just gone off, and after twenty-five years and a marriage apiece, that was all Judith and Joe could hope for. The annulment that Joe had told Judith he'd applied for had proved unnecessary; his first wife's previous bouts with wedlock had nullified the Las Vegas JP's service in the eyes of the Catholic Church.

Once he had obtained his civil divorce in late May, Judith launched a whirlwind of plans. At that late date, no ordinary mortal could have secured Our Lady, Star of the Sea Catholic Church for a Saturday afternoon wedding the last weekend in June. But Judith's extraordinary status as a parishioner-cum-sleuth had moved the appropriate mountains. Father Hoyle was only too glad to accommodate Judith in gratitude for helping solve the Holy Saturday murder in the parish hall. The fact that Homicide Lt. Joe Flynn had been the official investigating officer hadn't hurt anything, either.

Judith had worn champagne silk, draped across the bosom, nipped in at the waist, with soft little pleats falling over the hip. Gone were seven of the ten pounds she'd been determined to lose, but at five-nine, it only showed when the zipper of her dress closed without her tugging and gasping. Her new hairdo, with short waves of frosted raven tresses, had obliterated the premature gray that Dan had insisted she live with for most of their marriage. "Beautiful," Joe had whispered at the altar, and Judith's heart had turned over. He wasn't quite accurate, but with her well-defined features and careful makeup, she definitely felt fetching. But then Joe always had a knack for making her feel attractive.

They had been joined in Holy Matrimony before a church virtually packed with family and friends, who had flown in from various points of the compass. Joe's diplomat brother, Paul, had come from London; Andrew, the oil rig engineer, flew up from Houston; and the eldest Flynn, Tom, who called himself a soldier of fortune, claimed he'd commandeered a private plane out of Burundi. Judith couldn't boast any relations with such exotic backgrounds, but she was mightily pleased when Aunt Ellen and Uncle Win showed up from Beatrice, Nebraska. She was just as happy that Cousin Renie's Uncle Fred hadn't gotten permission to leave the Rocky Mountain High Rest Home in Denver for the occasion. Uncle Fred, whose current reincarnation was Louis XV, had sent his regrets and a picture of Madame de Pompadour cut out of a French history book.

"It was fun, wasn't it?" said Judith, after her ruminations about the wedding and their morning amatory adventures had run their course.

"What was?" Joe asked slyly, plugging in the coffee maker.

Judith gave him a look of mock reproach, then secured the ties of her new blue terry cloth robe. "The wedding. And the reception, too. But I don't think Uncle Al should have sold chances on the cake."

Joe shrugged. "It was only for the top tier. Besides, Uncle Vince won and didn't even know it. He was asleep under the gift table."

"True," said Judith distractedly. It was Monday morning, and although the wedding celebration had taken place less than forty-eight hours earlier, in some ways it seemed quite distant. Maybe it was because they were almost two hundred miles from home, looking out over the vast Pacific Ocean, with the smell of salt in the air and the sound of breakers in the background. Judith gazed through the picture window of the beach cottage and watched half a dozen seagulls circle the sands. She smiled. It didn't seem quite right to be so happy, not after all those years of hardship with her lazy, bad-tempered first husband. Dan might have been a good father to their only child, Mike, but he had been no provider. Indeed, while Judith worked two jobs to make ends meet, Dan had seemed determined to eat up any profits. Literally. It was no wonder that he weighed over four hundred pounds when he died at age forty-nine.

But Judith had survived that marriage, even triumphed over her tribulations, when she'd converted the old family home into a successful bed-and-breakfast establishment. Next to Mike, Hillside Manor was her pride and joy. She hoped that its running would be safe for a week in the hands of her capable, if erratic, neighbor, Arlene Rankers.

"Breakfast in," Joe announced, delving into the well-stocked refrigerator. During his off duty hours, Joe Flynn relaxed by honing his culinary skills. He had insisted on cooking for Judith at least a few times during the honeymoon, and breakfast was his first foray into the kitchen. The cottage was a perfect retreat, set high on a bluff overlooking the ocean, with wooden steps leading down to the beach. The exterior was weathered blue shakes, with windwhipped juniper trees sheltering the small garden. Judith couldn't believe her good fortune in getting a weeklong reservation on such short notice. But Mrs. Hoke, the owner of the cottage, had struck Judith as a bit eccentric. Or at least not a very sound businesswoman. Judith had discovered Pirate's Lair only by accident, at a meeting of bed-and-breakfast owners. It was not, her informant had told her, a B&B, but a self-contained guest cottage, with a wonderful view, a complete kitchen, a boathouse, and two bedrooms. Still in a prenuptial daze, Judith couldn't imagine the need for more than one, but took the phone number down. To her surprise, Pirate's Lair was available for the last weekend of June through the Fourth of July. Of course it hadn't come cheap, but Judith didn't ever expect to go on a honeymoon again.

Over breakfast, they made plans for the day. Judith and Joe had spent their wedding night in the bridal suite of downtown's most lavish hotel, less than ten minutes away from Heraldsgate Hill and the B&B. It was a fitting celebration site. Twenty-five years earlier, before Joe had gotten drunk and eloped to Las Vegas with the thrice-married Herself, the hotel's downstairs bar had been a favorite retreat. On one particularly memorable evening, attired in formal evening clothes, they had actually asked to see the honeymoon suite. But the puckish bellhop who had shown them up to the top floor had assessed their semidrunken state and pointed them to the door to the roof. The joke had fizzled when Judith tripped in her four-inch heels and fell, landing on a balcony just below the roof level. Joe had carted her home in a battered and bedraggled condition, explaining to Gertrude that they'd been mugged while visiting the zoo.

The day after the wedding they had driven down to Oregon, arriving in Buccaneer Beach just before dinner. The sun was still up and the wind was down, but clouds had inched across the horizon. They had eaten at a surprisingly good Continental restaurant on the edge of town and watched a sketchy sunset. Summer had not yet arrived full-blown on the Oregon coast.

Judith and Joe didn't care. Typical native Pacific Northwesterners, they weren't fond of hot weather. A nice ocean storm would suite them fine, especially since the cottage had a fireplace and all the driftwood they could burn.

"There's plenty to do and see around here," remarked Joe, skimming through the tourist brochure that Mrs. Hoke had left for their perusal. "Buccaneer Beach got its name from English pirates. Hey, this sounds right up your alley." He grinned at her over the brochure and began to read. " 'In the early part of the eighteenth century, English pirates roamed off the West Coast of North America. The likes of Captain Kidd and Blackbeard, with a bottle of rum in one hand and a blazing pistol in the other, preyed upon Spanish merchantmen, driving them back to the sanctuary of their coastal mission. For almost three hundred years, rumors have persisted that some of the pirates' plunder was hidden along the Oregon coast, particularly in the Buccaneer Beach area, which derives its name from visits made by those legendary seagoing brigands.' Want to get a shovel and start digging?"

Judith gave Joe an off-center grin. "Sounds like a lot of puffery to help promote their Fourth of July Freebooters' Festival. The only thing I want to dig around here is clams."

Joe consulted the brochure once more. "Kite-flying is big here this time of year. Or we could drive down to the dunes and ride a buggy around," he suggested.

"Renie and I did that once with Uncle Cliff," recalled Judith, savoring Joe's excellent French toast. "He went about a hundred miles an hour. At least it seemed that fast."

Joe gave her a dry look. "I don't think you can go over thirty in a dune buggy. From what I remember of Cliff Grover, everything he did seemed like an adventure."

Judith smiled and nodded. Cousin Renie's father had been as different from her own as two men could be, despite the ties of brotherhood. Cliff Grover had been a merchant seaman, periodically arriving home with a month's growth of beard and a delicate jade figurine. He was the kind of man who always had to see what was around the next bend or on the other side of the hill. Donald Grover, Judith's father, had been a high school teacher, content to explore the world from his favorite chair with the floor lamp shining just so on whichever book he was devouring for the night. It was no wonder that Judith's first calling had been as a librarian.

"Sounds like fun," said Judith. She took the brochure from Joe, who was topping their orange juice with just a dash of champagne. "I haven't been down here on the coast since I was in college. Let's take our time and stop at all the little touristy spots, especially the scenic viewpoints."

Joe handed Judith her glass and raised his own. "To being suckered by the Oregonians. To all the lighthouses and sea lions and myrtlewood souvenirs." He clicked glasses with Judith, then kissed her cheek. "To us."

Judith sighed, smiled, and sipped. "Dune buggy for two?" She put down her fork and rested her chin on her hands, gazing at Joe. The sun was peeking out from behind pale clouds. The waves crested, then ebbed on the sands below. "Dare I say this is perfect?"

Joe grinned as he poured more coffee. "It sure beats my last honeymoon. I put two hundred bucks on one blackjack hand, then went down for double, and got a deuce. With luck like that, I should have bailed out then."

"Where was Herself?" Judith could ask the question freely now. The old rivalry was ended; Judith had won.

Joe gazed up at the kitchen ceiling, hung with fisher-

men's nets and glass balls. "Oh—probably in the bar. The
only game she ever played was Bourbon-on-the-Rocks.
You can't beat it, but she's never figured that out. Poor
fool."

"Poor fool," echoed Judith. And wished she could feel
sorrier for the woman who had held Joe Flynn in temporary custody for a quarter of a century. "I'll settle for another cup of coffee. And a dune buggy for two."

"Hey, Joe," Judith yelled over the roar of the wind and
surf, "aren't we going too *fast*?"

He turned slightly in his place behind the wheel of the
dune buggy. "That's what you probably told Uncle Cliff,"
he shouted back. The words were muffled, however, because of the handkerchiefs they wore over their mouths.
Judith and Joe were also attired in goggles, required wear
for dune buggy drivers and passengers. The little Jeep-like
vehicle sped over the rounded sand dunes, up and down,
higher and higher, then dropped dizzily onto flatter
ground. Here and there, the keepers of the dunes had
placed an appropriate skull or a treasure chest. Judith
smiled behind her kerchief—when she wasn't grinding her
teeth in fear.

The breeze whipped their clothing. The sun, flirting
with the clouds, occasionally blinded them. To their left,
they could glimpse the ocean, relentless, powerful. Atop
the highest dunes, shore pines grew twisted with the wind.
Beneath them, scrubby bushes lined the buggy's path. An
occasional gnarled root protruded from the sand.

"Hey, Joe, watch out for those . . ." Judith's voice was
lost in the roar of the waves.

Joe saw the big root, almost a yard long, and six inches
above the ground. But he was too late. The dune buggy
struck the obstacle, bucked like a bronco, and crashed onto
its side. Judith screamed. But at least they'd stopped. The
wheels were still spinning. She adjusted her goggles and
turned to look at Joe. He was grimacing and reaching for
his left leg.

"Are you okay?" Judith asked when she finally got her breath.

Joe's face contorted with pain. "Are *you*?" he gasped.

She was fumbling with her seat belt. "Yes, I think so. Joe . . ." Now she gazed at him in real alarm. "What's wrong?"

With effort, he moved his head just enough so that he could meet her worried black eyes. "Damn," he breathed, then his expression grew almost sheepish. "Damn, damn, damn!"

Judith put a hand on his shoulder. "Joe, what is it?"

The green eyes with the gold flecks that Judith always found so magnetic flickered and closed. "I broke my freaking leg. Do you want an annulment?"

With a little shriek, Judith clutched at Joe's shoulder. Then she sucked in her breath. Joe had passed out.

But he was smiling. Sort of.

The good news was that Joe would recover. The bad news was that he would be laid up in Buccaneer Beach Community Hospital for at least five days. He had suffered a compound fracture of the left tibia and could not be moved until the bones began to knit. The doctors were kind, seemingly competent, and Joe was resting comfortably. But for now, the honeymoon was over.

Disconsolately, Judith paced the visitors' waiting room. She should have never said it was *perfect*. The word had hexed them. Nothing was perfect. She and Joe were married; they would, God willing, enjoy many years together. But their wonderful seaside honeymoon had been sabotaged by a dune buggy. And under the no-refund lease, Judith was out seven hundred dollars.

Or at least most of it. She wandered from fake-leather chair to fake-leather sofa to myrtlewood lamp to blank TV set. She should stay in Buccaneer Beach, of course. She couldn't leave Joe alone in the hospital. But what would she do for the rest of the week by herself?

Not that Judith was unaccustomed to filling her spare hours on her own. It was just that she'd had so few of them over the years. During her first marriage, there were the two jobs, during the day as a librarian and working nights in the bar at the Meat & Mingle. Then came seeing Mike off to college, moving back in with her mother, renovating the old Edwardian house on Heraldsgate Hill, and starting up the B&B. The truth was, Judith was a novice at recreation. She could read herself to sleep at night or take in an occasional movie, but that was about the extent of her independent leisure. Staying alone in the honeymoon cottage meant for two was beyond her. Judith's statuesque figure slumped against the outdated magazines in the wooden rack at her back. There was only one solution.

Judith left the visitors' waiting room, marched to the row of pay phones in the hospital lobby, and called Cousin Renie.

TWO

RENIE SAID *NO*. She was sorry about Joe's accident, she really felt bad that their honeymoon was ruined, she even commiserated about the seven hundred dollars. "But," Renie asserted in the businesslike voice she usually reserved for her graphic design clients, "I'm up against deadline on the artwork for the Franciscan monks' calendar, I have a symphony brochure to complete, and most of all"—Renie took a deep breath and a considerable amount of umbrage—"there is no way I can leave our mothers. You stuck me with the job of getting your mom settled in with my mom. Next to sizzling in hell for all eternity, I can't think of anything more gruesome."

Judith was assailed by a pang of guilt. She had not wanted to leave the Resettlement of Gertrude entirely up to Renie, but with the start of the tourist season at the B&B and the wedding preparations, she hadn't had much choice. Besides, Renie had volunteered, arguing that as long as their mothers were going to be living together in Aunt Deb's two-bedroom apartment, it was her responsibility as much as Judith's.

"What's the matter?" Judith asked into the phone. "Mother's been there almost a week. I thought she was getting used to it."

Renie snorted. "Has marriage made you soft in the head, coz? Your mother has caused two fires, booby-trapped the toilet, and insulted the milkman. My Mother the Martyr is on the verge of *complaining*. That's how bad it is."

Judith grimaced. "I knew this wouldn't be easy. But Mother swore she wouldn't live under the same roof as Joe."

"Right, right," agreed Renie, rather testily. "But you must have figured out that she thought it would be Joe who would have to compromise, not her. Listen, coz, we should have guessed there'd be problems when she locked herself in the attic."

"It's not an attic any more, you dope, it's the third floor family living quarters, and you know it." Judith had raised her voice, gaining the attention of an orderly, two nurses, and a Pink Lady at the desk. She had to simmer down. Renie was right—it was too good to be true to think that Gertrude would surrender her place in the family home without a whimper. But in fact, she *had* moved in with her sister-in-law and sometimes arch-rival, and Judith had prayed that the matter was settled. With Mike away in Montana on a job with the Forest Service, Judith had hoped that she and Joe might experience a serene summer. Except, of course, for the horde of guests who would be tramping in and out of Hillside Manor. Business, however, was business.

"Anyway," Judith went on, dropping her voice, "I don't think Mother locked herself in deliberately. She just got a little muddled. Change is really hard on old people."

"It's hard on this middle-aged one, too," griped Renie. "And the day your mother gets muddled, I'll tap-dance down the freeway during rush hour. Nude."

"Okay, okay," muttered Judith, fearing that she and Renie might be on the verge of one of their rare quarrels. As close as sisters but without any sense of sibling rivalry, the cousins had always meshed like ham and eggs. Or so the voracious Renie would have put it. "I'll try to sort it out with Mother when I get home. Meanwhile," Judith went on in a wan voice, "I'll go out and walk the beach alone and fly a kite alone and eat at all these terrific restaurants alone."

There was a short pause. "Restaurants?" Renie's voice had also changed, but it was far from wan. "Bill and I haven't been down there for a long time. Have they really got some good places to eat?"

Judith could hear Renie's lips smack. "Loads. Last night I had pasta with Dungeness crab and Joe got beef Wellington in a pastry so flaky that . . ."

"Stop!" Renie sounded as if she were being tortured by the Spanish Inquisition. Judith half-expected to get drool in her ear. "Hey, coz, let me run over to the apartment and see if they're both still alive. The monks and the symphony can wait. St. Francis was a very patient man, even if Maestro Dunkowitz isn't. Bill left last night for some numbnuts conference in Champaign-Urbana," she explained, referring to her husband's post as a clinical psychologist and university professor. "The kids—sniff—don't need me as long as I leave them money, so let me think about it, okay?"

It was, Judith thought, a good thing Renie couldn't see her sly smile. "It's up to you," she said. "I wouldn't force you into coming down. Oh!" she exclaimed in mock surprise. "It's almost noon, low tide. I'm going down to the beach and dig some butter clams. I hope I can carry them all by myself. Bye-bye." Chortling, she hung up and went to check on Joe.

Since Joe had been given enough pain medication to knock out an elephant, he wasn't much fun to be around. Leaving him snoring like a walrus, Judith decided she might as well live up to her word and headed back to Pirate's Lair to try her hand at clamming.

The garage, where Joe had parked his aging but still handsome MG two-seater, was crammed with cartons, gar-

dening tools, and firewood. Judith and Joe had been thankful that the MG hadn't needed much space. She prowled
around, finding a bucket and a shovel resting between two
crates. Judith eyed them curiously. Mrs. Hoke, who report-
edly lived on the edge of town, must use the garage for
storage. The idea struck Judith as odd; why would she lug
junk all the way across town? The distant ringing of the
phone reached Judith's ear, interrupting that line of
thought.

It was Renie, announcing that she could catch a south-
bound train leaving at 2:00 P.M., arriving in Salem around
9:00. She would rent a car there and drive out to the coast.
No, countered Judith, she would make the drive inland and
collect Renie at the depot. Renie didn't argue.

"I'll eat on the train," she told Judith.

"Of course you will," replied Judith. "How are our
mothers?"

"Mothers? What mothers?" It was Renie's turn to chor-
tle.

Judith was just heading back outside when a big Buick
pulled into the drive and parked next to a black van. Pirate's Lair was situated in a cul-de-sac, with paved roads
leading back up a hill to Highway 101. While there were
several permanent and rental houses in the immediate vicinity, the cottage itself was flanked on both sides by commercial enterprises, a large motel to the left, and a posh
resort to the right. Judith wondered how Mrs. Hoke had
managed to withstand the real estate developers.

Waiting by the garage, Judith watched as the newcomer
emerged from the car. Judging from her air of proprietor-
ship, Judith guessed it was Mrs. Hoke.

"Hallooo," the woman called, waving a long, gangly
arm. She was tall, in her fifties, with springy dark hair going gray in patches, and bright gray eyes. "Is everything
all right?"

"Well, sort of," replied Judith, coming forward and ex-
tending her hand. "I'm Judith Flynn. My husband had an
accident this morning." Judith explained about Joe and the
dune buggy. Mrs. Hoke commiserated as they went inside.

"Such a shame," she clucked, setting a roll of paper towels and a box of plastic garbage bags on the kitchen counter. "But you say your cousin is coming down to stay with you?" The look she gave Judith suggested something improper.

"My cousin *Serena*," Judith emphasized, setting Mrs. Hoke straight. "It seemed a shame to rent the place and stay here alone."

Mrs. Hoke made a stabbing gesture at her hair. "Oh, I don't know. Solitude is a good thing." She darted a glance through the kitchen window which looked out toward the motel where a curly-haired young man was struggling with a dragon-shaped kite in the parking lot. "Oh!" Mrs. Hoke grabbed her eelskin purse and began to rummage through the contents. Her spare figure was attired in a wrinkled blue corduroy jumper and a black turtleneck top. "Your receipt . . . it's here some place . . ."

"That's okay," Judith said in a soothing manner. "I'll have my canceled check with my next bank statement."

But Mrs. Hoke seemed intent on finding the receipt. The more she looked, the more she fluttered. "Oh! I saw it . . . It's on yellow paper . . . I know I've got it . . ."

A surreptitious glance at her watch told Judith that it was almost 12:30. The tide would soon start coming in again. It was all she could do to keep from tapping her foot.

"Ah!" Mrs. Hoke produced the yellow slip of paper as if it were an original copy of the Magna Carta. "Here, Mrs. Flynn. I knew it was in there all along!"

"Swell," said Judith, a trifle dubiously. "Thanks," she added, smiling. Being addressed as Mrs. Flynn was still a novelty. And a thrill. "I take it you don't live on the beach?"

Mrs. Hoke's gray eyes widened. "The beach? Oh—the beach!" She giggled, an unmusical sound that jarred Judith's ear. Why had she asked? Judith was anxious to be off with her bucket and shovel. But the genuine interest in other people that had helped make her B&B such a success was hard to put on hold. "The family home is actually a farm," Mrs. Hoke explained, still bubbling with girlish glee. "It's above the town." She gestured with a long, thin hand. "My parents owned it. They started a creamery years ago and then built a cheese factory. Ogilvie's Cheese was once a household word."

It had, in fact, been a common commodity in the McMonigle house, Judith recalled. But somewhere between an eviction notice and a threatening letter from the IRS, Ogilvie's Cheese had disappeared from the local grocery. About the same time, the store also stopped permitting the McMonigles to pay by check. Judith wasn't sorry those days were behind her, but now that she thought about it, she missed the cheese.

"Good stuff," said Judith, edging toward the door. "Did the family sell out?"

Mrs. Hoke twirled her springy hair into strange little coils. "Well, sort of. This state was hit hard by a recession about then . . ." Her voice, the bubbles now deflated, trailed off.

Judith knew about Oregon's Hard Times that had begun more than a decade earlier. Long before the rest of the nation had nervously mouthed the word "Recession," Oregon's timber industry had been particularly hard-hit. Parts of the state were still fighting an uphill battle in what was optimistically called a Recovery Mode. But back in the late 1970s, Judith had enough economic disasters of her own. She gave Mrs. Hoke a sympathetic smile and pushed the door open.

Her landlady seemed reluctant to leave. "You're sure you have everything?" she asked, standing first on one foot and then the other. Judith noted Mrs. Hoke was wearing red knee-sox with hiking shoes. It was not a fetching combination.

"Yes, the cottage is wonderfully well furnished." Judith kept her smile fixed in place.

"Oh, good." Mrs. Hoke's gaze lingered on the cozy kitchen with its nautical decor. The cupboards, like most of the room, were finished in knotty pine. "What about wax paper?"

"Huh?" Judith's smile slipped. "Wax paper? I don't think we've needed any yet. There's aluminum foil, though. That should do it."

Mrs. Hoke's angular face turned eager. "I can go get wax paper at the store. I'll be back in ten minutes."

Judith tried not to look pained. "Actually, I was just going down to dig some clams . . ."

The springy hair hopped up and down as Mrs. Hoke nodded vigorously. "That's all right, I have a key. I'll just leave the wax paper on the kitchen counter. And Drano. I'll bet you're out of Drano."

"Heaven knows I'd hate to be out of Drano," said Judith, wondering if Mrs. Hoke knew something she wasn't telling about the plumbing in Pirate's Lair. Grabbing the bucket and shovel from next to a sealed carton marked "Fragile," Judith bade Mrs. Hoke farewell and walked in her long-legged manner across the front lawn to the wooden staircase that led to the beach.

It was a long way down. Judith counted the steps which made several zigs and zags before reaching the flat, gray sand. One hundred forty stairs in all, a serious workout as far as Judith was concerned. Especially since she would have to climb them going back. Luckily, she was suffering no ill effects from the dune buggy accident except for a headache and a slight stiffness in her back.

Briefly, she assessed the stairways that led up from the beach on each side of Pirate's Lair's narrow wooden set. Those belonging to the We See Sea Resort were concrete, with landings and benches about every twenty steps. The Best Ever Over the Waves Motel boasted a tram. Judith was tempted, but assumed it probably came out in the lobby or some other place where a nonguest could be easily spotted. She resigned herself to the return climb and set about the business of clamming.

The breeze felt fresh on her cheeks and the sound of the ocean was music to her ears. Some ten yards from the staircase, nestled at the foot of the bluff, stood the old boathouse, of a much older vintage than the cottage. The little structure obviously had been neglected and was apparently unused. Or so Judith assumed until she saw a man's silhouette in the small murky window. Judith paused and frowned. The confirmation letter that she had received from Mrs. Hoke had stated that everything on the property was at the newlyweds' disposal, including the beach rights which permitted clam digging and the building of a fire under safe circumstances. There had followed a couple of paragraphs of legalese which Judith now found incongruous with the flighty, disorganized, Alice Ogilvie Hoke. But of course her landlady had probably sought a lawyer's advice when it came to renting the cottage. Should Mrs. Hoke be informed that someone was inside the boathouse? Judith considered, then shrugged. With or without Joe, she was on her honeymoon. As long as whoever it was didn't bother her up at Pirate's Lair, she'd ignore the interloper. Judith had had enough of mysterious events in the past year and a half to last her a lifetime.

The clam harvest was meager. The tiny holes that indicated a clam was close to the surface often proved to be decoys, made by some other sort of sea creature. After an hour, Judith had dug up only a couple of dozen clams, but more than enough to make herself some chowder. The tide was coming in, the kiteflyers were out in force, and the beach was overrun by children building sand castles, youngsters on mountain bikes, dogs fetching sticks, and couples strolling hand in hand. Briefly, Judith felt envious. She and Joe should be out there, kicking at the sand and watching the waves edge ever closer.

But at least she and Joe finally belonged to each other. Judith smiled at the thought and started up the beach toward the wooden staircase. The stiffness she had noticed earlier had worsened, bringing on a headache. Her bucket seemed heavier with every step and she noticed that she'd skinned her fingers in several places when she'd abandoned the shovel for chasing after her elusive prey with her bare hands. She should have worn gloves.

Halfway up, she paused to catch her breath. Even living in a four-story house hadn't prepared her for quite this much exertion. But the view was spectacular. The ocean seemed so vast, so endless, so dominant. A lonely trawler bobbed out on the horizon. How far away, Judith mused? The sun was no longer directly over head, and was now sitting on top of a row of fluffy white clouds. Down on the beach, the vacationers ebbed and flowed like the tide itself. Judith switched the bucket and shovel from one hand to the other, then resumed her ascent. She had reached the next landing when a movement almost directly below caught her eye. It was a bearded man in what appeared to be a baggy sweater and rumpled pants, staring up at her. She could just make out his uneven footprints in the sand. They led from the boathouse.

"Big deal," she muttered to herself. "At least he's not carrying out a TV and a VCR." Judith continued up the steps.

Back in the garage, she went to put the bucket and shovel where she had picked them up and hoped the garden hose would reach that far so she could wash down the clams. But something wasn't quite right. Judith paused, frowning. The carton marked "Fragile" was gone. Mrs. Hoke must have taken it with her, Judith told herself. And why not? It was her house.

Inside, she looked for a box of cornmeal to shake into the clam bucket to help get rid of the sand. Sure enough, the wax paper, Drano, and a huge pink kite sat on the butcher-block kitchen table. Judith smiled. Maybe she'd try her hand at flying the kite later. Everybody else in Buccaneer Beach seemed to think it was a wonderful pastime. But for now, she was off to visit Joe.

The drive to the hospital took only five minutes. The sprawling structure apparently had started out as a clinic shortly after World War II, and, like the rest of Buccaneer Beach, had grown helter-skelter. Judith found Joe awake, but not exactly alert.

"Guess what?" she blurted, startled by the big cast, large sling, and complicated pulleys, "we've got Drano."

"Run him on a third party ticket," murmured Joe, making an attempt to get comfortable. Judging from his grimace, the effort was not a success. "Maybe he can beat Nixon."

Judith gingerly sat in the visitor's chair which was heaped with fresh linen. "Uh ... Joe, it's the nineties. We're in Buccaneer Beach."

For an instant, the green eyes came into focus. "What for?"

Judith sighed. "Never mind. How do you feel?"

He was still squirming, though the sling hampered him severely. "Rotten. Where's my wife?"

Judith froze, staring at Joe. "*I'm* your wife, you knot-head!" she bristled. "We're *married*, Joe. We're on our *honeymoon.*" Her voice had risen, eliciting a rustling sound from behind the curtain in the room's only other bed. Flushing, Judith tried to compose herself and put a hand on Joe's upper arm. "Joe, it's me—Jude-girl." She had never cared for the nickname he had given her so long ago, but now she clung to it, hoping to jog his memory. "You're ... ah ... fuddled."

His eyes were closed and he'd stopped wiggling. For the first time, Judith noticed a bruise on his left forearm and a couple of scratches on his neck. She could hardly believe that except for the headache and stiff back, she'd escaped unscathed. Judith took in Joe's misery and felt contrite.

"You go to sleep," she whispered, patting his shoulder. "I'll come back after dinner."

His eyes opened. "Okay." He managed a feeble smile. "See if you can get the nurse to come in here."

Judith smiled back. "Sure." She started for the door.

"And," Joe called after her, his voice surprisingly strong, "keep away from the bottle! I'm tired of having to stick your head under the shower to sober you up!"

The sound of more rustling could be heard from the other bed. Judith fled into the corridor, almost colliding with a young doctor. Glancing at his name tag, she noted that the flaxen hair, fresh face, and hazel eyes belonged to Rolf Lundgren, MD. He didn't look a day over twenty-two; Judith guessed he was an intern.

"Excuse me," she apologized, automatically brushing him off as if he'd been Mike, "I wasn't looking where I was going."

Dr. Lundgren's smile was wry as he glanced into the room Judith had just vacated. "A lot of women run out of D-204. We're getting used to it since Mr. Beezle was admitted. Maybe we need a stop sign for the staff."

"Mr. Beezle? Is he the one in the other bed? I'm Mrs. Flynn," Judith added in explanation.

Dr. Lundgren acknowledged Judith's introduction with a casual nod. "Oh. That's quite a fracture your husband suffered. I've never seen one like it. The orthopedic surgeon, Dr. Scott, says it's a wonderful learning experience for me."

"Maybe for my husband, too," murmured Judith, thinking it might teach Joe not to drive so fast. At least not in a dune buggy. "You're an intern?"

"Right." He nodded again. "I've only been here two weeks. Usually, we're assigned to larger hospitals, in bigger cities. But Buccaneer Beach is very shorthanded, especially during tourist season. I'm glad, though—it's a nice place. I feel at home."

Judith had felt that way, too, at least until Joe had broken his leg. She exchanged a few more words with Dr. Lundgren, mostly about Joe's prognosis. The intern had already learned to be reassuring yet vague. Adopting a philosophical attitude, Judith took herself to dinner at a small diner about two blocks from the hospital. She'd save the serious eating for Renie's arrival.

When Judith returned to the hospital shortly before seven, Joe was sleeping like a log. She waited about ten minutes before deciding it was useless to stick around and watch him sleep. Or worse yet, have him awaken and imagine again that she was his ex-wife, Herself. She was reaching for her handbag when the curtain on the other bed was snatched away by a gnarled hand, and a cherubic face beamed at her.

"You got any with you, sweetheart?" The old man was beaming toothlessly at Judith.

"Any what?" asked Judith, trying to look dignified.

"Hooch." His expression was ingenuous. "I could do with a drink. Haven't had one in almost a week." He thrust the gnarled hand in Judith's direction. "Jake Beezle here. How's by you?"

Reluctantly, Judith angled her way around the end of Joe's bed and shook hands with Jake. "Judith Flynn. My husband's out of his head."

"So am I," replied Jake cheerfully. His hospital gown had slipped over one bony shoulder. "At least that's what everybody says." Jake started to lift the covers. "Want to see my hip replacement?"

"Ah . . . no, thanks," Judith responded hastily. "I hate blood. And stitches." She gave Jake a sickly grin. "Nice view," she said, searching wildly for a change of subject. "Very attractive parking lot."

Jake glanced out the window. "Huh? Oh, yeah, sure is, especially when some of them nurses drop something and have to bend over. Heh, heh." He gave Judith a leer which didn't quite mesh with his cherubic features. "Is it in your pocketbook?"

Nervously, Judith looked around. "Oh—my handbag? What?" Jake Beezle had her justifiably confused.

Jake turned faintly reproachful. "The hooch. I hope it's bourbon. Back in Prohibition, I used to run Canadian rye down the coast. Good stuff, but not so smooth as Kentucky mash."

Judith started backing away. "No hooch, Mr. Beezle. My husband is having delusions. Nice meeting you. I have to meet a train."

Jake Beezle chuckled and wheezed. "That's what they all say, sweetheart. Who's the engineer—Jack Daniels?" His laughter followed her out into the corridor. Judith was getting tired of fleeing her husband's hospital room. *Marriage wasn't supposed to be like this*, she thought with a helpless sensation.

But it was still an improvement over the first time around.

Renie's train was fifteen minutes late, which was just as well, since Judith hadn't taken into account the winding road that led inland from the coast. Neither had she considered the handling of the MG, which she hadn't yet driven on the open highway. Judith had trouble keeping the sports car under sixty-five, a speed Joe considered cruising.

Her cousin arrived with two suitcases and a garment bag, insisting that the late June weather was too unpredictable to know what type of clothes to pack.

"So you brought all of them?" Judith inquired, hoisting the garment bag over her shoulder and feeling her lower back give a twinge of pain.

Renie gave Judith an arch look. "Hardly. I could have brought almost everything in the big suitcase if Bill hadn't taken it with him to Champaign-Urbana."

It was almost dark as they drove through patches of wispy fog. Renie asked after Joe; Judith inquired about their mothers.

"My mother acted as if I were going with Admiral Byrd to the South Pole on a five-year expedition," replied Renie. "Your mother said it was too bad Joe didn't break his neck instead of his leg."

"In other words," Judith said dryly, "they're both fine."

"They're themselves," replied Renie. "My mother says yours smokes too much. Your mother gripes that mine talks too much. Before I left, they were arguing about what to have for dinner. My mother wanted to warm up some green Spam she's been saving in the fridge for about three months and yours wanted me to run down to the public market and get pickled pig's feet. Fortunately, Auntie Vance and Uncle Vince called to say they were coming down from the Island with a vat full of chicken and noodles. They're staying for dinner."

"Good," said Judith, braking for a curve. "Did Mike call from Montana?"

Renie gave Judith a vexed look. "Not that I know of. He didn't leave until yesterday. He's probably just getting in about now. Stop fussing." Still eyeing Judith's strong profile, Renie's face softened. She knew her cousin was feeling guilty about a lot of things—for sending Gertrude off to live with Deb, for not paying more attention to Mike's summer plans and the upcoming fall semester at school, even for finally getting what she wanted by becoming Joe's wife. The cousins' minds were so in tune that Renie understood how Judith could feel both elated over her newly-married state and yet undeserving. There had been so many years of obstacles and discontent that Renie realized Judith felt unworthy of happiness.

"Boy, are you lucky," said Renie brightly. She didn't wait for Judith's response, which was just as well since an ancient RV was swaying dangerously in front of them and forcing a slowdown to forty-five. "You've only been married for two days and you've already had your first bad break. Break? Get it? Ha-ha."

Judith kept her eyes on the road. "I'm sure glad I asked you to come down. You're always so positive, you twit."

Renie ignored Judith's remark. She knew how glad Judith was to have her. And Renie was glad to tag along. It was Judith who put their feelings into words as she finally got onto a straight piece of road and was able to pass the lurching camper.

"Strange as it seems, coz, my honeymoon wouldn't have been complete without you."

Renie grinned. "Gee, somehow I'd hoped it would be. Then again," she added in an unusually thoughtful voice, "maybe I didn't."

THREE

EVEN IN THE dark, Renie was charmed by the cottage. They had parked in the garage, but Judith insisted on taking Renie around to the front so she could get an un-obstructed moonlight view of the ocean. The cousins stood on the bluff watching the silver waves in silence. Although the kites had disappeared for the day, the beach still beckoned strollers and even a few joggers.

"Nice," said Renie at last. "Very nice. I can see why you didn't want to waste the rental."

They had turned back to the house. Judith started to speak, then let out a exclamation of surprise: "Hey—I didn't turn on any lights. It wasn't dark when I left and I never thought about it."

The cousins stared at the picture window in the living room. A single floor lamp was aglow, and in the doorway to the kitchen, they could see two people standing very close together.

"What on earth . . . ?" Judith rocked on her heels. "Are we being burgled?" she asked, lowering her voice.

"I don't think so," answered Renie, whose distance

vision was better than her cousin's. "Look—they're, uh, hugging."

"If I want to see anything far away, I have to get up closer," said Judith, moving carefully but purposefully toward the cottage. Within six feet of the window, they ducked down, trying to conceal themselves behind the rhododendrons, azaleas, and Oregon grape which grew in a border against the house. "Egad," gasped Judith, "it's our landlady!"

"Who's she landed?" Renie whispered back.

Judith peered through the shrubbery. "I don't recognize him. It's not the guy I saw at the boathouse this afternoon."

"What guy?"

"Never mind that now." Judith felt her short, frosted black hair get caught in the spiny Oregon grape. Mrs. Hoke and the man who held her in his arms were profile-to-profile, apparently exchanging affectionate words. "I feel like a window peeper," Judith said under her breath.

Renie was kneeling on the ground, now damp with dew. "He looks a lot younger than she does. But I guess older women and younger men are all the rage. I knew I should have tried to seduce Dooley on his paper route."

Judith motioned for Renie to shut up, but the couple had disappeared into the kitchen, arm in arm. "Great," muttered Judith, still trying to extricate herself from the Oregon grape. "Now what do we do, go for a ride?"

The idea didn't strike Renie as particularly strange. "We could get root beer floats," she suggested, making a pass at wiping off her linen slacks. "Hey, it's not eleven o'clock yet."

"Well—maybe," Judith said dubiously. "This isn't exactly the Big City, you know." Walking over to unlock the MG, she saw two cars that she hadn't noticed earlier parked out at the edge of the road next to the black van. One was Mrs. Hoke's Buick; the other was some sort of four-wheel drive. Since Pirate's Lair was squeezed in between the resort and the motel, people tended to park everywhere in the cul-de-sac.

"That's nervy," Judith complained as she backed out the driveway. "I mean, it's her house and all that, but she shouldn't be bringing her boyfriend over for the evening. I should have known there was something flaky about this place."

Renie gave a shrug. "Thirty minutes and one root beer float apiece and they should be gone. If not," she said composedly, "we'll roust them. Just because one-half of the honeymoon is in traction doesn't mean you don't want to use the cottage."

"Right," agreed Judith, driving up the short, steep hill that led to Highway 101. "Maybe Mrs. Hoke just came by to drop off some more stuff. She's already been at the house twice today."

"Nosy, huh?" Renie gave a little sniff. "Who was the other guy you were talking about?"

Traffic was still fairly heavy on the highway, but most of the storefronts were dark. Judith drove slowly, though the car seemed to fight her every inch of the way. "It was nothing," Judith said in dismissal. "There's an old boathouse down on the beach that belongs to Mrs. Hoke. I doubt if it's been used for years, but some man was hanging around there this afternoon. He's probably one of the locals. In any event, he looked a lot older, at least as far as I could tell."

"Which you can't, without Dooley's telescope," noted Renie, then bounced in her bucket seat as she spotted a neon sign that read "Del's Diner" dead ahead.

Judith pulled off the highway and into the vacant parking lot. She had her hand on the ignition key as the neon sign went blank. "Drat," she muttered, "we'll have to go further up the road."

They did, all the way past the city limits. Growing annoyed, Judith pulled into a darkened service station and turned around. "We'll try the other end of town," she said, heading back into Buccaneer Beach.

The city had grown in a north-south sprawl along the ocean, with its best real estate on the west side of the highway. There was a shopping center to the north and an out-

let mall to the south. In between was a six-mile stretch of
other businesses which served the regular population of
seven thousand and the tourists, who numbered almost as
many at any given time during the summer months. Judith
drove past all four of the town's stoplights. At last, on the
far side of Buccaneer Bay, they came to a drive-in. Judith
pulled up to a plastic Jolly Roger which made muffled
noises at her.

"Ask them if they've got hard ice cream," said Renie.

Judith did. They didn't. Renie looked as if she were
pouting. "Well?" demanded Judith testily. "Do you want a
float or not?"

"You know I don't like soft ice cream," Renie replied
peevishly.

The Jolly Roger was getting surly. "Then to hell with
it," said Judith, slamming the gears into reverse. She had
hit seventy by the time they reached the outlet mall.

"I don't get it," said Renie, with a whine. "This is supposed to be a town that caters to tourists. It's almost the
Fourth of July. Why isn't anything open?"

"How do I know?" snapped Judith. "Do I look like the
Chamber of Commerce?"

Renie fell silent, then suddenly brightened just as they
reached the center of town and the turnoff to Pirate's Lair.
"Why don't we go to a grocery store and get some vanilla
ice cream—the hard stuff—and root beer and make our
own?"

Judith was already taking a left-hand turn. "Why don't
you go dig a hole in the sand and stick your head in it?
The grocery stores around here close at ten."

"Oh, good grief!" It was almost too much for Renie to
bear. She slumped in the seat, her short chin disappearing
behind the collar of her silk blouse.

"Cheer up, coz," soothed Judith, taking pity on Renie.
"I've got buttermilk. I could make *grössita* for breakfast."

The thought of fluffy chunks of German pancakes did
much to restore Renie's spirits. As ever, Judith marveled at
her cousin's capacity for eating everything in sight without
getting fat as a pig. Metabolism, Renie always said, and

Judith mournfully had to admit that her cousin was probably right.

They arrived just as Mrs. Hoke was coming out to her car. Judith's sense of self-righteousness returned. She braked at the edge of the road and rolled the window down, calling to her landlady.

Mrs. Hoke's lanky figure came toward the MG. "Mrs. Flynn! Oh! How nice to see you! I was just leaving! Oh!" She giggled, again jarring Judith and this time rattling Renie. "I had to get my dulcimer."

Judith gritted her teeth. "You play the dulcimer? How . . . arcane."

Mrs. Hoke was leaning into the car, all elbows, shoulders, and hands. "I don't play it well, but it's such a quaint old instrument. Oh!" She gazed at Renie. "Is this your cousin?"

"Right, Serena Jones, Mrs. Hoke." The two women acknowledged each other while Judith racked her brain to come up with a tactful way of telling her landlady to keep away from Pirate's Lair. "By the way," Judith lied, hoping as she always did that her fabrication was in a good cause, "my husband might be getting out of the hospital sooner than we thought. He'll need complete quiet when he comes back here."

"Oh!" Mrs. Hoke looked both surprised and puzzled. "But of course! You certainly won't have me bothering you." She laughed merrily. "I've got unexpected company."

"How nice," said Judith. "Family?"

Mrs. Hoke simpered and hugged her angular frame. "You might say that." One eyelid dropped in an exaggerated wink. "Let's just say it's someone to whom I feel especially *close.*" She giggled some more.

"Good," said Judith, putting the MG back into first gear. "I hope your guest enjoys the dulcimer. Good night."

The cousins left Mrs. Hoke laughing her head off.

Joe, unfortunately, was wide-awake. He was uncomfortable, if not in pain, and extremely bored. The food was

wretched and the nurses spent all their time sitting on their
fat duffs gossiping and eating saltwater taffy. His doctors
knew as much about modern medicine as Hippocrates.
He'd called police headquarters back home to inform them
of his accident and had not received an adequate amount
of sympathy.

"Woody wasn't even there," he complained, referring to
his subordinate, the taciturn but kindly Officer Price. "He
was off on some damned drive-by shooting. They ought to
let Vice handle that crap," he said in an unreasonable tone.
"It's all drug-related. Sometimes I think the Chief has his
head up his . . ."

"Gee, Joe," Judith said quietly, trying to plump up the
pillows behind his head, "aren't you glad Renie came
down? I am. She only complains about root beer floats."

"Or the absence thereof," put in Renie, trying to pull the
room's second chair up to Joe's bed without waking Jake
Beezle. She failed.

"Hey, sweetheart," chirruped Jake, "you shrank! Did
you bring the good stuff this time?"

"Over here, Mr. Beezle," called Judith. "That's my
cousin. She's a teetotaler."

"Awwww . . ." Jake groaned as Renie scooted out of his
line of vision. "Hey," he yelled, jerking back the curtain,
"you got any cards?"

"Afraid not," said Judith, trying to keep Joe from yank-
ing on his pulleys.

"Cards?" Joe stopped squirming.

"I've got some," said Renie.

Aghast, Judith stared at Renie. "You do?"

"Sure." She delved into her enormous handbag and
came up with two decks of Bicycle playing cards. "You
know how Bill hates for me to read in bed because it
keeps him awake. I read in the bathtub and if I run out of
books on a trip, I play solitaire on the bathroom floor."
She slipped the red deck out of its box. "Oh!—these are
for pinochle. *That's* why I had so many red queens."

"Pinochle!" exclaimed Jake.

"Pinochle!" cried Joe.

"Pinochle!" moaned Judith.

"Four-handed?" inquired Renie.

Judith made a face at her cousin. "At nine in the morning? Are you nuts?"

Jake had pushed the curtain aside and somehow managed to reach the edge of the bed. "You can clear off this here stand thing and one of you girls can sit behind it and the other one between the beds." He patted his mattress and leered at both Judith and Renie. "Real close like, okay? Looks like Flynn over there and me will have to be partners, seeing as how we can't move around so good. Deal 'em."

Renie did, wedged in between the wall and Joe's combination table and tray. Judith hauled her chair over and glared at Renie. "I can't believe we're doing this," she said between clenched teeth. "Haven't I suffered enough from those cribbage sessions with my mother?"

"Good game, cribbage," said Jake, who had jammed an unlighted cigar in his mouth. "If those porker nurses hadn't locked up all my money, we could play some stud." He grinned around his stogie and jabbed Judith with an elbow. "Stud's my game, stud's my name. Get it?"

"I already got it from Renie," muttered Judith. "Bid or bunch."

"I'll say two hundred," said Joe, looking considerably more cheerful. "Hey, Jake, you got another cigar?"

"I forget," said Renie, who was never at her best before 10:00 A.M. "What's a good bid for four-handed? Three-ninety, four hundred?"

"Right," said Jake, reaching under the mattress and pulling out a battered box. "Here, Flatfoot, have a cigar. Pity we can't light 'em in this booby hatch."

For the next two hours, the foursome played three games, two of which were won by the men. Judith, whose back was giving her fits in the low-slung visitor's chair, finally announced that she had to go fly a kite.

"Mrs. Hoke brought us one," she said, replacing Joe's water carafe and trying not to knock over his IV stand.

Jake stopped buzzing for the nurse to bring him a bedpan. "Hoke? Alice Hoke? Strange woman. Spooky. Haven't seen her in years."

Judith felt like saying she wished she could be as lucky. "Mrs. Hoke *is* a bit different, but her beach house is charming. It's the giggle that gets me."

"Giggle?" Jake made a scornful gesture with his gnarled hand. "I never knew that woman to smile, let alone giggle. She's a real sourpuss."

"Whatever," murmured Judith, bending down to kiss Joe good-bye. Seeing the bleak expression on his round, faintly florid, face, she was overcome with remorse. "Oh, Joe, this is such a rotten thing! In the fall, let's fly down to San Francisco and paint the town red! Remember all our old haunts? We'll stay at the Fairmont and go to the Top of the Mark and Fisherman's Wharf and the Blue Fox and out to North Beach and . . ."

Joe was looking pitiful. "How can I climb those hills on crutches? Just put me in a ground floor room on Mission Street and I'll watch the bums beat each other up for a pint of muscatel."

Jake popped up from his pillows. "Muscatel? Somebody got some vino fino over there? Hey, you guys, pass it around!"

Judith gave Jake a thin smile, then turned her attention back to Joe. "You'll be fine in a few weeks. I talked to Dr. Scott this morning. Really, Joe, he strikes me as quite competent. And that intern, Dr. Lundgren, seems very dedicated." She kissed him again. "Renie and I'll be back this afternoon."

"Promise?" Joe was growing more wan by the minute.

"Sure. I love you." Her voice had dropped to a whisper.

"Me, too," said Joe, and closed his eyes.

"Honestly," said Renie when they were out in the parking lot, "men make the most dismal patients. I told Bill the next time he got a cold I was getting him a Do-It-Yourself-Last-Rites-Kit. Did I ever tell you about the time he hyperventilated in the middle of the night and I woke up to find him sitting there in bed with a paper bag over his head?"

"Dan did that once," said Judith, "but it was a grocery bag. He'd eaten all the groceries first. For the week." She sighed and got into the car. "By the way, ditch those cards, will you? I'm not going to spend the week playing pinochle with Joe and that crazy old coot, Beezle. I was married too long to one semi-invalid to put up with that."

Renie jumped a little as Judith banged the car door shut. "I don't know about that," said Renie as Judith revved the engine with a vengeance.

"About what?" Judith's strong features were set.

"It seems to me," Renie said lightly, but with meaning, "that maybe you've been single too long. Could it be that you've forgotten what marriage—a real marriage—is all about?"

Judith didn't answer. But as they drove down 101, she was thinking very hard.

The kite-flying was not a success. The cousins discovered that it took more than a good wind and a lot of strong string to fly the sophisticated kites of Buccaneer Beach. They wouldn't give up, however, and decided that next time they'd find somebody who would teach them. Not, Judith noted, the curly-haired young man from the motel who still couldn't get his green dragon off the ground. A more likely prospect was a ten-year-old boy with a kite shaped like a giant black and gold butterfly. His kite had soared, dipped, swooped, and circled with all the grace of a ballet dancer. Judith and Renie were duly impressed.

"A lot of them are practicing for the annual kite-flying contest," Judith explained over dinner on the bay at Chuck's Chowder House. "It's part of the July Fourth Freebooters' Festival. That's what all the banners are for along the main drag."

"That's a week away," said Renie in mild surprise. "We could still be here for that if Joe's not out of the hospital."

Judith grimaced. "We're only paid up through Saturday night. If we have to stay on, we'll have to rent one of those cardboard boxes in the carport. I can't afford another seven hundred bucks."

Renie was watching the waves and looking wistful. "I could pitch in. It wouldn't be for a whole week, anyway. Unless I succumb to an attack of guilt over my neglected clients, we could be here for all the festivities." She crumbled a handful of crackers into her chowder. "It might be fun. There I was, feeling sorry for myself, with Bill gone, and Tom and Tony running off on a sailboat, and Anne flying down to L.A. for the holiday. Buccaneer Beach would sure beat lighting sparklers for our mothers and letting them spell out insulting names for each other."

"Let's just be thankful all four of our kids have jobs for the summer," said Judith, referring to Mike and the three Jones offspring. "Joe's daughter, Caitlin, may be coming back from Switzerland for Christmas."

"That'll be nice," agreed Renie as their waiter brought them each a shrimp Caesar salad. They waited for him to perform with the giant pepper mill. Chuck's Chowder House was crowded, a large, noisy eatery where customers sat family style on benches. Judith and Renie, having returned from another round of pinochle at the hospital, had arrived shortly before seven. The line at Chuck's had reached far into the jammed parking lot. The cousins had not been seated until just before eight, or, as Renie put it, about two minutes short of her demise from famine.

But the wait was worth it. The salad was crisp, the creamy chowder lived up to its reputation, and the sockeye salmon steaks almost brought tears to Renie's eyes.

"Much better than green Spam, huh, coz?" grinned Judith over a Coffee Nudge.

"You bet." Renie smacked her lips. "And don't you feel virtuous for entertaining Joe and Jake this afternoon?"

Judith dropped her eyes. "I guess." She paused, making circles with her forefinger on the smooth tabletop. "Maybe you're right. In over four years, I got used to being single."

Renie inclined her head. "Joe was smart. He figured you needed time to know your own mind." She regarded Judith with what her cousin called her serious Boardroom Face. "Even with Joe, it won't be easy, coz."

"True." Judith gave Renie a crooked smile. "We're not exactly off to a carefree start."

"Maybe that's just as well." Above the rim of her Spanish coffee, Renie gave Judith a fond look. "You get through this honeymoon, and the rest will be easy."

Judith laughed. Renie was right. Nothing was ever easy. The combination of Renie's company and the excellent meal soothed her soul. She gazed out over the bay where half a dozen pleasure boats headed for home in the gathering darkness. There was no sunset, for rain clouds had blown in with the afternoon breeze. Directly below the windowsill a little creek tumbled through large boulders, making its way to the sea. Several children, and almost as many dogs, scampered on the sands. Smoke from a beach fire curled up into the twilight. Judith watched the waves and felt at peace.

A soft mist had settled in on the MG's windshield when Judith and Renie reached the parking lot. The air was cool and damp, but the wind had died down. It was almost ten by the time they returned to Pirate's Lair. To Judith's relief, the house was dark, but she had remembered to leave a light on in the garage. The faint sound of music could be heard drifting from the We See Sea Resort next door. Judith decided they should build a fire in the cottage's stone fireplace. The cousins gathered wood and kindling to bring inside. Judith noticed that more boxes seemed to be missing from the garage. She gave a mental shrug—if Mrs. Hoke were moving her belongings, that was fine—as long as she didn't keep popping into the house itself. Maybe, Judith thought with a wry smile, she'd taken home a crate of dulcimers.

Renie was already in the kitchen, flipping on the lights. "Have you opened the damper yet?" she asked, heading for the living room.

"No," replied Judith as Renie switched on a table lamp by the beige sofa that sat across from the fireplace. "Let's make sure we do it right. I wouldn't want to set off the smoke alarm."

The words were hardly out of her mouth when Renie set

off her own alarm. A piercing scream brought Judith vaulting around the sofa and across the floor. Renie stood frozen, the kindling clutched in her arms like a newborn baby. At her feet was Mrs. Hoke, long arms and legs at awkward angles. At her side was the bright pink kite the cousins had tried to fly in vain that afternoon.

And around her neck was the long, strong string. Her face was a ghastly shade of purple and the gray eyes bulged up at the cousins.

Judith and Renie knew she was dead.

FOUR

Mrs. Hoke, alas, was not the first body the cousins had encountered. After their initial shock, Judith volunteered to summon help. Unable to figure out if the area had 911 emergency service, she called both the Buccaneer Beach police and the Juniper County Sheriff. Still dazed, Judith replaced the phone and immediately questioned her own judgment.

"Drat," she groaned, slumping onto a kitchen chair. "Now we'll have both the police *and* the sheriff here. What a mess!"

"Let them sort it out," said Renie, rummaging in the cabinets for brandy or some other calming source. "Jeez, coz, how could we possibly end up with another dead body?"

Judith gave Renie a gimlet eye. "We live in violent times," she murmured. Leaning so far back in the chair that she almost tipped it over, Judith swore in frustration. "Having Joe break a leg was bad enough, but now this! Why couldn't that goofy woman get herself killed some place else?"

Having failed to find anything stronger than orange

juice, Renie poured them each a glass and collapsed at the table. "That's a good question. Why here?"

Judith blinked. "It's also a callous one. I think marriage has turned me into a miserable crank." She took a sip of orange juice and shook her head. "Poor soul. Here I'm carping about my honeymoon and she's dead. Why don't I just go rent a broom instead of a kite and fly back to Heraldsgate Hill?"

Renie couldn't sit still. She was pacing the kitchen, glancing out toward the cul-de-sac every time she went by the window. "Where's her car?" asked Renie.

"I didn't see it." In her mind's eye, Judith pictured the scene as they approached the cottage. A van, a pickup, a beater, and a couple of compact cars had been parked along the road. But no Buick. "You're right," said Judith. "Why did she come here to get herself killed?"

Renie stopped pacing and leaned on the back of a chair. "Maybe she was meeting the boyfriend here again."

Judith considered, then shook her head. "Unless Mrs. Hoke reserved this place for her assignations—and for all I know, she might—it seems pretty odd that she'd show up two evenings in a row when she knows we might be here or coming along at any moment. It would also be risky for whoever killed her. If we hadn't had to wait so long at Chuck's Chowder House, we might have been here an hour ago. Oh, dear!" Judith shuddered. "If we had, maybe we would have been in time to stop the murderer!"

"Well, we weren't here," Renie declared. "You can't beat yourself over the head for that." She stiffened as sirens sounded in the distance. Then more sirens, coming from another direction. Renie grimaced. "Shoot, where will they all park?"

"That," said Judith, getting up, "is their problem. At least they aren't pulling up in front of Hillside Manor and scaring off the clientele."

Through the window, the lights from the emergency vehicles flashed around the kitchen. Renie started for the back door but Judith heard a vigorous rapping at the front.

Avoiding Mrs. Hoke's body, Judith raced out of the kitchen to let in half a dozen police and firemen.

"Sheriff," said a tall, lean man in his late forties, barging past Judith.

"Chief of Police," said a short, stocky man about the same age rushing with Renie from the kitchen area.

"Where's the body?" The two law enforcement officers made a duet of the question, but it wasn't music to anybody's ears. Indeed, they had both stopped in back of the sofa, glaring at each other.

"Who called *you*?" demanded the police chief, bristling.

"What's it to *you*?" snapped the sheriff. "Take a hike, Clooney."

"The hell I will!" retorted the police chief, fists on hips. "We got called over here. This is my jurisdiction. You're out of your league, Eldritch. As usual."

The sheriff loomed menacingly over the police chief. Eldritch had sunken blue eyes with deep hollows and a lantern jaw. "When was the last time you caught a perp, Clooney?"

The police chief shoved his stomach at the sheriff. "The last time you let one slip through your knock-knees, Eldritch. I always get my perp, you twerp."

Judith and Renie exchanged dazed looks while the various emergency personnel milled around as if they were looking for canapés at a cocktail party. "Excuse me . . ." Judith shouted, but nobody heard her except Renie.

"Hey!" yelled one of the firemen from the middle of the living room. "There's a dead woman on the rug!"

The argument between the sheriff and the police chief ceased. Grimly, the two men marched toward the corpse.

"Hell's bells!" breathed Chief Clooney. "She's dead, huh?"

"As a dodo," agreed Sheriff Eldritch. "What color is that anyway?"

"Puce," snapped Judith, coming up behind the sheriff. "This isn't an art exhibit; it's a murder victim. Would you people please do your duty?"

The two men turned surprised faces toward Judith. Eldritch seemed bemused; Clooney bristled a bit. "You the one who called me in?" the chief asked, hitching his belt over his paunch.

"I called both of you," Judith replied, her gaze avoiding the corpse. "I wasn't sure who had authority in a small town. That's why there's such confusion. I'm sorry about that, but you're lucky I didn't call the State Police, too."

Chief Clooney didn't look as if he felt so lucky, but at least he stopped bristling. His square face was flushed and he ran a beefy hand through the sparse brown hairs atop his head. "Okay, let's get on with it. Looks to me like the lady's been strangled." He glanced quickly at his rival law enforcement official. "Well?"

Eldritch had turned back to the body. "Is that kite string?" He saw the pink kite next to Mrs. Hoke and straightened up to glower at Clooney. "Kite string! Now that's real ugly!"

"So are you," snarled the police chief. He gave a start as he bent down to examine the victim. "So who *is* this?" He stared hard at Judith with small hazel eyes.

"Ha!" crowed Eldritch. "You don't even know your own citizens! Some police chief! I'll bet you wouldn't recognize the mayor!"

Judith was trying not to gnash her teeth. "It's Alice Hoke and she owns this house. My husband and I rented it from her for the week." She had wedged herself between the warring police chief and sheriff, standing with her arms folded across her breast and her chin thrust out. "My cousin and I came home shortly before ten o'clock and found her like that. Dead."

Clooney and Eldritch both gazed down at the grotesque form of Mrs. Hoke. The time that had passed since Renie's grisly discovery had not improved the landlady's appearance. Judith looked away, her knees shaky and her lower back aching.

"Bull," said Clooney, hauling a bent notebook from his back pants pocket. "Maybe you found her like this, maybe you didn't." He smirked at Judith. "But I'll tell you one thing." He smirked some more, now looking at Eldritch, then across the room at Renie who had climbed up on a stool for a better view. "Oh, yeah, sure, you came in and fell over a body all right. But it's not Alice Hoke. It looks sort of like her, but it's not. And I ought to know—Alice and I are going steady."

An hour later, the cottage was cleared of everybody but Sheriff Josh Eldritch and Police Chief Neil Clooney. The scene of the crime had been photographed, measurements taken, floors vacuumed for evidence, surfaces dusted for prints, and the corpse taken away. The pink kite was removed, too.

Judith and Renie, who had been relegated to the spare bedroom at the rear of the cottage, waited for permission to emerge. Renie, who was staying in the guest room anyway, changed into her purple velour bathrobe and smeared brown cream on much of her face. Judith was tempted to tell her she didn't look a heck of a lot better than the putative Mrs. Hoke.

During their interval of seclusion, the cousins didn't go too far beyond expressing their amazement over Chief Clooney's startling announcement. Renie had asked if the victim had actually claimed to be Alice Hoke. Judith had thought back to their meeting the previous morning. The woman who had shown up in the Buick hadn't introduced herself, but she'd certainly answered to the name of Mrs. Hoke and had definitely acted as if she owned the place.

"She even told me about her family's cheese factory," Judith told Renie. "Ogilvie's Cheese, remember?"

Renie cocked her head. "I think so. Big chunks of cheddar, right? They put out a Colby later but it wasn't as good."

Judith was sitting on the edge of the bed in her stocking feet. There was sand in the durable carpeting, sand on the flowered bedspread, sand just about everywhere, including between the cousins' teeth. Beach living had its drawbacks, the ubiquitous sand being one of them. Now, it seemed, a corpse was another. Judith surveyed the cozy

room with its bleached pine furniture and green voile curtains. Murder seemed incongruous. But then it usually did.
In the brief silence, Judith could hear the roar of the ocean
coming through the open windows.

"Whoever she was," said Judith, "she had a reason for
pretending she was Mrs. Hoke. I just hope she didn't make
off with my rental money."

"I thought you sent a check," said Renie, putting on a
pair of mules.

Judith nodded. "I did. I sent it to a different address.
The family farm or whatever, I suppose. This woman had
a receipt for it." She stood up, running a hand through her
waves of frosted hair. "I wonder where I put it? My purse,
I suppose. The address should be on it some place."

Before Judith could speculate further, the cousins heard
a rap on the door. Sheriff Eldritch asked them to come
back into the living room. Judith winced at the disorder
caused by the law enforcement people, but decided that
any housekeeping tasks could wait until tomorrow.

Chief Clooney was sitting in the big blue rocker while
Sheriff Eldritch draped his lanky frame over a high-back
chair. Judith and Renie sat across from them on the sofa.
The two men were still exchanging hostile glances, but at
least they seemed temporarily inclined to put personal dif-
ferences aside and tend to business. Both now had note-
books and pens at the ready. Judith couldn't help but
wonder if the absence of any assistants was the result of
an argument, like a pair of duelists disputing the reputa-
tions of their seconds.

For openers, Eldritch deferred to Clooney. "You say you
rented this place?" the police chief asked.

Judith nodded. "My husband and I did. I'm Judith
Flynn, Mrs. Joseph," she added with a note of pride, "and
this is my cousin, Serena Jones."

"Mrs. William," put in Renie and yawned.

After noting hometown addresses and phone numbers,
Clooney asked where Mr. Flynn might be. Judith didn't
see the need to explain that they were on their honeymoon.

She wasn't anxious for any more smirks from Chief Clooney.

"He wrecked our dune buggy and broke his leg," said Judith. "He's in the local hospital for a few days. That's why I asked Renie—my cousin—to come down and stay with me. It seemed a shame to rent the house and then have to stay here alone." She paused, allowing time for both men to make notes. Clooney wrote very fast; Eldritch took his time. Renie stood up and offered to make tea.

"I'd rather have coffee," said Clooney.

"You got any seltzer?" inquired Eldritch.

"We don't even have root beer," said Renie in an aggrieved voice. "I'll make tea *and* coffee." She headed for the kitchen, looking like a purple grape in her big velour bathrobe.

"So," said the sheriff, apparently taking his turn as interrogator, "how did you meet the victim?"

Judith explained how the ersatz Mrs. Hoke had shown up the previous day with household supplies and the receipt. "She was here again last night," Judith continued. "She had a man with her."

"Who?" interjected Clooney, edging forward in the rocker and making the springs creak.

"I don't know." Judith gave a little lift of her wide shoulders. "According to you people, I don't even know Mrs. Hoke. Who was that woman?" She gestured at the outline of the body on the carpet. "Did either of you recognize her?"

Clooney's eyebrows twitched. "We're asking the questions here, Mrs. Flynn. Why did *you* think she was Alice Hoke?"

Renie had returned, carrying the rest of her orange juice. Judith told the lawmen how the woman had acted as if she was Mrs. Hoke and had even talked about the family cheese factory. "I've got the receipt in my purse," she said, getting up. "I'll show it to you."

Her brown suede handbag was still on the kitchen table where she'd left it upon returning from dinner. Judith flipped through her belongings, but couldn't find the yellow slip of paper. She dug into her wallet, then the zippered inner pocket. The receipt wasn't there. Biting her lip, she tried to remember if she'd put it somewhere in the house. It wasn't on the counter or in the drawer by the phone.

The teakettle whistled and Judith went through the motions of making tea and instant coffee, but her mind was on the receipt. She must have mislaid it. Perhaps it was in the bedroom or the living room. But the police or the sheriff's men would have come across it. Judith made an exasperated face. She hadn't really looked at the yellow paper; she'd just dropped it into her purse. Maybe it had fallen out. Then again, maybe it had been taken out . . . But by whom? And why?

She was still looking vexed when she returned to the living room. "I can't find it," she said, setting four mugs, a ceramic teapot, and a carafe of coffee on the table next to the couch. Renie went out to fetch cream, sugar, spoons, and napkins. "Your people didn't pick it up, I suppose?"

Eldritch glanced inquiringly at Clooney who shrugged his burly shoulders. "We'll find out. When was the last time you saw this woman alive?"

"Last night," said Judith, handing Clooney a mug of coffee and offering tea to Eldritch who declined. "About eleven-thirty. She was just leaving. We didn't see the man, though. He must have already left."

Eldritch was looking longingly at Renie's orange juice. "Let's back up. Are you saying this woman came here with a man? They were here together? What are you talking about?"

Judith explained how she and Renie had returned from Salem and seen the so-called Mrs. Hoke and a man through the window. "I don't want to imply that they were in a passionate embrace," Judith emphasized, "but they were standing very close together. Let's call the scene 'intimate'—in the real sense of the word."

"Intimate, huh?" said Clooney, slurping coffee and obviously conjuring up more lurid images than Judith had intended. "So you went away and let them go at it?"

Judith lifted her chin. "We went away," she said with dignity.

"And a lot of good it did us," put in Renie, sounding surly. "How come nobody in this stupid town stays open after ten o'clock?"

"What for?" asked Eldritch.

"What do you mean, 'stupid'?" countered Clooney.

Renie wasn't about to be put off by a mere sheriff and a chief of police. "I mean whatever happened to *Open All Hours*? This is almost the twenty-first century. Don't you yokels have a 7-Eleven? I can get three kinds of root beer at 3:00 A.M. at the one on Heraldsgate Hill."

"Hold it," rumbled Clooney, looking dangerous. "This is a murder investigation, lady. Let's not get sidetracked."

"Sidetracked?" echoed Renie, rolling her eyes. "You're the one who was picturing that poor woman frolicking on the carpet with some young stud. We just said we saw them. Together. For all we know, he was her dentist, making a house call. I think people in small towns must have dirty minds. If they kept longer hours, they wouldn't have time to think bad thoughts." Renie looked uncharacteristically prudish, a fair imitation of Gertrude at her most narrow-minded.

Judith put aside mental comparisons with her mother and intervened. "Look! All we can tell you is that I saw this woman twice—three times, if you count through the window—and that she was in excellent health when she left here last night around eleven-thirty. She may have been here again today to get more boxes or dulcimers or whatever, but we didn't run into her."

Eldritch sat up a little straighter. "More what?"

Judith waved a hand. "She claimed she'd come back last night for her dulcimer." Seeing the blank expressions on the lawmen's faces, she went on, "It's an old-fashioned musical instrument. Like a guitar. Except she didn't have it with her. But somebody has been taking boxes out of the garage for the last two days. They're stacked to the rafters." Folding her hands in her lap, Judith tried to strike a calmer note. "Really, that's all we know, except that she drove a fairly new Buick. I dealt with Mrs. Hoke—or whoever rented this place to us—only by mail. I'm sorry we can't be more help."

Clooney was tapping his ballpoint pen on his notepad. "It's Alice's house, all right," he said, more to himself than the others. He was silent for a moment, then turned wearily to the sheriff. "Well, what do you think, Josh?"

Eldritch looked pleased at being asked. "I hate to say it, but you're probably right. You know the family better than I do. You're older," he added slyly.

Clooney snorted and stood up. The rocker creaked again. "Not by much, Big Fella. But at least I know Alice." He looked smug.

Eldritch unwound himself from the chair and also got to his feet. He looked down at the cousins. "You're not going anywhere for a few days, I take it?"

"No," replied Judith, with a distasteful glance at the victim's outline on the carpet. "How long do we have to put up with that?"

Eldritch shrugged. "A day or two. You can walk on it."

"Gee, thanks," said Judith faintly.

"By the way," said Clooney, turning around in the doorway, "where'd that kite come from?"

Judith and Renie were both standing now, too. "Mrs. Hoke brought it," said Judith, then took three long strides to confront the sheriff and police chief. "I can't keep calling her Mrs. Hoke. I gather you two may know who she is. Why the secret?"

Clooney gave Judith a condescending look. "You're right, we're pretty sure who the dead woman is, but we're waiting for positive ID. Police procedure, you know." He gave an indulgent little laugh. "Actually, you *wouldn't* know. Trust us, we yokels have our methods, even in a *stupid town like Buccaneer Beach.*" He bit off the last words and glared at Renie.

Judith stopped her cousin just in time by stepping on her foot. Renie jumped, her mouth half-opened, but the words she was about to utter died on her lips. Sheriff Eldritch and Chief Clooney took their leave. The cousins could hear them arguing all the way back to their respective emergency vehicles.

"You should have told them," Renie insisted, shaking her head.

"Are you crazy? We've got enough problems without me admitting my husband is a big city homicide detective." Judith headed back for the living room to clear away the coffee and tea items. "Listen, coz," she went on as she handed the teapot and carafe to Renie, "Joe may be in the hospital, but I'm still on my honeymoon. It's not my fault that some woman I don't even know got herself strangled in the living room of Pirate's Lair. It's not my beach cottage, it's not my town, it's got nothing to do with me. I'm sitting this one out." She gave Renie a long, level stare.

Renie batted her eyelashes. "Oh. Okay, you're right. It's midnight, let's head for bed. Maybe we can go to the outlet mall in the morning."

"Sounds good," said Judith.

" 'Night," said Renie.

" 'Night," said Judith.

At one in the morning, Judith was still awake, wondering who had been murdered in the living room at Pirate's Lair. At two, she was still puzzling over the missing rental receipt. At three, she was wishing she'd gotten a better look at the young man she had seen through the picture window. And at four, she finally drifted off to sleep, but dreamed of a furtive figure, rowing a boat and sinking slowly in dry sand at the foot of the staircase that led to the beach.

Judith knew she was sunk, too.

FIVE

JUDITH TRIED TO pretend it was an ordinary day at Buccaneer Beach. Mike called from Whitefish, Montana, shortly after eight-thirty. He'd only gotten in the night before because he'd spent Monday with his girlfriend, Kristin, and her family on their wheat farm in the rolling hills of the Palouse. It had been over ninety degrees on the other side of the mountains, and they'd sat around all day, drinking lemonade and beer under the shade of a big weeping willow. He hadn't yet seen his supervisor in the Forest Service, so didn't know exactly what his assignment would be. He promised to call back in a couple of days, either at the beach or when Judith got home.

"How come you didn't tell him about Joe's accident?" asked Renie, looking semialert over ham and waffles.

Judith didn't meet her cousin's bleary-eyed gaze. "Oh—I didn't want to worry him. He'll have a lot on his mind with a new job."

Renie started to say something in response, but decided to drop the subject. There were few topics the cousins avoided, but the relationship between Joe and Mike struck Renie as one of them. At least for the moment.

"We ought to call our mothers tonight," Renie said instead.

"Right," Judith agreed without enthusiasm. "And I should check in with Arlene and make sure everything is going okay at the B&B." She poured syrup over her waffle and gave Renie a surreptitious glance. "I think we'll skip the pinochle session this morning."

"Oh?" Renie's reaction was one of innocence. "How come, coz? Did you want to spend a lot of time at the outlet mall?"

"The least we can do is find out who got killed out there in the living room," said Judith, her mind in gear and her thought process assuming its usual logical order. "I turned the radio on this morning when I got up, but this town doesn't have a local station. The weekly paper comes out today, so it was probably printed before we found the body. After we go see Joe, we ought to stop by the police department—or the sheriff's office—and see what we can find out."

"Okay," agreed Renie. "Then what?"

Judith considered. "I'd like to check out the boathouse. For all I know, that man I saw lives there. Maybe he's a homeless person."

"And?" Renie was stuffing her mouth with waffle.

"I wish I'd noticed the license number on that Buick. I know it was an Oregon plate and it had some fours in it." She started to cut up her ham, then realized that Renie was taking the sudden plunge into detection much too complacently. "Well?" demanded Judith. "Aren't you going to try to talk me out of getting involved?"

Renie, whose mouth was still full, shook her head. Judith was faintly exasperated; she despised being so predictable. A hammering at the back door prevented Judith from defending herself.

A young man with flaming red hair and a dusting of freckles stood on the threshold with a tape recorder and a notebook. "Terrence O'Toole, *Buccaneer Beach Bugler*," he said with an eager, gap-toothed smile.

"So where's your bugle?" asked Judith, who assumed he was identifying himself.

"No, no, sorry, no music, no magazines, no encyclopedias," he said, looking apologetic and wiggling his unruly red eyebrows. "I mean, I'm not a salesman, I'm a reporter from the *Buccaneer Beach Bugler*. The local newspaper?" He eyed Judith as if he weren't sure she'd know a newspaper if she found one in her mailbox.

"Oh. Well . . ." Judith glanced over her shoulder at Renie and found no help. Renie was pouring spoonfuls of batter into the waffle iron, onto the counter, and over her shoes. Judith decided that her cousin wasn't as awake as she'd pretended.

"I'm covering the murder," said Terrence O'Toole, hitching up the navy blue suspenders he wore over a freshly pressed white dress shirt. He was tieless, and his open collar revealed a bright blue T-shirt. Judith wondered if Terrence was going for the Clark Kent–Superman look all at once, but hadn't yet figured out how to hold up his pants. "I hear you found the body. How do you feel about that?"

"Grim," replied Judith, wondering how to discourage the press tactfully. "Excuse me, I'm just a tourist and have no . . ."

"But that's the point!" exclaimed Terrence, beaming at Judith even as he inserted a foot in the doorway. "Kite-flying, beachcombing, waterskiing—everybody who comes to Buccaneer Beach does those things. They're a cliché. But you found a body!"

"Don't I always," murmured Judith. Behind her, she could hear Renie snicker. "I don't even know who got killed. Look, Mr. O'Toole, my husband is in the hospital and I have to go . . ."

Terrence's sky blue eyes widened under the unruly brows. "Hospital?" He wedged himself between Judith and the doorjamb. They were eyeball-to-eyeball, and Judith found herself fascinated by the gap between Terrence's teeth. "Wowee! Did he get attacked? Is this a conspiracy?"

Judith, whose nature, not to mention her livelihood, allowed for an open-door policy, relented and stepped aside. "Hardly. My husband wrecked a dune buggy. Or it wrecked him." She ushered Terrence to an empty chair. "We'll give you five minutes and a cup of coffee. If you can tell us who the victim is, we'll divulge our deepest horrors."

"Let's leave our mothers out of this," muttered Renie, dutifully pouring coffee for the reporter.

Judith gave Renie a baleful look, then turned to Terrence. "Have you an ID?"

"Of course. Given the situation, I understand your need for caution. I even have a press card so I can park by the dock where they launch the crab boats." Terrence flipped out his wallet.

Judith put up her hand. "Not *your* ID—I mean for the woman who was killed here last night."

The blue eyes again grew wide. "Oh! Wowee! Sharp question! Yes—her name was Leona . . ." He paused, consulted his wallet, realized his mistake, and opened his notebook. Judith began to worry about Terrence O'Toole. "Leona Ogilvie. She's somebody's sister."

Judith's brain clicked. "Alice Ogilvie Hoke's sister?" She exchanged quick looks with Renie. If Alice and Leona were sisters, that might account for some of the confusion. It would also explain why the police chief thought the victim looked familiar.

Terrence nodded, just a shade doubtfully. "Right. Extremely sharp. I think." He picked up the coffee mug Renie had handed him and took a big gulp. "I graduated from OSU last semester. I haven't been in Buccaneer Beach very long." With an air of regret, Terrence dumped a heaping teaspoon of sugar into his coffee. "Neither was Leona Ogilvie."

Judith arched her dark brows. "Oh? But was she from here originally?"

Terrence nodded. "There was a big difference between

Leona and her sister, Alice. In personality, I mean. Leona
went away a long time ago. To be a missionary in South
America. My editor told me she must have just got back.
Weird, huh?"

"She would have been safer with the pygmies along the
Amazon," remarked Judith, thinking that Leona's recent
return might explain all the boxes in the garage. Perhaps
they were her belongings, shipped back from South America. "Was she staying with her sister, Mrs. Hoke?"

Terrence didn't know. Indeed, after a few more inquiries, Judith came to the conclusion that except for the
victim's name and occupation, Terrence O'Toole didn't
know any more than the cousins did.

But the youthful journalist was determined to proceed
with the interview. "How did you react to murder in your
living room?" Ballpoint pen at the ready, Terrence's bright
blue eyes roamed from cousin to cousin.

Judith considered. "Shocked, of course. Upset. Violence
is always disturbing, especially when it intrudes under
your roof. Your rented roof, that is," she added hastily. She
felt crass, but the truth was, Judith had encountered death
so often in the past year and a half that she had built up
defenses to shield herself. The words tripped out as if by
rote, having had far too many opportunities to sort out her
reactions before setting foot in Pirate's Lair. "Any life
taken willfully is a life wasted," she declared, looking unduly solemn.

Terrence O'Toole regarded Judith with something that
bordered on awe. He wiggled his eyebrows at her. "Deep.
Very deep. Wow-*ee*." His lively gaze shifted to Renie,
who was complacently finishing her third waffle. "And
you, ma'am?"

Renie waved her fork. "Me, too," she said with her
mouth full. Her brown eyes veered up to the kitchen clock,
whose crab claw hands pointed to nine forty-five, and very
close to her traditional time for becoming fully alert. "First
of all, you're writing on your wallet," she said after taking
a big swallow and waiting for Terrence to notice his error.
"Then I'd say it's tragic, and wonder how Alice Hoke is

taking her sister's untimely demise. What do the law en- forcement bozos tell you about Leona's survivors?"

In the wake of Renie's unexpected statement, Terrence O'Toole all but reeled. "Not much," he replied in a faint voice. "They don't tell the press everything they know."

"But we have," said Judith with a smile. She stood up, hoping the young reporter would construe her move as the signal for his departure.

Luckily, after taking the cousins' names and addresses, Terrence also took the hint. With a final gap-toothed grin, he headed out the door and jumped onto a red motor scooter. Judith and Renie hurriedly cleaned up from break- fast.

"You're right, coz," remarked Judith as she loaded the dishwasher. "Where was Leona staying? Was she merely helping her sister out or really impersonating her? The problem is, we don't know much about Leona or Alice, except that their parents owned a cheese factory that made great cheddar."

Renie nodded. "And according to Terrence O'Toole, Leona spent most of her life converting quaint natives in the Andes or up the Amazon. Somewhere down there." She gestured vaguely in the direction of the Oregon- California state line.

"I think we'd better call on Alice Hoke." Judith pressed the button on the dishwasher and raised her voice over the machine's din. "Let's go see Joe first and then pay our condolences to Mrs. Hoke."

"Okay." Renie gathered up her huge handbag and light- weight summer jacket. The sky was fitful, with a breeze blowing off the ocean. "But won't she think we're sort of pushy?"

The cousins were at the car, with Judith unlocking the door on the driver's side. She hesitated, her shoulders slumping. "Of course she will. We don't even know the woman. It would be utterly tasteless to waltz in on her at a time like this. What are we thinking of?"

"You mentioned going to see the sheriff or the police chief," Renie reminded Judith. "They must know something about Leona, especially since Clooney is seeing Alice."

"Nobody else sees much of her from what I hear," said Judith, still standing disconsolately next to the MG. "Damn, coz, we don't need to turn ourselves inside out. I paid seven hundred dollars to rusticate with Joe in this blasted cottage. Instead, I get you—but that's okay," she said, ignoring Renie's wince, "at least it's a vacation. Why am I beating myself up over a woman I'd never seen in my life until Monday?"

"Because we found her corpse on Tuesday?" Renie rattled the handle of the car door. "Come on, open up. And stop being a dork. You know you thrive on this sort of mayhem. Or at least on the solving thereof."

But Judith was shaking her head emphatically. "You make me sound like a ghoul. There's a lot to do and see around here. We can poke around in the tourist shops, visit the galleries, collect shells . . ."

"And go fly a kite." Renie rolled her eyes at Judith. "Hey, coz, let's face it, all those things sound like fun in the brochures but the truth is, they bore both of us stiff. Heck, your one attempt at playing tourist put the Great Love of Your Life in traction."

Judith grimaced at Renie. "He drove like your father." She unlocked the door, but didn't get into the car. "Wait a minute." Judith marched over to the cartons piled at the end of the carport. "Look," she called to Renie, "some of these are stamped by Lufthansa."

"So?" Renie was now leaning on the roof of the low-slung sports car. "Who do you think sent them—Hitler?"

Judith ignored her cousin's flippancy as she studied the boxes. "It just seems odd that . . ." Pausing, she turned one of the smaller cartons upside down. "Whoever this stuff belongs to didn't want anybody to know about it. The mailing labels have been ripped off."

Resignedly, Renie approached Judith. "What do you think is inside? Drugs?"

The cousins exchanged sly glances. "There's one way to find out," said Judith. "Come on."

They marched back indoors, each carrying a box. Judith used a butcher knife to slit open the carton she'd set on the kitchen table. Crumpled newspapers in a foreign language filled the box. Judith carefully rummaged inside; Renie held her breath.

With a frown, Judith displayed the first item her fingers had touched. It was a serving bowl, in a pretty pink and yellow flower pattern. Then came a platter to match, two cups, three saucers, and a soup tureen. Judging from the chips and cracks, the set was well-used. Renie attacked the second box with the knife, but found only a pile of women's clothing, also well-worn.

"No drugs," she said, checking the linings just in case. "This must be Leona's—or somebody's—household stuff. Shall we plunder the rest of the boxes out there in the carport or just content ourselves with minor vandalism?"

"I feel like a dope," said Judith, repacking the dishes. "See if there's some tape in that drawer over there. The least we can do is seal these boxes back up."

"If they belong to Leona, she won't be needing them right away," Renie said with a grimace. "Of course, they might be Alice's. But why rip off the shipping labels?"

Judith shrugged. "Who knows? I'll be darned if I'm going to open all the rest of those cartons, though. If there's something mysterious about them, we'll leave it up to the police. And the sheriff."

Ten minutes later, the cousins were at the hospital, listening to Joe's litany of complaints about the staff, the food, and his discomfort. Judith tried to cheer her husband as best she could; Renie's eyes glazed over.

"... to make oatmeal taste like toenail clippings and dilute the orange juice so that you might as well be drinking ..."

"... a corpse." Judith had been trying to interrupt Joe for some time. Finally, her words registered. Joe's green eyes stared at her and his mouth clamped down.

"In the cottage? What the hell are you talking about?" He struggled with pulleys, ropes, and cast, trying to sit up further in the bed. "Is that what ... One of those dim-witted nurse tubs said something about a murder, but I didn't think it was here, in Buccaneer Beach. What the hell is happening, Jude-girl?"

Judith explained, watching Joe's self-pity turn into as-tute professionalism. He picked up the unlighted cigar from the nightstand and stuck it between his teeth. Renie glanced over at the other bed and noticed that Jake Beezle was gone. Joe caught her curious gaze and mouthed the word, "Therapy." Judith concluded her narrative.

"Well, well," remarked Joe, chewing on the cigar and linking his hands behind his head. "So you've got another murder on your hands, Jude-girl. It's out of my jurisdic-tion; it's off your turf. How much good will it do to tell you to keep out of it?"

Judith turned wide black eyes on her husband. "None. I've got the outline of a corpse on our rented living room rug. Can you really think I'd ignore all this and look the other way?"

Although he wished otherwise, Joe couldn't. Experience told him that the victim must have known her killer. Yet somewhere deep down in the layman's part of his mind, he was hoping for the nameless vagrant who was moving on down the road by now. At least that way Judith would not be in any danger.

Joe gnawed on the cigar and frowned. "You and Renie form a human chain, okay? I don't want either of you tak-ing chances." He saw Judith nod and Renie salute. "Do you know that a lot of us cops figure that if you don't find the killer in the first forty-eight hours, you might as well give up?"

"It's only been twelve," Judith replied dryly. "Where do you suggest we start?"

"Her nearest and dearest," said Joe, relenting a bit. His bride and her cousin were at a distinct disadvantage trying to solve a crime in Buccaneer Beach. On previous occa-sions, Judith had known the people involved, even when she was out of town. But here on the Oregon coast, her chances of running up against the murderer were remote.

He took out the cigar and examined the well-mangled end. "Look for motive, opportunity, means." He uttered a short laugh. "What am I saying, I'm talking to my bride, the Bed-and-Breakfast Sleuth. Just get me a notebook and keep me posted. Check out that boathouse first—Alice Hoke can wait. If she's as bereaved as she ought to be, you won't find out much this soon anyway. In fact, I'd keep away from the family in general. You might check to see if anyone else has shown up in town in the last few days who could have a connection. Buccaneer Beach is small enough that word would probably get around."

"Gee," grinned Judith, "thanks for not giving me any advice. Do you want a written report or will verbal do?"

The gold flecks danced in the green eyes. "Not verbal, oral." He grabbed Judith by the wrist and pulled her close. "The next time Jake goes to therapy, dump Renie and lock the door," he whispered. "I miss you, Jude-girl. This is a hell of a honeymoon."

The tide was almost out when they reached the beach fifteen minutes later. As usual, the kiteflyers trod the sands, as did the walkers, the joggers, the children, and the dogs. Clouds were drifting out to sea, and there was genuine warmth in the late morning sun. Judith and Renie approached the boathouse warily.

"Why are we acting like a pair of fugitives?" asked Renie. "You said the boathouse was part of the package."

"Because the guy who was hanging around down here wasn't," replied Judith, who had paused to examine the sand some twenty feet from the small structure. "It looks as if the tide never gets any further than here, so there's not much in the way of clear footprints. The sand's too soft and dry."

"I don't know why you're looking for footprints at this late date," said Renie, as they moved slowly up to the four steps that led to the tiny porch. "And even if you found some, there are so many people all over this beach, nobody could possibly sort out one set from another."

"True. Alas." Judith jiggled the doorknob. To her surprise, the door opened easily. The cousins edged inside.

The boathouse looked much better from the inside than the outside. Although the furnishings were worn, even tattered in the case of the floral sofa, it was apparent that somebody was keeping the place tidy. Judith took in the rest of the small room, with its two easy chairs, a large cherrywood coffee table, a pair of floor lamps, and a magazine rack which she noticed held the latest issues of *People* and *Good Housekeeping*. The sagging floorboards creaked beneath their feet, reminding Judith of her house on Thurlow Street.

Straight through the small sitting room was a kitchen, with two stools pulled up to the counter, a stove, sink, refrigerator, and even a microwave oven. There were no windows and the far wall was covered with nautical charts. A coffeepot was plugged in, a casserole dish was covered with aluminum foil, and the sink contained half a dozen dirty dishes.

"The lived-in look," murmured Renie.

Judith glanced down at the linoleum which displayed a starfish pattern and looked comparatively new. "The man I saw might be whoever's living here," she remarked, feeling the ever-present sand underfoot. "He might also be coming back, since the coffee's on. There's no rear entrance. We'd better scoot."

"Right," agreed Renie as they exited the little kitchen. She stopped to open one of the doors on each side of the open entry into the sitting room. "A half-bath," she said. "Sink, toilet, shower. Clam shells on the shower curtain. Or are they abalone?"

Not to be outdone, Judith tugged at the other door. It was a small closet, housing clothes for both genders. Judith arched an eyebrow. "My Mysterious Stranger has a girlfriend. Unless he gets a kick out of wearing ugly dresses and pantsuits."

"Takes all kinds," said Renie, coming to look over Judith's shoulder. "Gee, I haven't seen that much corduroy since Grandma Grover used to make all of us cousins jumpers for school every fall."

"And corduroy party dresses with mother-of-pearl buttons from collar to hem. I always looked like a can of Crisco and you looked like a bean pole." Judith smiled in reminiscence. "Cousin Sue insisted she was too old for the jumpers when she got to high school but Grandma made her one anyway and stitched a picture of the team mascot on the back."

Renie's brown eyes twinkled. "Do you think Grandma was serious?"

Judith grinned. "Was she ever?" No one could have been more of a pixie incarnate than Grandma Grover. Judith lived by two of her axioms, "It's always better to laugh than to cry" and "Keep your pecker up." Renie preferred "It'll all be the same a hundred years from now." But the real heritage Grandma Grover had passed on was the gift of laughter, which Judith considered the rarest form of courage.

"You know," Judith mused as they started out of the boathouse, "there are times when I can actually hear Grandma saying something in my ear, like . . ." She stopped, her hand on the rusty door knob. "Corduroy! That's what Leona was wearing when I first met her. A corduroy jumper."

Renie stared at Judith, then inclined her head. "So now we know where the deceased was staying." She gestured at the little sitting room. "Cozy, huh?"

"Sort of." Judith gave the room a last look, then tried to open the door. The knob resisted her twist, then the door pushed inward, almost toppling Judith into Renie.

"Burglars! Help, police!" A middle-aged man with a graying beard seemed to take up most of the doorway. With a deft movement, he reached down and picked up a baseball bat that was stationed just inside. "Get back, you devils! Back, I say! You're in my power!"

Judith obeyed, staggering slightly, but trying to smile. The bat made a wide arc, coming dangerously near her head. She stopped trying to smile and ducked. "Wait a minute! We rented this place! Seven hundred bucks says we're not burglars, you crazy loon!"

The bat cut through the air again, but with less force. He braced himself, seeming to favor one leg over the other. "What do you mean? I live here! Who are you?"

Judith tried to explain, no easy task, since every sentence was punctuated by a swing of the baseball bat. Renie had retreated behind the sofa, showing minor signs of alarm. At last the man lowered the bat, his flinty blue eyes resting on each cousin in turn. "Alice Hoke's got no business including this boathouse in the rental deal," he huffed. "I been living here for some weeks now. The old girl's off her rocker."

Judith felt like saying that Alice wasn't alone in that regard, but took another look at the bat and decided to be tactful. "Alice didn't handle any of the business in person. Her sister—poor thing—acted in her stead." She spoke the words innocently, awaiting the man's reaction.

Except for a fleeting expression Judith couldn't fathom, there wasn't any. "Doesn't matter. I want you both out. And stay out." He banged the bat on the floor for emphasis. Under the faded hooked rug, the boards seemed to shudder.

"No problem," said Judith, starting once more for the door. "We were just looking for a . . . boat. In the boathouse." Her smile finally made its way to her mouth. "By the way," she said, turning and trying to talk over Renie, "who are *you*?"

"Me?" The man looked as if he weren't quite sure. "Titus Teacher, whether you like it or not. Good-bye."

The cousins took their cue. "I don't like it. Whatever happened to small-town friendliness?" inquired Renie as they plodded up the sand toward the long staircase.

Judith shook her head, hands jammed into her jacket pockets. "Damned if I know. Is everybody in this burg nuts?"

Renie bristled. "Of course. Small towns are the bastions of lunacy. I've never understood why big cities have such a tarnished reputation. At least they have stores that stay open late."

Judith ignored Renie's carping. "If Leona Ogilvie was living in the boathouse with Titus Teacher, why isn't he more upset?"

Renie, eyeing the uphill slant of the staircase with dismay, shrugged. "Maybe he is. Maybe he acts out with a baseball bat. Like José Canseco or something."

Judith made no further comment, saving her breath for the long flight of stairs. When the cousins reached the front yard, they saw two figures going toward the carport of Pirate's Lair. Judith shouted but the sound of the surf swallowed her voice. The visitors, who could now be discerned as a man and a woman, disappeared, apparently to try the back door. The cousins used up their spare energy to race across the lawn and go in the front entrance. Judith hurried to the back door and greeted the young couple who looked as if they might have enough brains between them to qualify as Normal.

"Hi," squeaked the young woman, whose unnaturally blond hair was not quite held in place by a huge polka-dot bow. "I'm Larissa, and this is Donn Bobb. He's a clown."

Leaning wearily on the doorframe, Judith nodded dutifully. "I'm sure he is," she said. "Where's his bozo horn? Or does he have a dulcimer?"

Larissa's wide-set gray eyes grew enormous. "A . . . ? He had the measles once. Three-day. You should have seen his butt!" She laughed immoderately.

Judith had the feeling that Donn Bobb's butt might be next. "Excuse me," she said, trying to be patient, "but are you here for a reason or did we just get lucky?"

Donn Bobb, whose long, sandy hair fell about his forehead, his shoulders, and even seemed to curl under his chin, lazily swatted his companion's bottom. "Now, Fruit Loops, don't go aggravatin' people. This lady's paid to stay here and she has a right to know why we've come." He made a surprisingly graceful bow, which somehow seemed in contrast with his burly body. "Larissa's auntie got herself killed her last night and she wants to pay her respects. As it were." He gave Judith a plaintive look, then put out a big paw. "Donn Bobb Lima, rodeo clown and all-around auto mechanic. I'm here for the pea-rade."

Larissa Lima laughed again, recalling the raucous sounds of her late aunt. "Donn Bobb's from Texas, that's why he talks funny. You ought to hear him sing! Why, one time, we were at this bar in Galveston, he got up there behind the chicken wire where they can't hit you with the beer bottles, and some of the crowd . . ."

Donn Bobb gave Larissa a semigentle shove and came into the kitchen. "The livin' room, somebody said. You ladies found her, right?"

"Right," agreed Judith, leading the way. "It was my cousin, Mrs. Jones, actually . . ."

They had all arrived in the living room except Renie, who had decided to forage in the refrigerator. Judith stepped aside as Larissa knelt down beside the chalk outline of Leona Ogilvie's body. Sudden, convulsive sobs erupted from the young woman's throat. She threw herself at her husband and grabbed him around the knees.

"Oh! Poor Aunt Leona! Oh! She was so sweet! All those years with the pygmies, devoted to Jesus! I never knew a kinder or more fair-minded person in my whole life!" She sobbed some more while Donn Bobb absently patted her artificially-colored curls and yawned. "You gotta sing at the funeral, Donn Bobb! Her favorite was 'The Old Ragged Cross.' "

" 'Rugged,' " murmured Judith, but didn't expect either of the Limas to hear her. They didn't. Instead, Larissa climbed Donn Bobb's frame until she had gotten to her feet, then flopped down on the sofa, a hand over her eyes. Mascara oozed onto her cheeks. Renie ambled in, munching on a piece of toast smeared with strawberry jam about a half-inch thick.

"There's no ham in that refrigerator," she declared. "Did we eat it all?"

Judith gave her cousin an arch glance. "*You* did. This morning." She eased herself into the rocker. "Your aunt was a missionary, I hear. Brazil?"

Larissa nodded. Donn Bobb sat down next to his wife, twiddling his thick thumbs and looking decidedly uncomfortable. There were dark circles under his heavy-lidded brown eyes. Larissa ran a hand through her tousled hair, wiped at the streaks of mascara, and hitched one thumb in the belt loop of her cutoff jeans. "I hadn't seen her since she got back. Auntie left for the jungle over twenty years ago, when I was just a tot. It's lucky we got to see her at all—we only came to town Sunday, Donn Bobb having been on the circuit in Redmond and Klamath Falls and . . ." She screwed up her face, which would have been pretty had it not been so vacant. "Where were we, Hot Spurs?"

"Sublimity," replied Donn Bobb, who seemed barely able to keep awake, "but only 'cause the pickup broke down." He cast his heavy-lidded eyes at Judith. "I never met Auntie. Guess I missed one fine person. Larissa's done nothin' but talk about her since she found out she was dead as a bag of dirt."

Wincing at the simile, Judith considered offering her unexpected visitors coffee, thought better of it, and asked more questions instead. "I understand she was living down in the boathouse."

Larissa's eyes got wide again. "Oh, no! She was up at the house with Momma. The boathouse is an awful wreck. I remember playing down there when my brother and I were kids and it smelled so *awful*. Like seaweed. Ugh." Her voluptuous figure shuddered inside the tank top and cutoffs.

Judith wore her most innocent expression. "It's not half-bad, really. Decent furniture, clean, sort of cozy. A man named Titus Teacher has been living there for awhile, too."

Larissa wrinkled her nose. "Never heard of him. Maybe Momma hired him as a caretaker." The idea seemed to strike Larissa after the fact. She turned to Donn Bobb. "A caretaker! That makes sense, right, Passion Chaps?"

Donn Bobb roused himself from his somnolent state long enough to look puzzled. "Right, what?" He nudged her in the ribs. "Hey, Thunder Thighs, your auntie didn't bring some fella back with her, did she? I thought she was all religious and holy."

Larissa frowned. "She was. She didn't eat breakfast unless the Lord told her to make bacon or eggs."

"But no ham," remarked Renie. She glared at Judith. "Are we out of ham because Christ was a Jew or because these stupid stores in Buccaneer Beach are only open for two hours a day?"

The Limas gazed blankly at Renie. "Christ was a Christian," Larissa said with a knowing smile. "That's how it all got started."

Renie rolled her eyes and went back into the kitchen. Unlike Judith, she did not suffer fools gladly. Or at least with patience. More to the point, the refrigerator was not in the living room. Judith cast about for a leading question, but felt at a loss. The Limas weren't exactly a fount of information.

"You mentioned a brother?" she finally asked for want of a better line of inquiry.

Larissa blinked. The long eyelashes might not have been false but the smeared dark lines etched on her eyelids were. "My brother? Oh—Augie!" Her crimson mouth turned down. "He's a jerk. Do you know he came to town the other day from Idaho just to ask Momma for a loan? After all these years, not so much as a phone call let alone a visit to Momma, then he comes mooching around with his hand out. Why can't he get a real job like Donn Bobb? Augie keeps saying it's all because of the Eeeconnnomyyy." She spun the word out as if it were a joke.

Judith passed over Larissa's impression of national stability. "He's in Buccaneer Beach?"

Larissa batted her eyelashes again. "Augie? Oh—yes, at a motel up the highway. He and Momma had a big fight. Seven years since they seen each other—imagine! Then they squabble. Augie's wife is a snot. All she can think of is money. She never misses a chance to buy a lottery ticket, neither." Larissa sniffed as if such desperate attempts at fiscal security were beneath contempt. "If," she went on with a sly glance at Donn Bobb, "Augie and Amy could figure out what causes her to have babies, they might be able to save ten cents." Larissa aimed her bosom at Donn Bobb's upper arm. *"We* know, don't we, Italian Scallion?"

"Scallion?" echoed Renie, returning to the living room with a handful of carrot sticks and celery. "I should be so lucky. I could have made a salad. Say, coz," she said pointedly, "don't we have a *lunch date?*"

Judith looked up. "Ah—well, yes, I thought we'd drive up the highway to that log cabin place with the fresh trout." Renie beamed; Judith turned back to her guests. "I'm very sorry about your Aunt Leona. How is your mother taking it?"

Larissa frowned, then looked at her husband. "Oh—sad, wouldn't you say, Lethal Weapon? Donn Bobb doesn't know Momma real well. It's our first trip back home since we got married, so he just met her. But you have to figure," she went on as both Limas got to their feet, "she can't be happy her sister got murdered, right? But Momma isn't much for sharing her feelings. She's one to keep to herself, too much so, if you ask me. At least she's finally come out of her shell lately, even got a beau. After Auntie died, I told Momma to let loose and just wallow around in grief like a pig in a trough."

Donn Bobb was nodding—or nodding off. Even though he was standing up, it was hard for Judith to tell. His long sandy hair all but covered his face. "I gather your mother has been a widow for some time?" Judith inquired.

Larissa jostled her husband's arm, making him twitch a bit. "Oh, yes, my daddy's been gone quite a while. He passed on after I got out of high school and moved away. He got himself drowned when he was still pretty young. Well, fifty or so." She didn't notice the effect of her vague disclaimer on the cousins.

"Very young," asserted Judith with a steely smile. "I take it you're staying with your mother up at the family home?"

Larissa's eyes roamed about the ceiling. "Well—in a way. We're actually in the RV. We hauled it up behind the pickup. Along with the boat and the bikes."

The idea of so much rolling stock all on one highway made Judith's head spin. Feeling inadequate to the task, she tried to pin Larissa down. "It must be nice for your mother to have company. Evenings get particularly lonely when you live by yourself. Do you play cards?" she asked, almost gagging on the word.

"Cards?" Larissa glanced at Donn Bobb for help. None was forthcoming as Donn Bobb stared on. "No, none of us play. Like I said, Momma's not real sociable. That chubby ol' police chief must have done some powerful wooing to get her to go out with him. We just watch TV in the RV. Momma sews. Quiet, like."

"In the house?" Judith felt like gnashing her teeth.

Larissa burst into laughter. "Oh! What did I say? TV in the RV! Oh! A poem! And you said Momma in the house! She could be in the yard! Sewing! Oh!"

Judith leaned on the back of the rocker for support. "She could be, yes. And we must be . . . gone." With effort, she started herding the Limas toward the back door. "We're so sorry about your loss. Do give our condolences to your mother. And your brother. 'Bye."

Larissa's laughter reached even gustier proportions, like a tsunami rolling in from the ocean. *"Mother! Brother!* Oh, my, you are a caution! Thanks for making me laugh! I needed that! Donn Bobb says I'm too *serious!"*

Judith evinced amazement. "No! And all along I thought you were giddy!" Still maintaining an astonished expression, Judith firmly closed the door behind the Limas. She could have sworn she heard Donn Bobb snore.

SIX

"I'M NOT UP to this one," insisted Judith after the cousins had taken off like a shot in the MG. "You're right, these people are all nuts. Now we meet a loon with a baseball bat and a narcoleptic rodeo clown. What next, a tap-dancing tuna fish?"

Renie, finding herself en route to a restaurant, was in a less frazzled humor than Judith. "Give yourself a break, coz, it wasn't a complete bust. You found out there's a brother. And a wife. You learned that while Alice Hoke was with Chief Clooney, the Limas can probably alibi each other. Besides, they're too dumb to commit a murder. What we need is a suspect with an IQ higher than his or her body temperature."

Judith kept her eye on the road but her mind on Renie's words. "I don't know—it doesn't take a nuclear physicist to wring somebody's neck with a kite string. Titus Teacher doesn't have an alibi. And we don't know about Augie or Amy. 'Nearest and dearest,' that's what Joe said, remember?"

"Right, right." Renie settled back in the bucket seat. "What we need is a motive. If Leona was a missionary, she probably didn't have any money. I wish we knew who the young guy we saw her with was. He was just an out-line through the window."

"He was a blur to me," said Judith, picking up speed as they left Buccaneer Beach's city limits. "At least I under-stand old Jake Beezle's remark now. He said Alice Hoke never smiled, much less giggled. But Leona and Larissa certainly do. Did," she amended in reference to the de-ceased. Judith glanced over at Renie. "I wonder if Jake knew Leona?"

"Probably." Renie leaned forward as she spotted a log structure up ahead on the right. "You can interrogate him when we go to the hospital this afternoon. Is that the res-taurant?"

It was indeed Larsen's Log House, part of a complex that included a motel and a small gift shop, also built of logs. The parking lot, however, was full. Judith pulled in next door, which was another motel, but much older and in considerable disrepair. The sign that swung over the office entrance read "Anchors Aweigh Inn and Apartments—Weekly/Monthly Rates."

The rusting, battered car in the next space had Idaho plates. It also had two infant safety seats and many toys strewn about the ripped upholstery. Judith paused next to the MG. "We don't have a reservation," she noted with a gesture at the log cabin restaurant.

"So?" Renie blinked at her cousin. "Even I can wait."

"So do it," said Judith, trying not to look sly. "I've got to see a man about a murder. I think."

Renie finally noticed the car with its telltale plates. "Oh, coz, there must be a zillion people down here from Idaho. What makes you think this is Augie Hoke and Company?"

Judith lifted her hands. "The state of the car. The kiddie stuff. The motel up the highway, or so Larissa said. I could be wrong, sure, but as long as we're here . . ."

". . . I'm coming with you," interjected Renie. "This place looks a bit seedy to me. I don't want you to get caught in the middle of a drug bust. Joe would be really annoyed."

The fat man with a day-old beard behind the desk confirmed that a Mr. and Mrs. August Hoke were registered at Anchors Aweigh. He would not, however, give them the unit number or deliver a message until Judith explained that she was from the Oregon State Lottery Commission. Swatting at a pair of flies, the motel manager offered to get word to the Hokes.

"Tell them to ask for Mrs. Flynn over at Larsen's Log House. We'll be lunching there before we head back to Salem." Judith's eyes narrowed slightly, as if the threat of their departure were imminent.

The fib, Renie insisted, was the reason for the forty-five minute wait. "God is punishing you for such an outrage," she said as they cooled their heels in the reception area off the main dining room. "But why me? I never tell tall tales like you do."

"They're always in a good cause," replied Judith, on the defensive. "Besides, I didn't say they'd won the lottery, did I?"

Renie gave a slight shrug. "They'd know it if they had, I guess. Unless they're as dumb as Larissa and Donn Bobb. I don't know much about it—I haven't bought a lottery ticket at home in years."

"Dan used to buy them all the time," recalled Judith, as the aroma of fresh fish and baked bread wafted their way. "Remember the time he got five out of the six numbers and the dog ate the ticket?"

"Barely." Renie was distracted by the scent of food. Before she could comment further, the hostess beckoned to them just as a young, careworn couple came through the door. Judith heard the man ask for Mrs. Flynn. Allowing Renie to continue on into the dining room, she felt forced to invite the newcomers to join them. They looked as if they could use a good meal.

"The lottery?" Augie Hoke bore a passing resemblance to his sister, mainly because of his blond hair and blue eyes. But by comparison, he seemed lackluster, painfully thin, and extremely shy. His wife, also on the lean side, but with hair so dark it was almost blue, seemed chronically breathless.

"*Pottery,*" said Judith, leading the way and trying to find Renie in the crowded restaurant. Spotting her cousin hiding behind a menu, Judith made the introductions. "We're here in Buccaneer Beach to look for unusual pottery. We heard your family had some interesting heirlooms." Judith paused briefly and licked her lips. Renie was peering over the menu with a bemused expression, obviously watching closely to see how Judith would extricate herself from this monstrous prevarication which was growing like Topsy. "We—that is, my husband and I—rented your mother's beach cottage. But before I could call on her and inquire about the pottery, your poor aunt got killed. I certainly don't want to bother your mother at a time like this." Judith gave both Hokes her most sympathetic gaze.

Amy Hoke was giving her husband a puzzled look. "Pottery? Augie, does she mean that old blue stuff your mother has been using since she was a kid? It must be pre–World War II. Lu-Ray, isn't it?"

Augie stared off into space, though it was not the vacant expression of Donn Bobb Lima or even Larissa. "I guess. It belonged to my Grandpa and Grandma. Momma inherited almost everything, including the cheese factory." His long face sagged. "There wasn't much left, though, after the rat got hold of it and ran it into the ground." He pushed the menu aside and leaned toward Judith. "Then you aren't from the state lottery?"

Judith's black eyes widened innocently. "My, no. The motel manager must be a little hard of hearing. You're right though—Lu-Ray pottery can be quite a collector's item." The statement made her pause; another thought leapt to mind, then fled. Judith frowned. "Go ahead, order lunch. It's on us." She kicked Renie under the table.

With a show of minor reluctance, the Hokes complied. Amy requested only a small salad; Augie opted for oyster stew. Renie got both, along with the trout. Judith settled on halibut cheeks and cottage fries.

"So how are the children?" Judith asked airily.

The children—all five of them, as it turned out—were still in Idaho, staying with Amy's parents. Under Judith's artful probing, she learned that Augie worked in cement, which was seasonal at best, and nonexistent at worst. Amy was a candlemaker, probably not in great demand on a year-round basis. It was no wonder, Judith thought, that Augie, father of five, had come home to mother to ask for a loan.

"I hope," remarked Judith in midcourse, "that you got to see your aunt before she died."

Augie sighed over his empty oyster stew tureen. "Just once. We came up to the house—Momma's place—Sunday afternoon. Momma was going to fix dinner, but she got too tired. She's not used to company."

"It's been terrible for her," Amy put in, not making it quite clear if she blamed or pitied her mother-in-law, "to grieve for so long. Sometimes I think she waited alone in that house for seven years, like that lady in the poem, hoping Mr. Hoke would come back from the sea. Isn't it true that if you don't find a body, you can't declare somebody legally dead for seven years?"

Judith started to say that was true under certain circumstances, but Augie spoke first. "She never doubted he was dead. I think she used it as an excuse to avoid everybody. Even us. Momma never did like people much. Aunt Leona was more shy, but she had real love in her heart. She was sorry we didn't bring the kids. Auntie was crazy about kids. It's too bad she never had any of her own." His pale skin flushed slightly, as if he were embarrassed at having said so much to a stranger. But as ever, Judith's open countenance encouraged confidences. Augie looked away.

"She never married?" Judith's expression was bland.

It was Amy who answered in her breathless voice, "No. She spent her whole life devoted to missionary work."

Judith felt Renie nudge her under the table. "Do you have any idea who Titus Teacher is?"

Both the Hokes' faces were a void. "Who?" asked Amy.

Judith took a sip of coffee. "He's living in the boat-house. I thought he knew your aunt."

Augie and Amy continued to appear mystified. "Never heard of him," said Augie. "Aunt Leona was staying with Momma."

"Really," Judith responded. "And your sister and her husband were in the RV on your mother's property, right?"

Augie nodded as Amy made a face of disapproval, apparently caused by the mention of her in-laws. "Momma doesn't like guests. That's why we haven't come home for all these years. She'd keep writing and putting us off," Augie explained slowly. "I don't know how she put up with Aunt Leona for this past month. Or vice versa," he added with a dark look.

The check had arrived and Judith knew that the interview was rapidly drawing to a close. She felt as if she were getting nowhere. "At least you got to see Leona on Sunday," she said, trying not to be too transparent. "I still don't understand why she came back to Pirate's Lair last night. I mean, it isn't as if she were staying there."

Augie gave Amy an inquiring look. "Didn't Momma say she had some of her stuff stored in the boathouse? Maybe she went back to collect it."

Amy nodded, a languid, yet convincing gesture. "Augie's aunt loved the beach cottage. That's why Augie's granddaddy relented and left it to her." Briefly, her dark eyes sparkled. "Everything else went to Augie's mother. Not fair, I'd say, except it's none of my business. Everybody's family is different, I guess."

Judith tried to sift through this particular bit of information. "So Aunt Leona actually did own Pirate's Lair? Did she handle the rentals?"

Augie again looked vague. "She couldn't have, since she was gone for so many years. I suppose Momma did it for her." He gave Judith a sudden, sharp glance. "Oh—you mean now, after she came home. Maybe. It would have been her right. And fair's fair. I have to agree with Amy— the way the money got divvied up in this family wasn't exactly right. But then there wasn't as much left as there should have been, after ... all was said and done." He caught Amy's warning look and turned away.

"Done by the rat?" Judith asked guilelessly.

Augie colored again, offering his wife an apologetic nod of the head. "Yes—the rat. Race Doyle. Heck, Amy, everybody in this town knows what happened. Race botched up the cheese business and then made off with the money that was left and skipped town." His face froze in a portrait of resentment.

Amy sniffed. "He's probably been living on the Riviera ever since, chasing half-naked women. I can't believe his nephew had the nerve to come back here and practice law!"

Augie stared at Amy. "And that Momma still uses the firm! Just because Bartlett Doyle was the Ogilvie attorney for thirty years! Bart may not have been a crook like Race, but I wouldn't trust any Doyle an inch." He slumped in his chair, as if the uncustomary outburst had exhausted him.

"What happened to Bart?" asked Renie, now surfeited with tiny oysters and rainbow trout.

"Bart died," said Amy, as if it served him right. She took a deep breath. "He got run over by a logging truck last year."

Judith shuddered. She swiftly changed the subject, to when the Hokes were heading back for Idaho. After the funeral, according to Amy, which was scheduled for Friday morning. There was no point in staying on, Amy continued with a meaningful look at her husband, as long as Alice Hoke remained so *impossible*.

The restaurant was clearing out rapidly, and when Judith's offer of dessert was declined, even by Renie, it was obvious that the time for departure had come. Judith still hadn't found a tactful way to ask if the Hokes had an alibi for Tuesday night.

"This has been very generous of you," said Amy Hoke, getting up and smiling at the cousins in a wan sort of way. "We don't eat out much. It costs a lot with all the kids. I'm just sorry we don't know much about Alice's pottery."

"Oh, that's all right," Judith began, still racking her

brain for a subtle inquiry into the Hokes' whereabouts of the previous evening. "Maybe I can write a letter after I get . . ."

"I suppose," interrupted Renie, hoisting her huge hand-bag and pushing back her chair, "you've got an alibi for last night? We do." She gave the Hokes a big smile.

"An alibi?" echoed Augie, looking startled. "You mean . . ." He stared first at Renie, then at his wife. "Oh—well. I suppose that's routine, right?" His gaze shifted to Judith.

"You haven't talked to the police?" asked Judith. "Or the sheriff?"

"One—or both—left calls," offered Amy, brushing at the wrinkles in her faded denim dress. "But we haven't seen anybody yet." She took her husband's arm. "Actually, we went for a drive up the coast last night. We stopped at some place about ten o'clock for milk shakes." Amy gave Augie a tight little smile. "Didn't we have a nice time, honey?"

He petted her hand. "We sure did. No kids. Just us."

The cousins watched them head back for Anchors Aweigh. Renie stood with her fists on her hips, handbag swinging at her side. "They may not be nuts, but they're lying," she said flatly.

"Huh?"

Renie turned to Judith. "Milk shakes at ten o'clock? In this part of the world? Ha!" With a twitch of her backside, Renie stomped off toward the MG.

By coincidence, the law offices of Doyle, Doyle, and Diggs were adjacent to the *Buccaneer Beach Bugler,* right in the middle of town. Both buildings were low, long, and level on top. An insurance agency, a counseling service, and two dentists shared leases with the attorneys. Judith marched up to the receptionist's desk and asked to see Brent Doyle. Taking up the rear, Renie waited to see what colossal fib Judith would come up with this time.

"I don't have an appointment," Judith told the chestnut-haired young woman at the desk, "because I'm only in town for a few days. I want to see Mr. Doyle about suing a dune buggy."

The young woman didn't turn a chestnut hair. "Mr. Doyle is in a meeting," she responded with a chipped-tooth smile. "Will you wait?"

Judith glanced at her watch; it was after two o'clock. Joe wouldn't expect her back at the hospital until about four. "Yes," she agreed. The cousins took up places on a leather couch that was flanked by a large fern at one end and a philodendron at the other.

"You probably could sue," Renie whispered when the receptionist answered the phone.

"For what?" responded Judith. "Joe drove like a sailor on shore leave."

"The root," hissed Renie. "Didn't you say he hit a root?"

Judith gave Renie a disparaging look. "It was about the size of a small redwood. He should have seen it. *I* did."

Renie's further arguments were cut short by the opening of a door at the far side of the reception desk. A tall, angular woman stalked across the carpet with a sour expression on her face. Judith and Renie exchanged quick glances. The resemblance to Leona Ogilvie was sufficiently striking to let the cousins know they were in the presence of Alice Hoke.

"Carlene," intoned Alice Hoke, tapping the smooth surface of the desk for emphasis, "I shall need another appointment with Mr. Doyle in about a week after he sets up the new power of attorney. This is a convenient day and time. See to it, please." Without waiting for a reply, she swept out of the office. The cousins might as well have been part of the decor.

Carlene scribbled furiously, then picked up the phone and spoke softly, presumably to Brent Doyle. A moment later, she ushered Judith and Renie into the attorney's inner office.

Brent Doyle couldn't have been more than twenty-five, with a red-gold crew cut, a pug nose, and a deep tan that probably owed more to the electric beach than the Oregon sun. He had a hearty handshake, an expansive smile, and a rack of white teeth. Judith dropped the lawsuit and fell back on candor.

"That," she said after proper introductions had been made, "was my landlady, Alice Hoke. I'd never seen her before."

Brent Doyle grinned at both cousins. "Nobody sees much of her. She's a bit of a hermit. I've been away at law school for the past few years, but I heard she was getting to be a legend around here." He shoved back in his comfortable padded chair and adjusted the jacket of his well-tailored suit. "Now what's this about a dune buggy?"

"Skip the dune buggy," said Judith, taking in her surroundings which were stodgy in a 1950s wood and plastic style. No doubt Brent Doyle had inherited the office from his father. The son's outgoing manner didn't mesh with the father's pale green paint and trailing ivy planters. "My cousin and I found Leona Ogilvie's body in the beach cottage where we're staying. Naturally, we're a little nervous. Do you think we're safe?"

The grin faded slowly from Brent Doyle's wide face. He picked up a pen and twirled it in his slightly pudgy fingers. "Oh—who can say? It could have been a drug addict. Or a burglar. There are so many unstable people these days, even in a small town. How are the locks on the doors at Pirate's Lair?" He had become very much the lawyer, noncommittal, cautious, asking rather than answering questions.

Yet his query was not without merit. Judith tipped her head to one side. "The house wasn't broken into. We assumed Leona Ogilvie let her killer in. Or that the murderer was waiting for her."

"Ah." Doyle lifted red-gold eyebrows. "Well, I hear she was like that. Naive. Gullible. Poor woman." He shook his head and fiddled again with the pen.

"How is Alice Hoke taking it?" Judith asked, wondering if lawyers and doctors both took the same course in avoiding direct questions.

Doyle seemed to consider, his gaze transferred to the plastic-covered overhead light which was mercifully switched off on this partially sunny afternoon. "Mrs. Hoke is a strong person. She'll be all right." His voice was a trifle dry.

"I gather she and her sister really weren't close," Judith remarked. "Leona had been away for years, I'm told."

"That's true." Brent Doyle smiled again. "I never met the woman. She must have headed for South America before I was born." His square-shouldered shrug seemed to dismiss Leona Ogilvie's entire life.

Renie decided to end her role as stooge. "What ever happened to your uncle? The one who made off with the cheese money?"

Brent Doyle turned pale under his tan. "Where'd you hear that?" His grip on the pen tightened. "Say—what are you two here for? I thought it was something about a dune buggy. If you've got a lot of crazy questions, go ask the cops. I'm a lawyer, and I've only been in practice here about six weeks." An angry pulse throbbed along Doyle's jawline.

In reply, Judith whipped a copy of the lease out of her purse. "I want a receipt. Somebody stole the one Leona Ogilvie gave me. And I also want two free days' rent for the inconvenience of having found a corpse on the carpet. You can make the arrangements with Mrs. Hoke and let me know by tomorrow." Judith tapped the lease with a fingernail. "Make a copy, please. I want to keep the original."

Although startled by Judith's demand, Brent Doyle obviously found himself on ground he could tread legally. "The receipt should be no problem," he asserted. "It's hard to imagine how it got stolen. Are you sure you didn't lose it?" He stared at Judith as if she were a hostile witness.

Judith wasn't sure what had happened to the receipt, but she didn't intend to admit that to Brent Doyle. "It disappeared last night. About the same time Leona was killed." She let the implication sink in on the young attorney.

Doyle made a disparaging gesture with the pen. "That doesn't sound right. Of course I wouldn't know. I wasn't even in town. We had a law review reunion in Eugene and I didn't get back until this morning." It was Doyle's turn to let his words penetrate his visitors' brains.

Judith stood up and Renie followed suit. "Just make the copy and call me by tomorrow," said Judith. "If my husband is laid up longer than we expect, I'm going to have to stay on in Buccaneer Beach. I don't think it's out of line to ask for two free days rent after all we've been through. This town is dangerous."

"And inadequate," put in Renie. "Are the courts open all day or on an appointment-only basis?"

Mystified, Brent Doyle stared at Renie. Deciding to leave him in his baffled state, the cousins made their exit, but not before the receptionist had produced a copy of the lease. Judith and Renie were heading for the car when Terrence O'Toole came dashing out of the *Bugler*'s editorial office.

"Hey—it's me! Press!" He wildly waved a newspaper. "We put out an extra edition! You're in it! I got a byline—'By Terrence O'Toole, Staff Reporter!' Wowee! Want to see it?"

Resignedly, Judith took the paper from Terrence O'Toole. The sun had finally come out in full force and Judith suddenly felt too warm in her green leather jacket. The stop press contained four pages in all, featuring a banner headline blaring "LOCAL WOMAN MURDERED—Killer Kite Kayos Cheese Whiz's Daughter." A two-column picture of Leona, taken so long ago as to be virtually unrecognizable, stared out from under the bold type.

"Page two," said Terrence helpfully.

Judith flipped the paper open. Sure enough, there was the story, with Terrence O'Toole's byline in boldface type. "Gruesome Death Mars Tourists," read the double-decker headline, causing Judith less uncertainty than it might for other readers. "How about 'Tourists Marred by Gruesome Death'?" she suggested, but caught Terrence's rapt expression as he leaned over her shoulder and realized that it was too late for editorial comment. Which, the cousins recognized, was a shame, because the lurid account that fol-

lowed did nobody, including Terrence, any credit. Judith
and Renie came off sounding like a couple of hysterical
nincompoops. With a sigh, Judith folded the paper and
handed it back to the young reporter.

"Terrence," Judith began patiently, "is this your first
murder investigation?"

Terrence nodded vigorously. "Yes, I never expected to
have one so soon! Not here in Buccaneer Beach! How do
you like the part about wasted lives and forbearance in the
face of dire danger? Ghastly, huh?"

Judith goggled. "It sure is." She screwed up her face,
then recovered quickly. "Well, I like those parts better than
where you said we were swooning and our teeth were
chattering and we were clinging to each other like ...
'parasite vines on a cottonwood tree.' Gee, Terrence,
wherever did you get a simile like that?"

Terrence beamed, eyebrows dancing. "I took a creative
writing class. We did similes all the time." He handed the
paper back to Judith. "You keep it. A souvenir."

Judith stared at the *Bugler* as though it were a rabid
dog. "Okay ... Thanks. My mother will love it."

"I can get you more," he said, beginning to backpedal
toward the newspaper's entrance.

"That's okay," said Judith with a kindly smile. "We'll
manage." Warily, she watched Terrence try to get through
the *Bugler*'s door without opening it, smack himself in the
kisser, and finally reel inside.

"I'll never criticize the daily papers again," moaned
Renie. "When they say 'cub reporter,' is it because they're
un-*bear*-able? Or is that what Terrence really meant by our
for-*bear*-ance?" She started to laugh at her own awful
puns, then saw that Judith wasn't listening. She was, in
fact, clutching the newspaper to her bosom and shaking
her head.

"What is it, coz?" asked Renie, suddenly solicitous.
"Are you having heat stroke?"

"No," replied Judith in a faint voice, then swerved
around and headed for the car. "I just remembered something that's been bothering me ever since we were talking

about pottery with Augie and Amy." She yanked open the MG's door and gazed across the convertible roof at Renie. "Those dishes that were packed up in the carport? In newspaper?" She slapped the *Bugler* with one hand. "They weren't printed in Portuguese or Spanish, but German. No wonder those crates had a Lufthansa stamp! All that stuff didn't come from South America, but Europe!"

Over the top of the sports car, Renie's brown eyes were unblinking. "So?"

"So?" Judith frowned at her cousin, then sighed. "You're right. It doesn't mean much, does it?"

Renie tried to look sympathetic. "Not to me."

Discouraged, Judith got into the MG. Renie was right. For all she knew, the crates could belong to a neighbor. Even if they were the property of Leona Ogilvie, their European origins did not a murder solution make. Judith drove off into the sun and tried to draw some logical conclusions.

As so often happened in life, she was dealing with the illogical. But that didn't mean she was on the wrong track. At least she was on the right road, headed for Joe and possible enlightenment.

Or, hopefully, a hug.

SEVEN

BY LATE AFTERNOON, Joe was in a much better mood. He and Jake Beezle were watching an old John Ford Western and eating graham crackers. Judith's initial attempts at recounting her sleuthing efforts were rebuffed by Joe who seemed completely caught up in John Wayne's efforts to wipe out a lot of bad men wearing dirty shirts. Only at the commercial break did Judith finally capture Joe's full attention.

"A son, a daughter, two in-laws, the family lawyer, and a local lurker, huh?" sighed Joe, resignedly jotting names down on a napkin. He should have known better than to try to rein in Judith's curiosity. "Not a bad day's work. You even got a glimpse of Alice Hoke. How about an alibi for this Teacher creature?"

Judith shook her head. "I can't figure out where he fits in. I'm guessing those are Leona's clothes down in the boathouse closet. But Augie Hoke said his aunt was staying up at the big house with Alice." Twisting in her chair, Judith turned to Jake Beezle, who was pulling stray hairs out of his puny chest. "Mr. Beezle, did you know Leona Ogilvie before she went to Brazil?"

Jake's bright little eyes peered at Judith. "Brazil!" He made circles at his ears and waggled his head. "Where'd that fruit basket go, Flynn? I'll put some bananas on my bean and play Carmen Miranda, what do you say?"

Renie gazed interestedly around the room. "Fruit?"

"From Woody and the gang at homicide back home. Woody sent a deck of cards, too. I gave the basket to the rotund nurses." He grinned wickedly at Renie. "They need to keep up their strength for my back-rubs." The devilish green eyes now roamed in Judith's direction.

Judith, however, was not to be diverted. "As you were saying, Mr. Beezle?"

Jake looked momentarily surprised. "I was? Oh, yeah—Leona Ogilvie. Better looking than Alice, but there was a real resemblance. Neither of them were what I'd call babes, though. Too skinny for my taste." He gave Judith an appreciative leer. "I like women with meat on their bones. Otherwise, you shake 'em out with the sheets."

"But Alice married Mr. Hoke," Judith pointed out. "What was he like?"

Jake stopped examining his scrawny chest long enough to reflect. "Run-of-the-mill homely guy—perfect for Alice. He was a builder. Houses, mostly. He put up the one at the beach after he tore down an old tavern that had gone out of business in the Depression and just sat there for twenty years. Terrible waste of a good view." Beezle shrugged himself back into his hospital gown. "Bernie came a cropper when everything in this state went sour a few years back. He tried to start over with that resort deal at the beach, next to the cottage. I forget now, maybe he was in on it and then some Californians took over. Anyways, Bernie's share went toes up and so did he. Took his rowboat out one night and drowned himself. Or so everybody figured. Bernie couldn't take it—no gumption, I guess. That's when Alice started acting queer."

Judith considered Jake's recital. It seemed pretty straight-forward, except for one thing. "But she must have come out of her shell if she's seeing Chief Clooney."

Jake chortled. "Loony Clooney! He's almost as dumb—

and twice as ornery—as the sheriff, Josh Eldritch. I don't know nothing about Alice having the hots for Neil Clooney, but if it's so, they deserve each other. Whew!" He wiped at his wrinkled forehead as if the mere thought of a romance between Alice Hoke and the police chief was too much to bear.

Shifting cautiously among the pillows, Joe looked at his notes. "What about this Doyle clan, Jake? Did you know Race or his brother, Bart?"

"Sure." Jake reached for his water carafe, discovered he'd put his unlighted cigar in it, and rang for the nurse. "Bunglers, both of 'em. At least Race was. He took over managing the Ogilvie cheese factory after Alice's pa died about fifteen years ago and ran it into the ground. No business sense, bad choice on the family's part. Then Race took off with the money that was left. Guess he wrote himself a lot of fat checks before anybody caught on. Anyways, nobody ever heard from him again. Not even Bart. Or if Bart did, he never let on. It caused an awful stink in this town and got the police chief fired because the local yokels felt Race had made fools out of everybody in Buccaneer Beach, not just the Ogilvies. I suppose Race went to Mexico or one of them foreign hideout places. Alice was wilder than a mule caught in a barbed wire fence. So was Bernie." Jake's face suddenly lighted up. "It probably helped send him over the edge and out to sea in a pea green boat. Except it was blue. I remember when the Coast Guard found it washed up down past the lighthouse. Gruesome, huh?" He wiggled his sparse eyebrows at the trio of listeners.

Jake's account was interesting, but Judith didn't see how it shed much light on Leona's murder. "Was Race married?" she asked.

Jake rang again for the nurse. "Nope. Perennial bachelor, like me. Had an eye for the ladies, though." He leered at Judith and Renie. "Also like me. In fact, I recall that he courted Alice early on." He frowned. scratching at his head. "Or was it Leona? I forget. Anyways, everybody said later it was because of the cheese. It sure wasn't their shapes."

Renie, who had been leaning out the door trying in vain to get a nurse for Jake, popped back inside. "So how long has Race Doyle been gone?"

"Seven years," Jake answered promptly. "Same time I had my gall bladder out. You should have seen those stones! I had 'em made into a necklace for a cute little trick I was seeing down in Depoe Bay."

Joe was still studying his notes. His green eyes looked up from the napkin to Judith. "You're avoiding the local law enforcement folks. How come, Jude-girl?"

Judith and Renie exchanged ironic glances. "They didn't strike us as very cooperative, I guess. I got the feeling they spend more time wrangling with each other than trying to solve crimes."

Renie sat back down in the chair reserved for Jake's visitors. "Your bride was reluctant to tell them her groom is a homicide detective. I think she's afraid they'll arrest you for being out of your jurisdiction." She gave her cousin an amused look.

"I think they're out of their league," Judith declared a bit huffily. "I can't imagine either Clooney or Eldritch doing much more than arresting a few drunken tourists or breaking up a brawl among the local loggers."

Putting his notes aside, Joe leaned back in the bed as far as the ropes and pulleys would allow. "Oh—I don't know. Some of these small-town cops are pretty sharp when it comes right down to it. You might drop in on one—or both—of them and see what kind of background they've got on the victim. It would be smart to let them know you're still around."

If Judith and Renie were calling attention to themselves by meeting the various suspects, Joe figured the police and sheriff should know what they were up to in case they needed protection. He gestured at the napkin which rested on the side table between the hospital beds. Joe wanted to steer the cousins into safer channels. "The most important thing you're missing is information about Leona herself.

Except for a bunch of boxes and a wad of German news-papers, she strikes me as a mystery alive as well as dead."

Judith sat up straighter; her back was still a bit stiff. "Nobody will tell us anything except that she's been gone for over twenty years and was a dedicated missionary. Al-though," she continued in a speculative tone, "I have the feeling Titus Teacher knows more than he's willing to say, if only we could ever catch him when he isn't swinging that damned baseball bat. Alice Hoke must know some-thing about her sister, too."

"Maybe you should try some of the other, more disinter-ested locals," suggested Joe, who had just realized that Renie had discreetly turned off the TV. He glanced up at the blank screen. "Hey, what happened to the Duke?"

"What happened to the nurse?" demanded Jake Beezle just as Dr. Rolf Lundgren entered the room.

"I was just passing through," said the intern with a nod for the visitors. "One of the nurses said you rang before she had to go on break."

"Break!" squawked Jake. "Don't those fat broads ever do any *work*? What do they do, waddle off to the grocery store and load up a cart every hour on the hour?"

"Not in this town," murmured Renie.

"Say," said Jake, squinting up at the intern. "How old are you, sonny? Does you mother know you're out by yourself running around in a white coat?"

Dr. Lundgren's smile was amiable. "Don't worry, Mr. Beezle, I'm a graduate of the University of Oregon Med-ical School. Those nurses have a lot of responsibility. There are only three RNs on this floor for twenty-six pa-tients. Many of them require critical care."

Jake wasn't appeased. "Critical is right! It's critical that I don't die of thirst! Imagine, two blocks from the Pacific Ocean, and not a drop to drink!" He scooted sideways in the bed, peering around Dr. Lundgren. "Hey, toots, did you bring any today? The good stuff, I mean?"

Judith started to demur, but the intern interrupted with a request to examine Jake's dressing. As Dr. Lundgren pulled the curtain around Beezle's bed, Judith stood up.

"Okay," she agreed, taking Joe's hand, "maybe we should go see Clooney. Or Eldritch."

"Or both," chimed in Renie.

Joe gave a single nod. "Good." He looked up at the big clock next to the TV. "It's almost five now. You probably should wait until tomorrow." He gave Judith's hand a squeeze, then lowered his voice. "Thanks for not mentioning my job to those locals. I wouldn't want them coming around here asking for free advice and making me crazy."

Noting that the color was restored to Joe's cheeks and that the glint was back in his eyes, Judith melted. "I keep pestering you for advice," she said, her voice curiously thin. "Do I make you crazy?"

Joe put his other hand on her hip. "You sure do." His grin was deliciously off-center. "But I love it."

"Good," breathed Judith.

"Good-bye," called Renie.

"Good grief!" shouted Jake from behind the curtain. "This here medico can't be more than twelve years old! Somebody get me a grown-up doctor!"

Judith decided it was time for her to say good-bye, too.

Judith reached Arlene Rankers at Hillside Manor on the first ring. The B&B was full up as expected, reported Arlene. The guests were happy, the larder was well-stocked, and more reservations were coming in. Judith was not to worry. Everything was going beautifully. Except for the explosion.

"Explosion?" Judith rocked as if fifty pounds of dynamite had been set off under her own feet. "What explosion?"

"It's nothing," soothed Arlene as the teakettle whistled in the background. Fleetingly, Judith could picture her high-ceilinged kitchen with the old schoolhouse clock and the comfortable captain's chairs pulled around the maple table. And probably all in a smoking ruin, she thought as she waited for Arlene's explanation. "It was Dooley," Arlene went on, referring to the teenaged newspaper carrier whose family lived directly behind Hillside Manor.

"He and some friends went to the Indian reservation to get fireworks and they set some of them off early." There was a pause as Arlene spoke to someone away from the phone. Judith presumed it was a guest. Or the bomb squad.

"And?" Judith encouraged, now sitting down as Renie watched curiously from the sofa.

"What? Oh," Arlene continued, "it was one of those M14s or whatever they call them—our Kevin used to shoot them off when the Hungarians lived down the street, remember?"

Mercifully, Judith didn't. Kevin and the Hungarians must have shot their wad during her years on Thurlow Street with Dan McMonigle. For once, Judith was grateful to Dan for allowing them to be shipped off to the decaying neighborhood in the south end of town. "So what happened?" asked Judith, trying to keep calm.

"To the Hungarians? Don't you remember, they bought that roofing business and moved over to the Bluff not far from . . ."

"No, no, no," interrupted Judith, shaking the phone and wishing it were Arlene. "The explosion. What blew up?"

"Oh." Arlene sounded faintly bored. "Not much. Just part of the fence between you and Dooleys'. And a little bit of your toolshed."

Judith was aghast. "The toolshed?" She shuddered. The toolshed was the repository for Dan McMonigle's ashes. Judith had always meant to give her late husband's remains a proper burial, but never seemed to find the right moment. Before marrying Joe, she had vowed to take care of Dan as soon as she got back to town. "Which part of the toolshed?"

"Which part?" Arlene turned vague. "You mean east, west? I'm not sure . . . the part where there used to be a roof."

Judith clutched at her head. Alarmed, Renie came to her cousin's side. But Arlene was now speaking swiftly. "Don't you fuss about a thing. Carl says he and our boys can fix it in an afternoon. Mr. Dooley offered to help, too.

It was only part of the roof and everything inside seems just fine."

Then, thought Judith, so was Dan. She hoped. Taking a deep breath, she made a dazed attempt to count her blessings. "You're sure . . . ?" she began.

"Of course." Arlene chuckled. "Honestly, Judith, you worry so! Boys will be boys. The couple from Japan just loved it! They thought we did it to welcome them."

Like Hiroshima, Judith reflected darkly. But to be fair, the damage didn't sound particularly devastating. And Judith had no doubts that Arlene was being the perfect hostess. "Hopefully, we'll be back by the weekend," said Judith, "but Joe's doctors won't say anything definite until Saturday."

"I already told Serena I could stay on the extra days," insisted Arlene. "Heavens, it's no trouble; I'm right next door. Besides, I enjoy it."

Judith knew that was true. Over the years, Arlene had done her own share of catering, especially for parish events, and she was an excellent cook as well as a top-notch organizer. Judith decided that a minor explosion was a small price to pay for a week's vacation.

"I'll check back with you as soon as I talk to the doctors," said Judith, beginning to calm down. "Any questions you need to ask?" She doubted as much, since Arlene was justifiably self-sufficient.

Judith was correct. "Not a thing. I keep telling you, stop *fussing.* Just enjoy yourself. Say hello to Serena for me. And take care of Joe. I must run, I've got to find Sweetums."

An image of glinting yellow eyes and dirty orange fur slunk through Judith's mind's eye. "Where is the mangy little creep? Out eating birds?"

There was a slight pause. "Well, I don't know exactly. He's out somewhere, that's for sure."

The uncertain note in Arlene's voice jarred Judith. "You mean in the yard."

"Noooo," replied Arlene. "I would have found him by now if he were there."

Judith's recovery slipped a notch. "What do you mean? How long has he been gone?"

Another pause. "Let me see—since Sunday? Oh," she raced on blithely, "you know how independent cats are. The fireworks may have scared him. Pets don't like all that noise. I suppose the little dickens is hiding some place, waiting for the Fourth of July to be over. Take care, Judith, I'll see you soon." Arlene hung up.

Renie was considerably more sympathetic than Arlene, although she couldn't resist teasing Judith a little about Sweetums. "Sometimes I really don't think you despise that cat after all," she said, handing her cousin a stiff scotch. On the way home from the hospital, they had stopped at the liquor store and the grocery store to restock. To Renie's surprise, both had been open.

"I'd hate to lose him after all these years," admitted Judith. "I wonder if my insurance covers the toolshed."

"Well, your roof doesn't cover it any more," grinned Renie, hoisting her bourbon in a toast. "Cheers, coz. Here's to calling our mothers." Judith groaned.

Renie volunteered to do the phoning. But after finding the line busy on three attempts, the cousins decided to wait until after dinner. Since the weather had gotten so much warmer, they had agreed to build a fire and eat on the beach. Sitting in the living room at Pirate's Lair, Judith glanced down at the outline which was still etched on the carpet.

"We've got to clean that off," she said into her scotch. "It's a bit creepy."

"I'll do it," said Renie. "You get the corn and hot dogs and stuff ready to take to the beach."

Judith rustled about in the kitchen while Renie used some damp rags to remove the chalk marks on the rug. "Where's the vacuum?" she called as Judith came in from the carport with a stack of kindling—and a crumpled newspaper. "What's that, the Berlin *Gazette*?" inquired Renie.

"Not exactly," said Judith, setting down the kindling

and smoothing the paper on the counter. "It's from Liechtenstein. Remember Vaduz?"

Renie cast back through more than a quarter century of
memories to the three-month tour of Europe the cousins
had taken before their respective marriages. "I do, actually.
We went through there on our Eurail pass. It was somewhere around Austria. Or Italy."

"In between," said Judith. "This paper is dated May 10
of this year. If those boxes belonged to Leona Ogilvie,
why were they packed up in Liechtenstein and sent to this
country by Lufthansa? That's a long way from Brazil,
coz."

Renie, whose knowledge of German was only slightly
better than Judith's, stared at the columns of long, guttural
words. "Do you think Brazil is a lie?" she finally asked.

"A recent lie, maybe." Judith put the mangled newspaper into a wastebasket. "We should check with Lufthansa
to see when Leona flew with them last."

"She must have had a passport," said Renie. "Do you
suppose it's up at the family home with Alice?"

"Could be. Since Alice isn't grieving all over the place,
we ought to call on her before the funeral." Judith idly fingered the stop press edition of the *Bugler* which also reposed on the kitchen counter. "Tomorrow, maybe." She
glanced down at the big, bold headline. "Poor Leona. I
wonder if anyone is seriously grieving about her demise,
except Larissa?"

"Larissa always was too serious," Renie remarked facetiously, then slipped the newspaper out from under Judith's
hand. "Jeez, look at this layout! Even for a rush job, it's
offensive. And I don't mean the copy! This is an art direc-
tor's nightmare!" She turned to the back page and shook
her head. "It looks as if the only ad they could muster up
on such short notice was from the Freebooters' Festival
Committee. They're having a treasure hunt. Want to join
in?"

But Judith declined. "We've got our own hunt. For a
killer." She sounded unduly somber. "Come on, coz, let's

haul our goodies down to the beach. We need to get the fire started."

Fifteen minutes and many matches later, the driftwood finally caught. Judith and Renie sat on a big log and watched the waves roll onto the shore. The evening was clear, with the sun a great golden ball dangling over the ocean. Down the coast, on a rocky point beyond the bay, they could see a lighthouse. Three small boats were heading in, probably fishermen, seeking safe harbor in the marina.

The wind was down, so the kiteflyers had gone in, except for the curly-haired young man from the motel who was still trying to cope with his green dragon. Judith and Renie watched him struggle with the string, then race along the sand, pulling the kite behind him. It bobbed, sagged, and finally fell to the ground. The young man tried again, this time going in the opposite direction. The dragon lifted slightly, swooped, and came to rest about ten feet from the cousins.

"We gave up," Judith called to the frustrated kiteflyer. She didn't feel it was necessary to mention that part of the reason was because their kite's string had become a murder weapon.

"You're smart," the young man called back. "There's a knack to this, and I don't have it." He approached Judith and Renie, carefully reeling in his green dragon. "I paid fifty bucks for this thing. I feel gypped."

"It's very beautiful," said Judith, aware that the young man was quite good-looking, too. Tall, broad-shouldered, and narrow at the hip, his angular face was framed with auburn curls. Unlike Brent Doyle's, Judith felt certain that his tan was the real thing. "You must be a tourist, too. Haven't I seen you at the motel?" She motioned behind her, toward the Best Ever Over the Waves complex high above them on the bluff.

"Right," he said with a wide smile. His Spandex shorts revealed well-muscled thighs; his bare chest revealed everything. "Are you staying there, too?"

Judith realized she was staring and felt vaguely embar-

rassed. She was, after all, a sensible middle-aged woman.
And a new bride. With a husband in traction. Judith bit her
lip and concentrated on Renie, who was threading hot
dogs onto a stick. The mental images conjured up by
Renie and her wienies didn't help much.

"No," Judith finally answered, returning her gaze to the
young man and tilting her chin up in an effort at dignity.
"My cousin and I are staying at the beach cottage next
door, Pirate's Lair."

"Oh." The bright smile fled. Grasping the reel of his
kite, the young man began to backpedal. "Cute place. I've
seen it from my room. Have a nice evening." He all but
ran down the beach, the green dragon bobbing behind him.

"You *will* make friends," Renie murmured, placing the
corn on the cob near the fire's glowing embers. "Couldn't
we go someplace just once and not have you meeting and
greeting anybody who strolls within six feet of us?"

Judith wasn't listening to Renie's misanthropic diatribe.
"That's odd," she remarked, more to herself than to her
cousin. "He took off like a shot when I told him where we
were staying."

Putting two potatoes on another stick, Renie gave Judith
a wry look. "What's so odd about that? I'm not sure I'd
want to cozy up to a couple of strangers who found a
corpse in their living room. For all he knows, we done it."

Judith started to argue, then shut up. Renie was right.
Given the circumstances, they were as good a pair of suspects as anybody else around. Maybe even worse—if the
young man had read the special edition of the *Bugler,* they
were also a couple of idiots. Judith turned her attention to
keeping up the fire.

An hour later, the potatoes still weren't done. Renie suggested taking them up to the cottage and putting them in
the microwave. Or better yet, to avoid climbing the long
set of stairs, sneak into the boathouse and zap them there.

"We can't take a chance," said Judith. "Titus Teacher
may be in there, counting corduroy."

Renie agreed, and in the end, they simply ate the potatoes half-raw. Still, the food tasted delicious, enhanced

by the fresh salt air and the scent of smoking driftwood. Lazily, the cousins lounged on the log and watched the parade of beachwalkers pass by.

"We've still got to call our mothers," Judith said, glancing at her watch, which showed it was well after eight. The sun now hung low over the water, casting amber shadows on the waves. The lighthouse blinked in the gloaming, and a single ship traversed the far horizon. A freighter, Judith guessed, bound for California. Around the bay, above them on the bluff, windows began to glow as lights were switched on to ward off the coming of night.

Judith looked over at the boathouse, which was dark on the inside. She wondered about Titus Teacher. Surely the sheriff or the police chief must know who he was. Or at least Alice Hoke should. After all, she was the boathouse's legal owner.

Judith was about to say as much to Renie when they spotted two figures strolling down the beach, hand in hand. The woman was half a head taller than the man, but he was twice as wide. The cousins recognized Alice Hoke and Neil Clooney at once.

"Hey," whispered Judith, though the couple was still out of hearing range, given the crash of the incoming waves, "where do you suppose they're going?"

"Why don't you ask?" replied Renie archly. "Don't you want to be buddies with Chief Clooney and not-so-tiny Alice?"

"Sure do," replied Judith, awkwardly getting to her feet. "Let's go pass howdy."

"Let's just pass," muttered Renie, but as usual, she complied.

"Hi," shouted Judith, stepping directly in front of the couple. "It's us. Mrs. Flynn and Mrs. Jones. We cleaned up the carpet. Is that okay, Chief Clooney?"

Clooney, who was dressed in a plaid cotton shirt and khaki pants, scrutinized the cousins with a baleful eye. "Huh? Oh—the chalk outline. Sure, no problem. I meant to talk to you two today but you weren't around when I called this afternoon." He felt the pressure of his companion's hand and pulled her forward with uncharacteristic deference. "This is Alice Hoke. She's in mourning, so I'm giving her the air."

"And more," said Renie in her aging ingenue manner. "I mean, there's so much of it down here, right? The ocean and all." She waved one arm like a windmill.

Alice Hoke did not offer her hand. Up close, her thin face revealed a slit of a mouth, pale gray eyes, an aquiline nose that Judith figured could cut cardboard, and a sour expression. While she could see the resemblance to Leona, Judith wondered if Alice ever smiled, and if so, if the sisterly bond would have been even more striking. Alice's eyes had narrowed at Judith. "Your check hasn't bounced. Yet," she added with a squint.

Chief Clooney laughed and slapped Alice's bony shoulder. "Hey there, honey-bunny, stop kidding around! These ladies are okay, just got some Big City ideas."

"They got nerve," said Alice, puckering what little there was of her lips. "Mrs. Flynn here wants two days' free rent just because her stupid husband ruined a dune buggy. We don't do business like that in Buccaneer Beach, Mrs. Flynn. You get what you pay for. If you want to stay on, it'll cost you a hundred and fifty dollars a night."

Judith, whose best room at Hillside Manor went for eighty-five and included breakfast, aperitif, and hors d'oeuvres, gaped at Alice Hoke. "That's ridiculous! And don't call my husband stupid! If you must know, he's a pol . . ."

"Polish sausage salesman," broke in Renie, jabbing Judith in the back. "Say, Mrs. Hoke, you must have talked to Brent Doyle. Did you find that missing receipt?"

Renie's defensive maneuver caught Alice Hoke off-guard. "What receipt? I never issued one. I don't know anything about it."

"You should," replied Renie with a note of reproach. "That's the way we do business in the Big City."

Alice Hoke's long, homely face set like stone. "You're a pair of chiselers. Maybe worse. For all I know, you killed my poor sister!"

Renie's taunting turned to outrage, but Judith intervened before her cousin erupted. Judith had gotten her own temper under control. No matter how annoying Alice might be, a quarrel would serve no purpose. "Look—let's all take it easy. The last twenty-four hours have been pretty nerve-racking." She turned to Chief Clooney. "If you thought my cousin and I were under suspicion, I'm sure you would have questioned us by now, right, Chief?" Judith didn't wait for Clooney's assent, but looked back at Alice. "Truly, we're sorry for your loss. I've never had a sister—just my cousin here—but I can guess how hard it must be."

Alice's contemptuous gaze indicated she didn't think Renie could be any loss to anybody, but she didn't say as much out loud. "Indeed." Alice slipped her thin hand back through Clooney's arm. "Let me know when you plan to leave." She gave the police chief a little nudge and the two of them resumed their stroll.

Judith and Renie returned to the log. The fire was almost out and the sun was slipping down behind the edge of the world. Absently stirring the embers, Judith watched Alice and Clooney disappear into the dusk.

"I'm not sure she's going to let us in if we go see her tomorrow," Judith said with a sigh.

"She'd probably prefer we didn't go to the funeral, either." Renie, who was sitting cross-legged on the ground, picked up a handful of sand and let it trickle through her fingers.

"Right," agreed Judith.

"Drat," said Renie.

For a few moments, the only sound was of the incoming tide. Overhead, a half-moon dappled the water with silver beams. Judith and Renie looked up at the same time. They both grinned.

"What time is the funeral Friday?" asked Judith.

"I don't know, but there was an obituary in that special edition of the *Bugler.*" Renie chewed on her lower lip. "Dare we?"

Judith felt her conscience rise up only to be dashed by

her curiosity. "Everybody will be at the funeral. It could be our only chance."

Renie hugged her knees. "They should add 'Breaking and Entering' to the local tourist attractions."

Judith chuckled. "The main thing is not to get caught."

"We can always say we're looking for the receipt."

"True." Judith slid down behind the log and signaled for Renie to be silent. A few yards away, they could just make out two people coming from the opposite direction. Even though darkness was settling in, Judith recognized Alice Hoke. But the man who was limping at her side was not Chief Clooney.

It was Titus Teacher.

They went into the boathouse.

EIGHT

As EXPECTED, RENIE's mother answered the phone. She expressed dismay at having missed her daughter's earlier calls. "I talked to Mrs. Parker up the street for only a minute. And to Auntie Vance to thank her for the lovely chicken and noodles. Oh, and Ellen, in Nebraska. They got home safely this afternoon."

Renie was accustomed to her mother's marathon bouts on the telephone. Deborah Grover loved the phone as much as Gertrude Grover despised it. Now, with the sisters-in-law under the same roof, Renie wondered if her mother didn't use the instrument not only as a source of pleasure but as a shield to ward off Gertrude.

Patiently, Renie listened to her mother's account of Aunt Ellen and Uncle Win's airline adventures, Auntie Vance and Uncle Vince's problems with the ferry schedule, and Mrs. Parker's dilemma with her miniature poodle, Ignatz, which had suddenly become un–house-trained.

"People certainly have their troubles," commiserated Renie, with a glance at Judith who was checking the newspaper for the funeral times. The cousins had agreed not to worry their mothers by mentioning the murder. "Are you and Aunt Gertrude getting along okay?"

The slightest hesitation caused Renie to frown. "Well—yes. All things considered."

Renie could imagine what all those things actually were, which mainly meant Gertrude being Difficult. "Do you think Aunt Gertrude is . . . adjusting?"

Deb's voice tightened. "She's adjusting the thermostat right now. I honestly don't think we need to have it up to seventy-five when it's *almost eighty outdoors.*" Her voice rose as she spoke, presumably for Gertrude's benefit. "She adjusted the refrigerator, too. Our milk froze. Then she adjusted the bathroom scale. I've lost ten pounds. Now she's adjusting the floor lamp. Gertrude, do you mind, dear? I'd really like to keep the bulbs in their sockets."

Renie blanched. "Mom—call somebody and get up a card game for tomorrow. You know how much Aunt Gertrude loves to play cards. It's too bad your church group doesn't meet for bridge during the summer."

Deborah Grover sighed, a martyr's last breath before the fatal blow delivered in the name of heresy. "If I do, you know who will have to fix the snack. Even in my wheelchair, *some* people expect to get waited on."

"Yes, well . . ."

"But don't worry about *me,*" Deb went on. "It's not too much trouble. It's just that my hands get so sore from pushing the wheelchair. It bothers my back, too. And my bad hip."

"Maybe one of the other players could pick up . . ."

"I thought about calling Dr. Clapp and making an appointment for next week, but I don't know when you'll be home. Besides, I so hate to bother you. You're always so busy with your little drawings."

As ever, Deborah Grover's cavalier dismissal of her daughter's graphic design career rankled, but Renie was used to it. Despite the fact that Renie usually stopped by her mother's apartment once a day and called at least twice, Deborah still resented the fact that her daughter felt compelled to *work*. Or at least do something with her time that didn't involve her mother.

Renie kept a tight rein on her patience. "Go ahead, call the doctor. I'm sure I'll be back by next Wednesday."

"Wednesday!" wailed Deb. "That's a week from today! You'll miss the Fourth of July! Why do you have to be gone so *long*?"

"Because of Joe," Renie replied in reasonable tones. "It all depends on when the doctors will release him."

Aunt Deb expelled another sigh, beyond martyrdom. "I don't see why you have to stay there for over a week, Serena." She was beginning to sound a bit cross. "Judith is a grown woman, she can be on her own for a few days. It would do her good. At least," she added darkly, "she doesn't have to put up with her mother any more."

"Yes and no," said Renie faintly. "Speaking of Judith, I'll put her on so she can say hi to Aunt Gertrude, okay?"

Thus began the long winding down of the conversation between Renie and Aunt Deb, involving many reassurances of mutual love, promises of keeping safe, and fulsome wishes for a happy reunion. Out of breath and almost out of patience, Renie gratefully handed the phone to Judith.

"Well, you horse's behind, what do you want?" rasped Gertrude. "I don't have time to gab my head off on this stupid telephone. I've got to go fix the temperature on the hot water tank."

"Just checking in, Mother. Are you okay?" Judith winced.

"Okay? What does 'okay' mean? I'm a crippled old woman shipped out of my house like some foreign leftover in World War II. DPs, they called them. I figure it stood for Dopey People, because they couldn't find their way home. *I* know where my home is. But I guess I'm not welcome there any more. A fine thing; I might as well be living over a heating grate outside the public market." Gertrude snorted loudly.

"Mother," Judith began on a familiar weary note, "it was you who insisted you couldn't live with Joe. We even offered to get one of those new condos a block down on Plum Street and run the B&B by remote control." It had, in fact, been a fleeting idea, but the impracticality of living away from Hillside Manor had dashed the plan. So had the three-quarters of a million dollar price tag on the luxurious new residences.

"Bull," replied Gertrude. "When are you getting home? My glasses need adjusting."

"Why don't you try adjusting?" Judith snapped, and was immediately repentant. "Sorry, Mother, I'm kind of beat." Briefly, Judith considered telling Gertrude about the toolshed. And Sweetums. Maybe her mother already knew. If she didn't, it might be better to save the news until Judith could deliver it in person.

"Beat?" growled Gertrude. "From what? Lying half-naked in the sun and getting sand up your nose? Or do you have to keep running over to the hospital to hold that shanty Irishman's hand?"

"Mother . . ."

"Forget it, kiddo. You've made your bed, now you lie in it. Of course," she continued at her primmest, "that's all you ever really wanted to do in the first place with that wild Irish rogue."

"Mother . . ."

"Got to go. Deb's whining about sitting in the dark. Lord, how that woman can go on! I'm putting my ears in storage for the summer. G'bye." Gertrude slammed the phone down so hard that Judith jumped.

Renie was standing by the picture window, watching the moonlight dance on the ocean. "We could take assumed names and stay here forever," she mused, slowly turning to face Judith.

Judith was shaking her head. "They're a pair, coz." She stood up and stretched. Her back was definitely better, but still given to occasional twinges. "What did you just say?"

Renie looked blank. "Huh? Oh—about hiding from our mothers. A joke, right?" Renie didn't sound too sure.

"Right." Judith's tone was also uncertain, but it had nothing to do with Gertrude and Aunt Deb. Dismissing the elusive thought, she pointed to the copy of the *Bugler* lying on the coffee table. "The funeral is at ten o'clock, Friday, Buccaneer Beach All Souls Are Us First Covenant Church, Tenth Street and Ocean Drive."

Renie made a face. "I kind of hate to miss it. What do you bet the Wailers show up?"

"The what?"

"The Wailers." Renie perched on the rocking chair. "When Bill and I lived in Port Diablo, there was a bunch of women who came to every funeral whether they knew the deceased or not. They sat together in the back row and wailed. It was God-awful. Maybe they do that in other small towns, too."

"Jeez." Judith rolled her eyes. "Let's not get sidetracked. Why do you suppose Alice Hoke went to the boathouse with Titus Teacher?"

Renie yawned. "Is this a riddle? If not, then my guess is that she: a) owns the boathouse so why shouldn't she go there with or without Titus Teacher; or b) wanted to collect whatever Leona had left there." Renie gave a little shrug.

"What about c?" asked Judith.

"There is no c. It's too late for c. I'm heading for bed."

Renie was as good as her word. Judith noted that it was almost eleven and decided to follow suit. Lingering at the window for one last view of the ocean, she tried to plan their activities for the next day. Thursday. Perhaps Joe was right—they should tackle the police chief and the sheriff.

Yet Judith felt discouraged. True, a mere twenty-four hours had passed since Renie had stumbled across Leona Ogilvie's body. Joe had said that if a murderer weren't caught in forty-eight hours, the case often remained unsolved. Judith felt the pressure of that statement. But she and Renie couldn't search Alice Hoke's house until Friday. And even when they did, Judith wasn't sure what they expected to find.

Suddenly aware that she, too, was very tired, Judith staggered off to bed. The window was open and the sound of the waves lulled her to sleep. She dreamed not of murder most foul, but of her mother, adjusting the ocean so that it ran down the drain and left nothing but an empty beach littered with bifocals.

Renie had found lamb kidneys in the local grocery store. She was elated, since Falstaff's Market on Heraldsgate Hill rarely had them on hand. "These yokels probably don't appreciate a good grilled kidney for breakfast," said Renie happily over coffee.

"Gack," said Judith, "I can't think why not. How about frying up some goat gizzards?"

"Goats don't have gizzards," said Renie with an air of dignity. "I never understood why Grandpa Grover didn't teach you how to appreciate good English cooking."

"Because it doesn't exist," retorted Judith, going through the phone book to find the address of the sheriff's office. She already knew where the police department was located, having passed it several times on Highway 101.

An hour later, after a brief visit with Joe in the hospital, the cousins were asking to see Josh Eldritch. His headquarters was situated in a no-nonsense one-story building at the south end of Buccaneer Beach on a side street near the high school and next to a shingle mill. The aroma of sawdust and smoke was pleasing to a pair of native Pacific Northwesterners.

Eldritch didn't keep the cousins waiting long. He had them ushered into his crowded office after about a five-minute delay, and warily eyed them both.

"You know something we don't?" he asked abruptly after they'd sat down on the other side of his desk.

"Probably not," answered Judith. "That's why we're here. To see if we've picked up any information that might be helpful to you." She gave the sheriff her most beguiling smile.

The sunken blue eyes turned quizzical. "What kind of information?"

Judith grew diffident, and not without reason. In truth, she and Renie had gone over their small store of facts at breakfast and realized they had learned very little. But Josh Eldritch didn't need to know that. Yet.

"Leona Ogilvie's stay in Vaduz, for one thing," said Judith, hoping that her guess was correct. "Did she intend to settle here or go somewhere else?"

Eldritch's lantern jaw dropped a jot. "What? Where's Vaduz? California?"

"It's the capital of Liechtenstein," Judith said at her most self-deprecating. "You know—that little country wedged in between Switzerland and Austria. A lot of people go there for tax reasons—and other peculiar purposes."

It appeared to be news to Josh Eldritch. "Europe, huh?" He rubbed at his long chin. "I thought she was in Brazil." Catching himself, he waved a sinewy hand. "I mean, I didn't know she'd been traveling in other countries."

"Her passport must say so," Judith remarked, still diffident.

"Her passport." Eldritch cleared his throat and looked down at the cluttered surface of his metal desk. "Yeah, sure it would. Alice Hoke probably knows where it is."

"It wasn't with her other ID?" Judith asked innocently.

Eldritch looked up. "Uh . . . No. We didn't need to check ID. Clooney was pretty sure it was Leona, once the old goof gave it a thought. The Ogilvie sisters look a lot alike."

"That's true," said Renie suddenly. "Leona had no purse. At least I didn't see it the night of the murder."

Judith gave her cousin a sharp look. "You're right. But she did carry one, an eelskin bag. I wonder if she left it in the car." She turned back to the sheriff. "By the way, where was her car? I know she drove a Buick, but there was no sign of it Tuesday night."

"Clooney's men found it parked up above the cul-de-sac, on 101," Eldritch said grudgingly. "She must have left it there and walked down. It was only about a block away."

"And her purse?" Judith asked encouragingly.

Eldritch waved his hand again, this time in impatience. "Don't ask me, I wasn't there. If you think Neil Clooney is going to share any information with us, you're dead wrong. What's her purse got to do with it anyway?"

"The passport. It might have been in there." Judith kept her tone amiable.

Eldritch pushed back from his desk, stretching out his long legs. "So what? She could have come from Timbuktu for all I care. What's that got to do with her getting killed?"

Judith had to admit she didn't know. "It just seems odd, since she let on she was in Brazil for twenty-odd years. It's even more odd that she also let on to me that she was her sister." Keeping her gaze fixed on Eldritch's long face, she let the words sink in.

"The woman was daffy," declared Eldritch. "Alice didn't think Leona was fit to let loose. It's a wonder Leona didn't think she was the Queen of Sheba or some damned thing." He pulled the chair back toward the desk and rested his arms on a stack of paperwork. "Look, this is probably just your typical screwball killing, some guy on drugs who wandered in from the highway looking for money and Leona Ogilvie happened to be in the wrong place at the wrong time. I don't go for Clooney's dumb-assed theory about buried treasure."

The sheriff's phone rang; he picked it up and asked the caller to hold. The request was obviously a signal for the cousins to be gone. He allowed them a parting shot of information. "Yeah, buried treasure. Every year we go through this with a hoked-up hunt put on by the Chamber of Commerce and some service organizations. And every year some crazy fool gets the idea that he can find a chest full of gold and jewels left over by the Spanish three hundred years ago. It's a bunch of crap, but people are gullible as hell. If it were a crime, I'd haul them in." He turned away and spoke into the phone. "Yeah—who's picking off seagulls with an AK-47?"

The cousins trudged out of the sheriff's office. "What now? Clooney?" Renie shielded her eyes from the bright morning sun. The forecast for the Oregon coast was a high of eighty-one. Summer appeared to have blown in on the western winds.

"I guess." Judith stood by the MG and surveyed the sawmill's dark dome through a stand of Douglas fir. "At least we can ask him about the buried treasure."

"That sounds like a crock to me," said Renie, getting into the sports car. "I'm with Eldritch on that one."

Judith figured her cousin was right, but having called on half of the local law enforcement chiefs, she felt obligated to talk to the other, too. Neil Clooney, however, was out. One of his subordinates told Judith and Renie that his boss wasn't expected back until just before lunch.

Out in the parking lot, Judith scanned Buccaneer Beach's main street. The police department was two blocks from the newspaper office. "We could ask Terrence O'Toole about the treasure hunt except that I don't think I can stand his feverish excitement."

"We could ask Neil Clooney," said Renie, pointing across the highway. "Isn't that him going into the coffee shop?"

It was. The cousins waited for a break in the almost endless traffic, then ran for their lives. By the time they reached the restaurant, which was built in the shape of a giant oyster shell, Clooney was already at the counter, teasing the pretty redhead who was serving him coffee and a sweet roll.

Judith and Renie climbed up on the empty stools on each side of the police chief. He evinced surprise, with just a touch of irritation. "I'm taking a break," he said, pointing to a clock with a picture of Elvis that hung above the confectionery cabinet. Elvis's arms showed that it was not quite eleven.

"So are we," said Judith. "Say, Chief, tell us about this treasure hunt. Is there really something buried from way back when?"

Clooney stuffed a chunk of sweet roll into his mouth. "Could be." His words were muffled as he chewed lustily. "There were pirates around here, that's for sure. But nobody's ever found any treasure." He washed the roll down with a big swig of coffee. "Lord knows they've dug up most of the beach from one end of town to the other and then some."

Judith accepted a white mug of coffee and let Renie tear apart an elephant ear for sharing. The cinnamon- and sugar-covered coil was about a foot in diameter. Judith hoped it tasted as good as it looked.

"It's interesting though," remarked Judith. "Especially your theory. Or did the sheriff get it wrong?" She sampled the elephant ear; it wasn't up to Begelman's Bakery's standards on Heraldsgate Hill, but it was pretty tasty.

"My theory? If you heard it from that moron, Eldritch, it's probably all screwed up." Clooney finished his sweet roll and waited for the redhead to pour more coffee. He gave her his most seductive smile. She gave him the cream. "I suppose our lamebrained sheriff is trying to steal my ideas. Again. My guess is that some nut was looking for the treasure and Leona got in his way. It's that time of year." He wiped off his mouth with a rumpled napkin. "There've been a lot of rumors over the years. A couple of them pinpointed the area around Pirate's Lair. The beach, I mean. There were supposed to be secret caves or passages or some damned thing where the pirates hid out. But when the resort was built and later, when the motel went up, nobody found anything. I figure it's all a bunch of hooey. If there's any treasure, it's probably someplace else." He drank more coffee, then tossed the napkin on the counter.

"But," persisted Renie, "people still believe in the tales?"

"Sure," said Clooney, swiveling on the stool and barely managing to steer his bulk between the cousins. "People will believe anything, especially when money's involved. Then they have this Freebooters' Festival and treasure hunt and all the old stories get trotted out again. Midsummer madness, I call it. Happens every year."

"But murder doesn't," Judith said quietly.

Clooney's small eyes got smaller. "No. You're right. It looks to me as if somebody got carried away this time."

He stood up and put a dollar bill on the counter. "Hey, Janice," he called to the redhead, "that's for you. I'll make it a five if you can bake me a sweet roll like Alice does."

"Alice bakes as well as sews?" Having latched onto the police chief, Judith was loath to let him go. "She sounds very accomplished."

Clooney nodded in agreement. "You bet. She can make just about anything out of cheese. But her sweet rolls are tops. Night before last, she put frosting *and* brown sugar on top. Mm—mmm." He closed his eyes at the delicious memory.

Renie looked up from her coffee. "That was the night of the murder?" She shivered. "Sorry—it just seems so strange. You and Alice were eating fresh-baked goodies while poor Leona was getting strangled. Life's full of ironies, isn't it?"

Clooney was quick to agree. "You bet it is. Hell, we weren't that far away when it happened. I almost wanted to turn in my badge when I got the call after I took Alice home. It made me feel like a sap to have a homicide so close." He wagged a stubby finger at the cousins. "But don't go telling Josh Eldritch I said so."

Judith's expression was puzzled. "When you took her home? Where was she doing all this baking?"

Clooney plopped his regulation cap on his heat. "At the boathouse." He winked. "We wanted to get away from Leona and Larissa and Billy Bobb Donn or whoever he is. Those goofy kids of hers kept tramping inside from the RV to use the bathroom. There's no hookup in Alice's yard."

Judith's puzzlement deepened. "I thought Titus Teacher lived in the boathouse."

Clooney gave a shrug of his burly shoulders. "That screwball? He comes and goes. I can't think why Alice let him stay there in the first place. If you ask me, he's a common vagrant. And a moocher. I guess she wanted to have somebody around to watch things during the tourist season." He looked up at the Elvis clock. "Hey—got to run. It's almost time for lunch." The police chief trotted out of the coffee shop. Apparently he wasn't required to pay a bill.

Judith gave Renie the rest of her elephant ear. "This case is a bollix," she declared. "What kind of procedures are these people using? There's no cooperation between the two agencies, and for all we know, they're putting obstacles in each other's way. They don't have any ID for Leona, they don't know who Titus Teacher is, and now Chief Clooney tells us he was a stone's throw away from the murder, stuffing himself with Alice Hoke's brown sugar buns."

"I'm sure he was," said Renie with a faint leer. "Why can't you get Joe to ask Woody Price to run these people through the computer at home? We might at least find out if they really exist. I'm beginning to feel as if I'm leading a rich fantasy life."

"Getting Woody in on this isn't a bad idea," agreed Judith. "Let's go back to the hospital and talk to Joe. I'm not hungry for lunch after eating that elephant ear."

For once, Renie didn't protest. The cousins drove up 101, noting that there were more banners, bunting, and reader boards in honor of the upcoming festivities. The brightly colored pennants which hung on every light standard gave the town a cheerful air. Given the death of Leona Ogilvie, Judith felt that a black wreath on City Hall might have been more appropriate.

Joe was surprised to see his wife and cousin-in-law so early in the afternoon. He was watching the noon news and eating some kind of food. It was, Judith noted, impossible to identify the little white and yellow mounds that adorned his tray. Jake Beezle, however, said it was pig slop.

"Back in forty-seven, I worked in a packinghouse in Portland. Those pigs weren't killed; they died from eating this stuff. Do you know I get to go home Saturday?"

Judith congratulated him. Fleetingly, she wondered where home was for Jake Beezle. Visions of a shingle-covered shack somewhere up in the woods crossed her mind. But no doubt Jake would be glad to be out of the hospital, no matter how lowly his real abode might be.

Eyeing his lunch suspiciously, Joe considered Judith's request. "Woody won't come up with anything unless these people have a record. Do you think Leona is a criminal?"

"I wasn't thinking of your regular data base," said Judith. "Doesn't Woody have access to Customs and Immigration information? Or even Social Security?"

Joe gave Judith a withering look. "In other words, you want poor Woody to exert every possible effort in tracking down this bunch of loonies?" Joe sighed. He was bored stiff, but that was no reason to tax Woody's patience. On the other hand, he and Judith had been married less than a week. She was probably bored, too. Or would be, if she didn't have a murder case to solve. At least her request kept her at a safe distance from the murderer. "I'll ask," he finally conceded. "If he's tied up on other stuff, we'll have to skip it."

Judith sprang out of the chair and bestowed a loud kiss on Joe's cheek. "Great! Renie and I are going to go lurk around the boathouse. We're convinced Titus Teacher knows more than he's telling us."

"He hasn't told you anything," said Joe. "Are you sure you want to skip the funeral?"

Judith and Renie hadn't confided in Joe about their plan to search Alice Hoke's house, but they had said they didn't think there was any point in attending Leona's services. Joe's remark gave Judith pause. "You mean we might learn something?"

Joe gave a little shrug. "I always send a man to the funeral of a homicide victim. If nothing else, you can watch how the survivors react."

Judith gazed at Renie. "Well . . ."

Renie grabbed Judith's arm. "It's okay, coz," she whispered. "They'll all have to go out to the cemetery for the interment. That'll still give us time to search Alice's house."

Joe was giving the cousins an alert, inquiring look.

"What's up? Did you say something about 'search Alice's house'?"

Caught off-guard, Judith rallied quickly. "Renie said 'Sir Charles' Souse.' It's an English-style pub down the road with terrific watercress sandwiches."

"Sounds tasty," said Joe, the green eyes narrowing. "Make sure you keep a watch out for the footman."

"Sure, Joe," said Judith brightly. In her haste to get away, she practically fell over Renie. "Actually, we're going to have the Ploughman's Platter."

"Actually," responded Joe with a stern gleam in his green eyes, "you're not. But don't say I didn't warn you."

Renie was already headed for the elevator. With a feeble wave and a frozen smile, Judith slunk out the door.

NINE

IT WAS ALMOST one o'clock when the cousins returned to Pirate's Lair to head for the beach. They agreed on a late lunch, and after the English pub prevarication, decided that foreign food sounded like a good idea for dinner. After a brief scan of the telephone directory, they made reservations for eight o'clock at a small French restaurant five miles out of town.

Judith was applying sunscreen when Renie called to her from the living room, "Hey, coz—this stupid chalk still isn't out of the rug. It's harder to remove than the sand. Alice Hoke is the type who'll charge us for damages if we don't clean it right. Have you got any 409 around here?"

Judith emerged from the bedroom. Renie was right—in the bright light of day, a faint outline of chalk still showed on the carpet. "Just scrub it with soap and water," said Judith. "I didn't see any heavy-duty cleaners in the cupboard."

Renie complied, using her usual brisk energy to remove the last vestiges of the crime scene markings. The chalk was finally gone, but the rug looked limp. "I got it too wet," she lamented. "Maybe I should put something underneath so it doesn't leave a water stain on the hardwood floor."

Judith went into the bathroom to fetch some towels. "Stick these under the carpet to protect the wood. Don't worry, it's so warm today that it'll dry out by night."

Renie pulled up the carpet, only to discover that instead of padding, layers of old newspaper had been used for protection. The single sheets were soggy. She tugged a handful out from under the rug and tossed them on the hearth. "At least they're in English," she said, pushing a couple of towels under the rug.

Judith gazed down at the yellowing papers. "Old copies of the *Bugler*. From 1983. The high school basketball team came in second in the state tournament."

Renie stood up, brushing lint off the skirt of her cotton sundress. "Hooray for Buccaneer Beach. Let's go look for Titus Teacher so that we can then go look for lunch."

But Judith was still bending over, perusing the old newspapers. "Hey, coz—look! It's a story about Race Doyle! 'Big Cheese Does Big Bunk.' "

Renie leaned over Judith's shoulder. "There's a photo. Is that him?"

According to the cutline, it was. Judging from the sunglasses, open-necked shirt, gold chains, long sideburns, and drooping mustache, the picture probably had been taken circa 1970. Race Doyle looked like a fugitive from a psychedelic freak show.

Judith and Renie flopped down on the sofa. " 'Local law enforcement officials are still on the lookout for Race Doyle, Ogilvie Cheese Factory manager, who left town abruptly after the company's closure last week,' " Judith read aloud. " 'Doyle, who had taken over his post from the factory's founder, the late Angus Ogilvie, is suspected of absconding with as much as three million dollars of the company's holdings. Family members have accused Doyle of making several large checks out to himself in a dummy bank account.' " Judith emitted a hiss that was intended to be a whistle. " 'Rumors of bankruptcy had circled around

Buccaneer Beach for the past two months, but attorneys for the cheese company, including Doyle's brother, Bart, of Doyle and Diggs, insisted that the firm was merely in the process of reorganization. Founded by . . .' " Judith stopped reading. "This is all background stuff, about Angus and the cheddar and all that." She swiftly read through the ensuing paragraphs. Only the final sentences recaptured her full attention. "Hey—listen to this—'Bernard Hoke, local builder and son-in-law of the late Angus Ogilvie, claimed that he and Doyle got into a fistfight in the cheese factory parking lot. Hoke said that after exchanging blows, Doyle started to run off, but he (Hoke) jumped into his car and ran the other man down. Before Hoke could get out and collar Doyle, he (Doyle) disappeared under the parking lot fence.' "

Renie looked bemused. "Except for the pronouns, it's a lot better written than Terrence's stuff. I suppose Doyle never showed up again after that."

"We could find out by going through other copies of the *Bugler* at the newspaper office," said Judith. "But what would they tell us? We're not looking for Race Doyle. Or," she wondered, "are we?"

"Probably not," admitted Renie, taking the damp old newspaper from Judith and giving it a shake to get a better look at Race Doyle's twenty-year-old photograph. She gave a little start as another piece of paper became disengaged from the back of the *Bugler* and fluttered to the floor. "What's that?" She bent down to pick up a four-inch scrap.

If the *Bugler* looked old, this snippet was ancient. Carefully, Judith fingered the fragment which appeared to be parchment. "It's a map," she said in an awed voice. "Good heavens, it looks like . . ." Suddenly silent, she held the bedraggled paper in front of Renie. "Incredible! I swear it's a treasure map!"

Renie fingered the torn edge. "That's absurd! But you're right—look, it says . . . gee, this is hard to read, the printing is so old-fashioned . . . but something about so

many paces and . . . a rock." She stared at Judith. "Is there
a magnifying glass around here?"

Judith didn't know. At least she hadn't seen one. They
checked the desk in the corner of the living room and the
bureau in the spare bedroom. "We'll have to get one," said
Judith. "We can run up to the mall after we get back from
the beach." She went into the kitchen, got a plastic sand-
wich bag from a box under the sink, and slipped the fragment of map inside. "I'll keep it in my purse," she said.
"How do you suppose it got under the rug?"

Renie shook her head. "It's impossible to know, except
that it's obviously been there for ten years. Maybe more—
the newspapers might have been replaced somewhere
along the way. When was this cottage put up?"

Judith furrowed her brow. "Thirty, forty years ago? I
can't remember exactly when Jake said Bernie Hoke built
it. But the map itself could date from the early seventeenth
century. If," she added, having sudden doubts, "it's au-
thentic."

"We could get it carbon-dated," said Renie, excitedly.

Judith arched her eyebrows. "In this town? We'll have
to rely on our hunches. Come on, let's go down to the
beach and look for Titus."

Titus, however, was nowhere to be seen. The cousins
even risked his wrath by knocking on the boathouse door.
They did not, however, have the nerve to venture inside.
After almost an hour, they were about to give up when
they heard their names called across the sands.

Judith turned, squinting against the sun. Augie and Amy
Hoke were heading their way, walking with slow, almost
painful steps. As they drew closer, Judith noted that Amy's
eyes were wet with tears. Augie helped his wife sit down
on the log the cousins had used for their picnic the previous evening.

"What's wrong?" asked Judith, her innate compassion
written large on her face.

Amy gave Augie a quick glance of warning. He
squeezed her hand. "It's okay, Amy. You have a right to be
upset. Especially with a new baby coming."

Judith glanced down at Amy, who looked rail-thin in her worn denim shorts and faded tank top. It appeared she wasn't far along with the pregnancy. Judith's sympathetic nature motivated her to ask the Hokes if they'd like to come up to the beach cottage for a glass of lemonade.

Amy eyed the long flight of steps with apprehension. "I'll be okay. I'd rather walk up the road past the motel than take all those stairs just now."

Judith understood. During her clam-digging expedition, she had seen the dirt road that led up from the beach past a big new home with solar heating and a large deck that looked as if it had a hot tub.

"You sure you want to walk that far?" Augie inquired solicitously. "It's almost half a mile."

"No, it isn't." Amy's thin shoulders were hunched together as she dabbed at her eyes with a Kleenex. "We've already walked a lot farther coming from the other way." She looked up at Judith and Renie, attempting a pathetic smile. "I'm sorry I'm such a mess. It's been kind of a rough day and I always get weepy the first couple of months that I'm pregnant."

"It can't be easy coming to Buccaneer Beach and having a family member get killed," said Judith, joining Amy on the log. "Once the funeral is over tomorrow, you'll have the worst of it behind you."

Amy started to cry again. Augie clumsily patted her shoulder and made soothing noises. "Come on, Amy, we never really counted on anything. Besides," he said bending down closer to her ear, "if Aunt Leona were still alive, we'd be right back where we started from."

"But we are anyway!" wailed Amy, grasping at her husband's arm. "Don't you see, the only good part of her dying like that would have been if she'd really left us the ..." Amy caught herself, and turned to Judith. "Oh, dear, I sound so awful! It's just that it's so hard being broke all the time. Kids are the most wonderful thing in the world, but they do cost money."

"They sure do," agreed Renie. "I'm still trying to figure out how you can put so much money into college tuition to educate them and make them independent so they can become mature adults with dependent laundry. Then they bitch about Mom shrinking their clothes and turning them gray. So they buy new ones—with Mom and Dad's money, because it was Mom's fault in the first place and Mom feels guilty. They tell her she's given a whole new meaning to the term 'small clothes.' And what she tells them isn't . . ."

Recognizing one of Renie's favorite tangents, Judith broke in, "I think Amy means when they're still little children, coz. Basics, like food and shelter, right?"

Amy nodded vigorously. "I didn't even think we could afford to drive over to Buccaneer Beach, especially since Augie's mother is so selfish about not letting us stay with her. After all, this is the first time we've made the trip since Augie's dad died. It's not as if we keep popping in and out, dragging the kids along, too. His momma just doesn't like people, not even her own family." Catching her husband's pained expression, Amy dabbed at her tears and waved a finger at him. "You know I'm right, Augie. Your mother is a good woman in her way, but she's heedless of others. I didn't know Aunt Leona really, but she seemed much more gracious. That's why Brent Doyle's news came as such a shock."

Augie Hoke gave Judith and Renie an apologetic look. "We don't mean to bother you with our troubles. Heck, our family has already given you a bad time. Not," he added quickly, "that Aunt Leona could help getting killed, I guess."

Judith, whose sympathy for Amy had motivated a half-hearted effort not to pry, cast discretion aside. "Lawyers usually try to be the soul of tact. What did Brent Doyle say to upset you so badly?"

The Hokes exchanged faintly furtive looks. Then Amy gave a toss of her long black hair. "It won't be a secret long in this town. It's a good thing people in Pocatello don't gossip so," she declared, as if challenging Augie to disagree with her. "Mr. Doyle read Aunt Leona's will this afternoon. We always understood she'd leave what she had to us and that silly Larissa." Amy waved her finger again. "Now don't go defending your sister, Augie, you know she doesn't have the brains of a bug."

"She *is* kind of flighty," Augie murmured.

Judith waited to speak until a trio pedaling beach cycles whipped past, using their legs instead of the nonexistent wind. "I didn't realize your aunt had much of her own. Being a missionary, that is."

Augie finally sat down on the other side of Amy. Renie, who was tired of standing in the hot sun, plopped down on the sand in front of the others. Augie leaned around his wife to address Judith. "My granddaddy was an atheist. He didn't approve of Aunt Leona's religion or her missionary work, so he cut her out of his will. Except for the beach cottage. I guess he didn't want her to be dependent on Alice for money."

"So actually Leona *was* our landlady," said Judith.

Amy answered this time. "It was arranged that as long as Aunt Leona was out of the country saving souls, Augie's mother would have charge of Pirate's Lair and any profits made through rentals. But Alice couldn't sell the cottage unless Leona died without a will. Alice got the cheese factory, of course, but except for the land, it turned out to be worthless because of that manager who ran off with all the money."

"What happened to the land and the factory?" asked Renie, as a lazy kite drifted high above her head and fell to earth nearby.

"Momma sold that off a few years ago. That's where they built the outlet mall," said Augie.

"Hmmm," mused Judith. "She must have gotten a good price for it. That's prime property, right on 101."

"She did. Even in Buccaneer Beach, real estate prices weren't that cheap four years ago." Augie's tone was bitter. "That's why I thought she wouldn't begrudge us a few hundred dollars. But she does." He picked up a small piece of driftwood and gave it an angry toss.

"All along," Amy explained, pushing the long dark hair off her pale face, "we were told that Aunt Leona would

leave the beach cottage to us and to Larissa and Donn
Bobb. Of course we didn't expect her to die so young, but
we thought she'd come home some day and sell it, since
most of that stretch of waterfront is commercial now. Then
maybe we'd get sort of ... an advance, to help us out
while the kids were little and we needed it most." Amy's
downcast expression indicated that things hadn't worked
out that way.

"So she never made out a will in your favor?" asked Judith.

Amy nodded slowly. "Yes, she did. Years ago, while she
was still in Brazil. But after she came back to Buccaneer
Beach, she had Brent Doyle write a new version." Her
face crumpled as she looked at Augie and held his hand.
"She left everything to some man we've never heard of!
Imagine! It's a farce!"

Judith and Renie exchanged glances. Titus Teacher's
limping image had popped into both their minds. "A ...
boyfriend?" breathed Judith.

Augie gave an incredulous shake of his head. "Who
knows? Momma doesn't. Neither does Brent Doyle."

"Who is it?" asked Renie.

Amy bit her lips, fighting more tears. "Darren Fleetwood. He lives in Malibu, California."

Judith showed surprise; Renie looked perplexed.
"There's got to be a reason," Judith said at last. "Leona
didn't just pick his name out of a phone book."

"Maybe," speculated Renie, "he's some clergyman she
admired. Or a coworker from the missions."

Judith gave Renie a glance of approval. "True. Or possibly he's an orphan she had someone adopt in this country. There could be a lot of explanations, really. I'm sure
Brent Doyle will find out."

Amy had finally dried her tears and turned sulky. "He
called Directory Assistance while we were in his office.
They gave him a number, but there was nobody home, just
an answering machine."

"Was it this Fleetwood guy?" inquired Renie, who was
digging her bare feet into the warm sand.

"The voice on the machine didn't say," Amy pouted. "It was a man, though."

"He's probably at work," said Judith, feeling the perspiration break out under her sleeveless top. "Maybe Brent can reach him tonight. Whoever he is, he probably doesn't know that Leona is dead."

Renie hoisted a pile of sand on one foot and let it spill back onto the beach. "If Leona made the will in the last few weeks, this Fleetwood may not know about that, either."

"Whoever he is," Amy asserted in a resentful voice, "he's undeserving. I'll bet he's one of those smooth operators who play up to older women and get all their money. Spinsters can be terribly gullible."

Judith caught Renie's conspiratorial look. "It's possible," Judith admitted, getting to her feet. "How did Larissa and Donn Bobb take the news?"

Amy sniffed and Augie snickered. "Like the pair of silly fools that they are," she said. "They pretend they're not interested in money. That's because they don't have any. No responsibilities, either. Not like us, with a growing family." Amy's disdainful manner was a blanket indictment of her in-laws' life-style.

The three-wheeled beach cycles raced by again. Renie eyed them with interest, but Judith poked her cousin in the ribs. "Forget it, coz. I lost Joe to a dune buggy. I'm not offering you up to an oversized tricycle. Bill would never forgive me."

Renie said she'd settle for lunch. The cousins made their farewells to the Hokes and headed up the long staircase. Pausing halfway, Judith gazed down on the beach. Amy and Augie were still sitting on the log, huddled together. Judith wondered what they were talking about. Money, no doubt. She couldn't help but speculate on how far they might go to get it.

Fish and chips with a side of cole slaw purchased at a take-out stand on 101 satisfied the cousins' appetites. Their curiosity, however, remained unassuaged.

"Do you really think this Darren Fleetwood might be the guy we saw Leona with through the window?" Renie asked, pitching the fast-food containers into a barrel at the intersection of 101 and Seventh Street. The cousins had strolled along the highway, past the kite shop, City Hall, several gift shops, and the Methodist church. They were now about half a mile from Pirate's Lair, gazing through the shore pines at the handsome modern house Judith had spotted earlier from the beach. The place had a deserted air, and Judith wondered fleetingly if anything so lavish might be merely a summer home.

"It could have been him," said Judith, getting back on track. "Maybe we should try that number tonight, too. We could call Malibu before we go to dinner."

"Whoever Darren Fleetwood is," mused Renie, admiring the sleek lines of the three-story house with its shake exterior and artfully angled rooftops, "he has the best motive for murdering Leona Ogilvie."

"The only motive, as far as I can tell," said Judith, staring not at the spectacular dwelling on the point but across the highway, at a souvenir shop made to resemble a lighthouse. "Come on, coz, let's try to get ourselves killed in traffic and go over there to squander our meager savings on cheap presents. I've got to find a picture of the Sacred Heart of Jesus made out of a clam shell for Mother."

Renie was game. Five minutes later, they were in the shop, browsing among as gaudy a collection of Oregoniana as they could possibly imagine. Judith didn't find Jesus in a clam shell, but she did come up with the Blessed Virgin shedding beams of light over the skyline of Buccaneer Beach. She also selected a myrtlewood salad bowl for Joe and a coffee mug for Mike inscribed, "Oregon Coast—It's the Most." Renie got one just like it for Bill, except that it read, "Where the Hell Is Yachats, Oregon, Anyway and How Would You Pronounce It If You Cared?"

"I'll get each of the kids an ornament at that Christmas shop at the other end of town," said Renie, about to overdose on vulgarity.

They were at the cash register when a squeal erupted

from the other side of the T-shirt rack. "Ooooh—Donn Bobb, look! It's a picture of Bamm-Bamm! I've got to get it! He's my favorite Flintstone!"

Donn Bobb was leaning up against a life-sized wood carving of Barnacle Bill or some other grizzled nautical type. "Go ahead, Sweet Cakes, we only live once."

Larissa Hoke Lima sidled up to the counter with her purchase. She didn't recognize the cousins until Judith turned around to greet her.

"What a coincidence," said Judith, accepting her change from the cashier, "we just ran into your brother and his wife. I gather you had quite a session with Brent Doyle this afternoon."

Larissa seemed more interested in Bamm-Bamm's propeller beanie than in the lawyer's pronouncement. "Huh? Oh, yes, Brent dressed like a stuffy old codger. He's the same age I am. Can you imagine why he'd want to look like his father? That man wore *wing tips.*" Her crimson mouth turned down in disgust.

Judith waited for Renie and Larissa to conclude their transaction. Donn Bobb continued to lean against the carving, his mouth slack and his eyes closed.

"Amy and Augie are quite upset about your aunt's new will," said Judith as they started out of the store.

Larissa hadn't bothered with a bag, but held the T-shirt up against her ample bosom. "Isn't this *sweet*?" She smiled broadly at the cousins. "I should have bought one of Pebbles for Donn Bobb!" The smile faded; Larissa whirled. "Donn Bobb! I left him in the store! Wait a minute!"

Judith rolled her eyes; Renie drummed her fingernails on the shop sign by the door. "Don't expect much," breathed Renie. "Those two lost the oars to their rowboat a long time ago."

Acknowledging that Renie was right, Judith felt compelled by mere politeness to stay put. Sure enough, a giggling Larissa emerged moments later, towing a sheepish Donn Bobb by the hand. "Love," she announced, "makes the world go 'round."

"My, yes," said a mystified Judith. She glanced at Donn Bobb. "Sometimes it can even keep you awake."

Larissa howled. "Oh, Mrs. Flynn! You're such a *scream*! I didn't mean Donn Bobb here, I was talking about Aunt Leona. And her will." She gave her husband's arm a yank. "Hey, Sugar Lips, you sure you don't want that Pebbles shirt? What about Wilma?"

"Your aunt's will?" Judith tried to intervene before they were drowned in a sea of TV T-shirt trivia.

Larissa's eyes grew wide. "Yes, isn't that what you were talking about a minute ago? She did it for love, there's no doubt in my mind."

And not much else, Judith thought unkindly. "She did it for someone named Darren Fleetwood," said Judith pointedly. "What makes you think it was for love?"

Larissa shrugged her bare, freckled shoulders. "The will said he was her 'beloved' Darren Fleetwood. She must have loved him, right? I bet he was the Man of Her Dreams." She gazed adoringly at Donn Bobb whose unconscious expression indicated he was indulging in dreams of his own.

Amy's theory about a handsome young scoundrel playing up to a gullible, repressed spinster made sense. Judith took advantage of a sudden lull in traffic to say good-bye. The cousins pounded across 101, arriving somewhat breathless by the road that led to the handsome modern house.

"We could walk down to the beach and then take the stairs back up," Renie suggested, though she didn't sound enthusiastic about the idea.

"It's too hot," replied Judith, drooping under the late afternoon sun. "Let's take the high road and stop for a cold drink."

The first cafe they tried didn't serve anything, even beverages, between two and five o'clock. The drive-in a block away had lost the services of its ice machine. Judith and Renie returned to the take-out stand where they'd bought their lunch. Both ordered large Pepsis which they carried to a bench that overlooked the ocean.

"Why kill a woman who is leaving her only real property to a stranger?" asked Judith, staring out at the heat haze that had settled in over the beach. "Unless, of course, you are the stranger who inherits."

"What if you didn't know the will had been changed?" Renie sucked up the last drops of Pepsi through her straw. "Augie and Amy didn't know. I doubt if Larissa and Donn Bobb did, either. Or Alice Hoke."

"The young Hokes and the Limas may have thought they had a motive," Judith noted. Two young boys on skateboards whizzed by, forcing the cousins to tuck their feet under the bench. Overhead, a red, white, and blue banner proclaimed the wonders of the Freebooters' Festival, June 30–July 4. "But Alice had no reason to kill her sister. Unless she wanted to sell the beach cottage—but it sounds to me as if she's pretty well off already. That sale to the outlet mall people must have paid her handsomely."

Six blocks up from the turnoff to Pirate's Lair, Highway 101 briefly ran along the oceanfront. The bluff sloped gently here in the heart of town, with a small stream known as Bee Creek meandering under a bridge before splaying itself out on the beach. Across the highway, an old railroad car had been turned into a diner, resting on an abandoned spur that had once led to a now-defunct sawmill.

Down on the sand, seagulls fought over the remnants of somebody's picnic. A family of five tried to launch a bat-shaped kite, but their efforts were doomed by the lack of wind. Out on the ocean, two teenagers on boogie boards rode the waves. The summer day seemed so ordinary, so carefree, yet Judith felt weighed down by Leona Ogilvie's murder. The sheriff and the police chief could be right—a crazed stranger might have killed Leona. If so, her death was needless; that made it even worse. Judith wanted a real motive for Leona's homicide. Her murder should at least make sense. It had to be, in Judith's own lexicon, a *logical* death.

"I suppose we have to scratch Alice because she was

with Neil Clooney," said Judith at last. "It's too bad—she's the most unlikable of the whole crew."

Renie raised her eyebrows. "You're keen on Titus Teacher? I can't say he's hitting the top of my personal popularity chart."

Judith lifted a helpless hand. "I can't fit him in. Where was he, for instance, while Alice and Clooney were playing bake-my-buns in the boathouse? More to the point, why did Leona come back to the beach cottage? I'm sure she was meeting someone there. But who? The young guy we saw her with Monday night?"

Renie considered. "Young guy—who could that have been? For one, Donn Bobb Lima." She started counting on her fingers. "Was it him we saw with Leona?"

Judith threw up both hands. "If you couldn't see, I sure couldn't. If it was Donn Bobb, maybe they weren't embracing—Leona was probably holding him up. Besides, Donn Bobb's hair is longer than mine."

"Augie Hoke?" Renie ticked of another finger.

"His aunt? They might be fond of each other, but why would they meet at the beach cottage?"

"Because Alice didn't want company?" suggested Renie.

"Alice wasn't home. She was at the boathouse." Judith's forehead puckered. "So much for the young guys. Who else have we got? Are we really sure the man we saw was young?"

"It sure wasn't Clooney—he's too fat. And Eldritch is too tall. Titus Teacher has a beard." Renie chewed on her plastic straw. "There's nobody left. Unless," she added with a sly, sideways look at Judith, "you count Brent Doyle."

Judith eyed her cousin appreciatively. "Well. Nice work. But why?"

Renie tossed her paper cup at a garbage can with an opening like a shark's mouth. She missed. "I come up with the names, you provide the motives. All I know is that he's about the only other young man we've run into who is connected with the case."

Unable to endure the sun's direct rays any longer, Judith got up. "Brent Doyle would only fit into it if he had trashed Leona's will and made up a phony version, with himself as the heir. All he gets out of her death is the fee for probate. That may not be cheap, but it's no reason to kill a client."

Renie had to agree. The cousins started back toward the side street that led to the cul-de-sac. They paused at the corner as a black van turned off Highway 101 in front of them and drove by at a too-rapid speed. Judith grabbed Renie's arm. "That van," she said, practically knocking her cousin off the curb. "It's the one that's been parked by the cottage. Did you see who was driving it?"

"No," answered Renie. "I was too busy making sure the damned thing didn't run over my feet."

Judith was smiling to herself. "This time my eyes worked better than yours, coz," she said smugly. "I got a good look at the driver." Judith started walking briskly down the little incline that led to the cul-de-sac. She turned and hissed at Renie over her shoulder. "Come on, coz—maybe we can head him off. That was Titus Teacher."

But when the cousins reached the bottom of the cul-de-sac, the van had vanished.

TEN

Judith stood with fists on hips, surveying the curving road that led into Pirate's Lair. "Now where the heck did that goofball go? I'm almost sure that was the same van I saw parked here the first couple of days after we arrived."

Renie surveyed the vicinity. The short driveway into the beach cottage lay directly in front of them. The turn-off into the motel parking area was on their right, and the tree-lined entrance to the We See Sea Resort was at the left. Behind them were three older houses which had the look of permanent, rather than vacation, dwellings. The road into the cul-de-sac continued in a winding, north-south direction, more or less parallel to Highway 101.

"He might have been turning around and just kept going to hook back onto the main drag," Renie offered, "or maybe he went into the motel or the resort."

Judith debated with herself. It was too hot to go traipsing around parking lots, but curiosity won out over comfort. "Come on," she said, "let's check the motel."

Even though the neon sign read "No Vacancy," the parking lot was only half-full, awaiting the travelers who were still on the road. A swift once-over revealed the black van, resting in a stall close to the office. Judith and Renie approached warily.

Titus Teacher was gone. The vehicle's doors were locked; there were no windows in the rear. Judith peered inside the cab, finding nothing of much interest—a Thermos, a flashlight, a plastic sack with the logo of a local variety store.

"So where did he go? Inside the motel?" asked Renie.

Judith passed a hand over her forehead. Her bangs were wet with perspiration. She noted that Renie was also suffering from the heat. Even the flowers on her sundress looked as if they were wilting.

"That's where I'd go," said Judith. "It's probably air-conditioned. Wherever he went, he got there pretty fast for a guy with a game leg."

"It's not so far." To prove the point, Renie walked the fifteen feet to the office entrance. It took her a moment to adjust her eyes to the tinted glass. "Nice place. But I don't see Titus Teacher in there."

Judith was growing impatient to find some shade. "Maybe he uses their tram to get to the beach. The stairs must be hard on his leg. Let's go, coz. We're late for our visit to the hospital."

The cousins were heading out of the parking lot when they heard a car door close behind them. Idly, Judith turned. The owner of the dragon kite was starting up a late-model sports car. The curly-haired young man ignored Judith and Renie as he drove away from the Best Ever Over the Waves Motor Inn.

Judith noted that the sleek red sports car had California plates.

So far, Woody Price's news was negative. None of the Ogilvie-Hokes or Titus Teacher had shown up on the computer. "Which means," Joe said over the gin rummy hand he was playing out with Jake Beezle, "that none of them has a criminal record. Just for the hell of it, I had him check on that Doyle character. He was wanted all right, but there's been no sign of him since he took off seven years ago."

"I don't suppose his nephew, Brent, has any idea what happened to him," Judith mused.

"Brent?" Jake Beezle looked up from the card Joe had just discarded. "He'd have been starting college back then. I don't think his pa and Race were all that close, anyway. Some family spat between the brothers that went way back." Jake drew from the deck, then cackled triumphantly. "Gin, Flynn!" He fanned out his cards as his face grew somber. "Gin's the game, gin's my flame. And I ain't got any." He sighed. "I'll sure be glad to get home day after tomorrow."

The shake-covered shack Judith had envisioned earlier now expanded to include a single room with plastic over the windows and a sagging floor littered with empty liquor bottles. She wondered if Jake would have enough food on hand, or if she and Renie should offer to shop for him.

Joe was shuffling the deck. "Woody will try to check out some other sources tomorrow, but he's pretty tied up right now." He chuckled. "I don't know what he'll do without me once he gets promoted."

Judith suppressed a smile. She could imagine the tactful, empathetic Officer Price sensing his superior's need to be needed. Woody wasn't the type to lay it on too thick, but he certainly knew which buttons to push. "You'll still be his mentor," Judith said in reassurance. The conversation made her think of Neil Clooney. She looked over at Jake who was sorting his cards. "You mentioned that the chief of police got fired when Race Doyle absconded. Is that when Clooney came along?"

Jake nodded, and picked up the card Joe had turned over. "The City Council was so blamed mad they didn't want to hire anybody who'd worked for the ex-chief, so they hauled Clooney in from Milton-Freewater. You wouldn't believe the wrangling and jangling. Must have took 'em almost a year to get Clooney on the job." He tossed out a three of spades. "Anyways, it worked out okay for Clooney because by the time he got to town, the whole thing had kind of died down. And people wouldn't expect a newcomer to catch Doyle after so long."

"What about Eldritch?" asked Judith.

"He's only been sheriff for about five years. The guy he replaced was so old and daffy that everybody knew he couldn't find a fly in his soup. Say, what's for supper, Flynn? Gin." Jake spread out his cards again.

Joe was bemused. "You lucky old son of a gun. I'm going to have to dip into my pension fund to pay you off."

Jake was fingering a small menu printed on a buff-colored card. "I checked the box for the turkey divan. What's that? You suppose they cooked up a sofa? Most of this food tastes like old upholstery." His sharp little eyes raked over the cousins. "How about some poker? Those lazy lard bucket nurses are late with our supper tonight."

Judith smiled at Jake, then reached for her purse. "Renie and I are better at bridge. Sorry, Jake, but we have a dinner reservation." She neglected to mention the fact that it was over two hours away. "We want to show you something—except that we forgot to buy a magnifying glass." She took the little scrap of map from its resting place in the handbag's inner pocket and gave Joe a querying look.

It was Jake who responded. "Mrs. Wampole in D-208 has one. She uses it to read with. Cute little trick, even if she is lying about not being a day over seventy." He chortled. "I ought to know, I read her chart."

Renie went to fetch the magnifying glass, the price of the loan being a five-minute conversation. "It's a good thing I went instead of you," said Renie to Judith. "You'd still be there, hearing all about her four children, seven grandchildren, and two great-grandchildren. I only got their names, ages, and addresses."

Judith examined the map with Mrs. Wampole's magnifying glass. "At least it's in English," she said. "Joe, write this down." Her voice grew with excitement. "Four paces . . . Actually the *p* is gone, faded, I guess . . . king and queen of something or other . . . a hundred miles of . . . I can't make it out, it's just squiggles . . . Follow the bridge . . . Hmmmm."

Joe, with his ballpoint pen poised over a copy of the hospital's daily menu, made a face at Judith. "I'm supposed to write down that gibberish? The only thing that makes any sense is the part about the bridge. Here, give it to me. I'll get Jake to pilfer a microscope."

Judith was reluctant to part with the treasure map, but if there was anyone she could trust—other than Renie—it was Joe. "The handwriting is very old-fashioned. Of course they were English pirates. I wonder what king and queen they're talking about?"

Renie was wrinkling her pug nose. "William and Mary?" Her minor at college had been in history; her heart was forever in England. "They'd be just a few years too soon for the early seventeenth century. Isn't that when these pirates were supposed to be chasing the Spaniards all over the coast?"

"I think so," said Judith who was vague about names and dates when it came to the British royal house. Her English passion was literature, especially Dickens and the Lake poets. "You read the brochure this morning," she added with a faint hint of reproach.

"Right," agreed Renie. "Early seventeen hundreds. Queen Anne, then George I, the first Hanover. His queen was shut up in some German castle because she'd been caught dallying with a Swedish count."

"No account, probably," put in Jake, who was getting bored with Renie's recital. "Nothing around here named for any of those royal majesties. This ain't Canada, toots."

Dinner, served by a waddling nurse with a surly expression, arrived. Although Joe and Jake had ordered different entrées, both plates looked exactly the same. "I've got sole," said Joe.

"I've got rhythm," said Jake. "I wish I had booze. Or at least some real turkey. Wild Turkey, maybe." He chortled, but his mirth faded as he tasted his food.

Judith and Renie announced that they had to get ready

for their own dinner. Joe gave his bride a bleak look. Jake offered to give Renie the bird—off his tray. The cousins made their exit.

"Next time," Jake called after them, "we'll play some poker. I'll swipe some pills to use for chips."

Judith hoped he'd remember to swipe the microscope first.

After Judith called Arlene to learn that Sweetums still hadn't shown up, Renie got Darren Fleetwood's number from Directory Assistance. When she dialed his residence in Malibu shortly after 7:00 P.M., a pleasant masculine voice came on the line. The recording announced that no one could come to the phone at present, but to leave name, number, and any message at the beep. Renie hung up, a perplexed expression on her face.

"Well?" inquired Judith.

"He sounded sort of . . . familiar," said Renie.

"Let me try," said Judith. She placed the call, then listened intently. "You're right. Unless we *want* him to sound familiar."

"Who does it remind you of?" Renie asked.

Judith fingered her chin. "I'm not sure. Yet."

Renie arched her eyebrows. "But you can make a guess?"

Judith tipped her head to one side, in the direction of the motel. "Maybe."

"I thought so," said Renie. "The Green Dragon?"

"Could be," said Judith. "But phone voices often lie."

"So do people," noted Renie.

"So they do." The cousins exchanged quizzical looks.

La Bastide had been inspired by a guest house in Provence, but built by none other than Bernard Hoke as a summer retreat for a Portland banker. Located a half mile off Highway 101 and five miles south of Buccaneer Beach, the banker had not opted to take advantage of the ocean view, but instead had chosen a site nestled among tall ev-

ergreens next to a creek that wound indolently through
lush ferns.

The small terrace featured planters overflowing with
bright summer flowers. Judith and Renie agreed to have an
aperitif outside but to dine in the main part of the restaurant. Renie in particular was not keen on eating *al fresco*.
She insisted that too often unwanted extras were added to
the food—like bugs. But at least it was cool on the terrace,
with the sun finally starting to slip behind the cedar, fir,
and cottonwood trees which surrounded La Bastide and its
small, well-tended garden.

It was Renie, perusing the appetizing, but brief menu,
who discovered that Alice Hoke's late husband had built
the house. A somewhat effusive paragraph on the inside
front cover related the establishment's history.

"Alice," said Renie, putting the menu aside, "is the only
person we really haven't talked to much."

Judith sampled the spicy *pâté en croute chaud* they had
decided to share for a starter. "She doesn't want to talk to
us, as far as I can tell."

"Or anybody else," agreed Renie. "At least we
shouldn't feel picked on."

"Or so the story goes," mused Judith. She twirled the
stem of her aperitif glass in her fingers. "Has it struck you
as strange that after seven years of apparent seclusion, Alice has come out of the woodwork?"

Renie considered. "But has she? Having her sister murdered sort of forces her to put on a public face."

Judith allowed Renie to finish the last of the pâté. "I
don't mean that so much as the fact that she started seeing
Neil Clooney, she allowed the Limas to park their RV on
her property, and she didn't prevent the younger Hokes
from making the trip from Pocatello. Why have all these
things happened now? And about the same time that
Leona Ogilvie shows up in town?"

A waiter, whose aura was more evocative of Anaheim
than Avignon, ushered them to their table in the *salon*.
Lace curtains fluttered at the windows; lace draperies de-
pended from the ceiling lamps. A mural depicting joyous

farmers under sun-drenched skies in the fields of southern France covered one end of the room. Dried flowers stood in various gleaming copper utensils. The cousins smiled their approval.

"So what you're saying," Renie noted after they'd given their dinner orders, "is that Alice Hoke played the hermit for what—seven years?—and suddenly emerges when her sister shows up? Psychologically, that might not be too hard to explain. Bill would say that when Leona returned, Alice had a need to establish her own identity so she . . ."

Judith waved a hand. "Don't give me Bill's deep-thinking crap, coz. Not," she added hastily, seeing Renie's face fall, "that there might not be something to it. But Alice reestablishing her identity wouldn't get her sister killed. I'm looking for logic. Facts. Motives."

Renie brightened at the sight of her big salad topped with warm chicken livers. "Were you saying that Alice refused to let her kids visit until now?"

Judith shrugged. "It sounds like it. From what I gather, neither Larissa nor Augie has been to Buccaneer Beach since their father died. Larissa and Donn Bobb may have been on the rodeo circuit. Augie and Amy were probably too busy having babies. But any normal grandmother would want to see the kids, even if it meant Alice going to Idaho."

Renie munched on crisp lettuce. "Alice is not normal. I don't need Bill to tell me that much."

"Right." Judith paused as the waiter returned to pour their house white wine, bottled by an Oregon vintner. "And I don't need anybody to tell me that if Augie and Larissa both insisted on showing up to see their mother for whatever reasons, Alice couldn't stop them from coming. But she *could* refuse to see them. And she didn't. Meanwhile, she's suddenly out running around with Neil Clooney. It's not right, it's not . . . *logical*."

"So," Renie speculated, "you figure something must have triggered all this social activity on Alice's part. The obvious something being the Return of Leona Ogilvie, who promptly gets herself killed. Which is *not* logical, because the sister with the money is Alice. Unless . . ." Renie leaned across the table, unwittingly garnishing her blouse with the remains of her salad. "Could it be? Was it really Alice who got killed?"

Judith rolled her eyes. "Hardly. Augie and Larissa would know which one is their mother, even if they hadn't seen her since their father died. Surely Neil Clooney could tell the difference. I remember that he gave quite a start when he saw the body, but that was probably because the resemblance is so strong. Even if they were all in on some sort of conspiracy, there would be other ways to prove the dead woman was Leona, not Alice. And why play out such a farce? It would work better the other way 'round."

The waiter was removing their salad plates. "I wonder," mused Renie, "who Alice's will is made out to. Do you think Brent Doyle would tell us?"

Judith was staring off in the direction of the rustic mural. "No," she replied after a long pause. "Weird."

"What?"

Judith shook herself. "Nothing. I just had the craziest idea. Lunacy must be contagious in this town."

"What kind of idea?"

But Judith declined to elaborate. "It's too bizarre. Let me mull awhile. Or at least try to make some sense out of it."

Renie was about to pester Judith, but the arrival of their entrees bought her silence. For the next half-hour, with breast of duck *au poivre* in front of them and a bottle of white wine beside them, the cousins agreed to put murder behind them.

The duck blew up at 3:00 A.M. Unaccustomed to such rich living for more than two or three days at a time, Judith's usually stable stomach rebelled. Luckily, she had stashed some antacid tablets in her suitcase, but by the time her digestive tract had settled down, it was almost 4:00 A.M. and she was wide-awake. She sat in a chair by the picture window, watching the first dim streaks of light over the ocean.

It was about five minutes later that she heard a vehicle in the cul-de-sac. Judith thought nothing of it at first, since travelers had a right to arrive or depart at any hour of the night. For all she knew, one of their neighbors in the nearby houses worked an odd shift. But moments later, a soft thud sounded from the vicinity of the carport. Judith tiptoed out through the kitchen. She considered turning on a light, but thought better of it. Peering through the window in the back door, she saw a figure move, but couldn't make out more than a vague outline. Quickly, she moved from the kitchen, to see if Renie might have awakened. Her cousin, however, was sleeping like a log. Judith returned to the back door, deciding that she had nothing to lose by flipping on both the kitchen and carport lights. As she did so, she heard an engine start up. Unlocking the back door, Judith nipped out into the carport.

In the murky predawn light, she could just barely identify the vehicle turning out of the cul-de-sac. It was the black van. Judith gazed around the carport. Everything looked all right. She blinked. Two of the cartons were back.

ELEVEN

"QUILTS," SAID RENIE. "Nice."

"Crazy quilts, as far as I'm concerned." Judith used a hammer to pound the nails back into the packing crate. "Sheets and pillows in the other box. Why bring them back at four in the morning?"

"Why do anything at four in the morning?" Even at almost nine, Renie wasn't fully awake. "You sure it was that black van?"

"Pretty sure," said Judith, heading back into the kitchen. The cousins had decided to attend the funeral after all, and were going to eat a light breakfast before the ten o'clock service. "I wish I'd gotten the license number. Woody could find out through the Oregon State Patrol who that van is registered to."

A knock at the door interrupted their coffee, toast, and juice. To Judith's dismay, Terrence O'Toole stood in the doorway. "Hi, I brought you some extra *Bugler*s. For your family and friends."

"Thanks, Terrence." Judith forced a bright smile. "We appreciate it." She gave him a nod, presumably of dismissal.

Terrence didn't budge. "I brought you a map, too. We printed them this year. Are you going to take part in the big hunt?"

Judith held out her hand. "I doubt it, but thanks anyway. When does it start?"

Terrence handed over the map, printed on what looked like a place mat. Sure enough, Judith noted that along with the weekly newspaper and the Chamber of Commerce, various local restaurants and other businesses were co-sponsoring the Buccaneer Beach treasure hunt. "Tomorrow," replied Terrence, waving at Renie who duly waved back from her vantage point at the kitchen table. "They tell me it's limited to public places, mainly the beach. On the back of the map, they show you where they've hidden the treasure over the years so there won't be any duplication, like looking in the wrong places and unnecessarily disturbing property. You might want to keep an eye out; some of the people may try to use your staircase to get down the bank. Any resemblance to real pirates is intentional."

Judith sorted out this information and took a deep breath. "Okay. We'll watch for trespassers. And pirates." Her smile was strained. "Thanks again, Terrence."

This time he took the hint, and after stumbling over his own feet twice, departed from Pirate's Lair. Judith closed the door, returned to the table, and set the place mat down. "Just what we need—more people tramping around at all hours. It's a good thing Joe and I didn't need serious privacy after all."

Renie had polished off her third piece of toast and was beginning to acquire her normal alert air. She had put on her perennially smudged red-rimmed glasses and was studying the place mat. "Hey, coz, this looks like fun. See, it's not so much a map, but a puzzle. 'A & C don't stand for me; take a bike or a hike and go due west. Look for the sign that was formerly wine; go down, me hearties, and find the chest.' What do you think?"

"I think it's bilge," replied Judith, cleaning up their breakfast clutter. "We've got a real treasure map to decipher. If we can ever read the blasted thing. Come on, coz, let's get dressed. It's almost nine-thirty."

The Buccaneer Beach All Souls Are Us First Covenant Church was a peculiar blend of architecture, featuring a crenellated stone roof, yellow siding, and square windows hung with stained glass plaques. The truncated steeple looked more like a wooden chimney. Inside, rose-colored, flocked wallpaper clashed with lighting fixtures made out of wagon wheels. A larger-than-life-sized portrait of Jesus hung in the sanctuary, showing a blond, athletic, smiling Savior, beckoning lost souls to come forward and find salvation. Or play a little one-on-one. Judith couldn't be sure. Accustomed to the subdued, traditional decor of Our Lady, Star of the Sea Catholic Church on Heraldsgate Hill, the cousins shuddered.

The pews were filling up rapidly. Black did not predominate, as it would have in an earlier era of strict etiquette. Indeed, many of the mourners had arrived in shorts and cutoffs. Judith and Renie had done their best, given the circumstances. Judith had brought along a black and white polka-dot summer dinner dress. Renie settled for beige silk with a black patent leather belt.

The cousins squeezed in near the rear, realizing after they'd sat down that Sheriff Josh Eldritch was just across the aisle and Brent Doyle was two rows up. As the organ, which had a surprisingly mellifluous sound, intoned the opening hymn, a grim-faced Alice Hoke took her place in front of the church with Larissa and Amy. Alice, dressed in a plain brown linen dress, frowned at her daughter's tear-stained face. Amy's attempt to pat her mother-in-law's shoulder was rebuffed. When Chief Clooney bustled up the aisle to wedge his bulk into the row behind the family pew, Alice barely acknowledged him. Clearly, thought Judith, Alice Hoke preferred to experience her grief privately, perhaps even exclusively.

The babble of conversation faded away as the organ intoned its first doleful notes. Augie and Donn Bobb accompanied the flower-strewn casket, serving as pallbearers along with four men Judith didn't recognize. Alice Hoke kept her eyes to the front, never so much as darting a glance at the approaching remains of her sister.

The funeral was a simple, if lengthy, affair, mainly due to the Reverend Roscoe Bumber's interminable eulogy, a classic case of a man who knew not of whom he spoke. In his defense, however, the family apparently had provided him with a sketch of Leona Ogilvie's missionary career and her zeal in seeking converts for Christianity.

"There, in the heat of the jungle, amid danger, strife, and disease, Leona May Ogilvie brought the Lord to those poor pagan savages who worshipped false gods," Reverend Bumber declared in sonorous tones and with many flourishes. "Paying no heed to pestilence, flying in the face of wild beasts, defying the ignorance and poverty she found in every bend of the Amazon, Leona May Ogilvie sought to convert these simple, innocent natives with their sordid sexual pleasures and immodest attire with naked loins and bare breasts and ..."

"Jeez," muttered Renie.

"Help!" breathed Judith.

The Reverend raged on. Fortunately, there were no Wailers. At intervals, a hymn was sung. Judith's favorite was Donn Bobb's rendition of "Throw Out the Anchor, Someone's Floating Away." The cousins didn't dare look at each other. Judith found her eyes roaming over the congregation. Alice Hoke remained rigid; Larissa wept copiously; Amy looked as if she might throw up. Judith didn't much blame her, since Reverend Bumber was now thundering away about the most depraved of pagan sexual practices, which seemed to have something to do with making love with the lights on. Or at least during the daytime. Judith's gaze wandered to the other side of the church. She poked Renie; Titus Teacher was sitting in the back row.

Next to him was the curly-haired young man from the Best Ever Over the Waves Motor Inn.

It was almost eleven-thirty before the funeral ended. Judith and Renie beat a hasty retreat to the MG, which they had had the foresight to park half a block away from the church on Ocean Avenue. They hadn't wanted to take any chance of getting blocked in the parking lot.

"The address is 1708 Orca Drive," said Renie, reading from the note she'd made before leaving Pirate's Lair. "According to the map, we go up Tenth Street to Myrtlewood Avenue, turn right, then Seventeenth to Orca. Tenth isn't cut through because of the power plant."

It sounded simple enough to Judith, and it was. Five minutes later, they were at the Ogilvie-Hoke family home, a white two-story late Victorian house complete with a wide veranda and a turret. The Limas' battered RV was conspicuously parked just off the sloping driveway.

"It's a well-kept house," Judith remarked, parking the sports car at the edge of the road. She noted, however, that the barn near the trees lining the property was somewhat run-down, as were a couple of other outbuildings at the edge of an untilled field. "It's been a while since they took their farming seriously, though."

Renie concurred. The cousins walked up the drive to the front door. Alice Hoke lived on the edge of town, mostly surrounded by forest. The slanted roof of a much newer house could be seen in the distance, but there was no other sign of nearby habitation. Except for the occasional passing car, Judith and Renie felt safe from prying eyes.

"This property must be worth quite a bit, too," remarked Judith, working the lock with a tiny screwdriver. "What do you figure, at least a couple of acres?"

"I'm no judge," said Renie. She watched admiringly as the door swung open. "Way to go, you common crook. You never lose your touch."

It was true. Judith's lockpicking skills, honed as a child when her boundless curiosity got the better of her, rarely failed. The cousins entered a long hall, with a staircase at one side, an old-fashioned parlor on the other. Judith led the way, and somewhat to Renie's surprise, headed up to the second floor.

"What," demanded Renie, speaking in an unnecessary whisper, "are we looking for?"

"I've no idea," Judith replied candidly, "except that whatever it is won't be downstairs. Let's try picture albums, for one thing. And a passport, for Leona Ogilvie, the woman without ID. I'd like to know why."

Picture albums weren't easy to find. The first bedroom was clearly the master suite, with a big canopied bed covered by a lace counterpane. The only photo the cousins found was of an elderly couple attired in their best finery, standing by a Christmas tree. It reposed in a plain silver frame on the dressing table. Judith guessed it was Mr. and Mrs. Angus Ogilvie, Alice and Leona's parents.

"No other pictures," noted Judith. "No children, no grandchildren, no Bernie Hoke. Interesting."

"No Alice, if it comes to that," Renie pointed out.

"Right," agreed Judith. "She's not the sentimental sort. Still, you'd think she'd have at least one picture of her late husband."

"Maybe they didn't get along," suggested Renie. "Alice must have been a pain to live with."

"I'm sure she was. Twenty years of Alice could have helped make Bernard Hoke sail off into the sunset." Judith gave Renie a wry look. "There were days with Dan when I felt like walking in front of a Metro bus."

The cousins progressed to the next bedroom, a much smaller, considerably more cluttered, affair. A pile of magazines stood next to the bed. Religious tracts were scattered around the room. A dozen photos were stuck to the wall with transparent tape. All of them showed a much younger Leona Ogilvie with smiling native Brazilians in various states of undress. The blue corduroy jumper Judith had first seen Leona wearing was thrown carelessly over a chair.

Renie studied the pictures, most of which were curling around the edges. At a touch, one of them fell off the wall. "Whoops," exclaimed Renie, retrieving the photo. "I should put this back up."

"It won't matter to Leona," said Judith, rummaging through the bureau drawers. She turned suddenly, staring

Mary Daheim

at Renie who had placed the fallen photo on the dressing table. "Hey—let's see that!"

Judith examined the photo, which showed the youthful Leona in a bush jacket and split skirt, standing next to three young Brazilians in front of a native hut. "This picture—all these pictures—have been on the wall a long time. Look." She pointed to the square of paint where the displaced photo had hung. It was much lighter than the rest of the wall. "Would Alice have put them up?"

Renie considered. "Doubtful."

"Right," said Judith, getting down on her hands and knees and reaching under the bed. She found a pair of fuzzy slippers, a heating pad—and Leona's eelskin purse. "My wacky idea is getting less wacky by the minute." Squatting on the floor, Judith methodically went through the purse: a crumpled handkerchief, a comb, a nail file, a roll of breath mints, a safety pin, a ballpoint pen, a coin purse with $18.37. There was also a plastic folder containing various cards. Eagerly, Judith drew out each one and studied it with care. She noted Leona's ID, with the Orca Drive address, her Social Security number, a membership in a missionary society, and a temporary Oregon State driver's license. The next day, July 1, would have been her fifty-first birthday. Judith felt like a ghoul.

"Damn," she sighed, scrambling to her feet, "murder is an awful business." She glanced down at the provisional license. "It's dated about three weeks ago. Maybe I'm crazy after all."

"Well, *I'll* never know," sniffed Renie. "Have fun arguing with yourself, and, as my mother would say, 'Don't worry about me.' "

Judith shot Renie a baleful look. "I'm not being coy, I just feel silly with a theory that ..." She gave another start, then clutched at Renie's arm. "There's no passport! No credit cards, no bank cards, not even a library card!" Letting go of Renie, she rifled through the magazines. "Look! Some of these are over a year old!"

"So am I," said Renie dryly. "So stop treating me like a nitwit baby."

Judith went to the window to make sure no one was approaching the house. The coast was clear. She sat down on the bed, clearing away a pile of stockings and some underwear to make room for Renie. "I don't think Leona Ogilvie got back in town only a month ago," declared Judith. "I'll bet she's been here all along, living like a recluse in this house."

Renie was understandably incredulous. "But why? What about Alice? Is being a hermit a family trait?"

Judith glanced at her watch. It was high noon, and, she decided, high time to escape before any family members returned to the house. "I haven't worked this all out yet. That's one reason I didn't want to say it out loud. I'm not even sure if it ties into the murder. But," she continued, getting up and heading out of the bedroom, "I'm pretty sure Alice was never a recluse. It was Leona, posing as Alice. I'll bet you fifty bucks Alice Hoke just got back from Liechtenstein a month ago. The next question is why she came home to Buccaneer Beach."

It was just as well, Judith thought, that Jake Beezle was off in therapy when they arrived at the hospital ten minutes later. She wanted to test her theory on Joe. He listened carefully as he spooned up the last of his vanilla pudding cup.

"I can check that on the phone," Joe volunteered, referring to the alleged reentry of Alice Hoke into the United States. "I'll do it when Jake's not around. There's no point in getting him any more involved than he already is. After all, he goes home tomorrow and this is a dangerous business." The green eyes bored into Judith's face. "You know that, I hope? You two won't do anything stupid, will you? Like breaking into anybody else's premises, including Sir Charles' Souse's houses?"

With a sheepish expression, Judith felt compelled to give her husband an assurance of discreet behavior. "Nobody knows we're trying to solve this case. They just think we're a couple of snoopy tourists."

Her response didn't entirely satisfy Joe, but he knew it

was hopeless to try to enlist his wife's full cooperation. He felt inadequate to protect her, and it rankled. The best he could do was help her find the killer—before the killer found her.

"Okay," he said with a sigh, "you've got Leona living in seclusion at the family home. Any casual caller could mistake her for Alice because of the close resemblance. The family members haven't been around in years, no doubt discouraged by Leona from visiting. When they finally do show up, Alice is right where she's supposed to be. Leona's there, too, suddenly back from Brazil." He made a note in the margin of the *Oregonian*'s sports section. "It'll take some digging, but I can find out when Leona Ogilvie really did come home from South America. Now tell me more about the clothing in the boathouse and all those mobile boxes."

Judith moved Joe's tray out of the way. "The clothes may have been planted in the boathouse to make it look as if Leona were in transit. Or perhaps she planned to move down there. Alice Hoke may not be a hermit, but she doesn't seem to like people much. She hadn't seen her own kids in seven years, yet neither Augie nor Larissa seem to find that too unusual. I'll bet she was the kind of mother who didn't want them underfoot, even when they were small. Having Leona around must have galled Alice. She may have latched on to Neil Clooney just to get out of the house. I doubt that she and Leona could have gone on living under the same roof for very long."

Renie was prowling around the room, looking out the window next to Jake Beezle's empty bed. "Somebody's living in the boathouse right now, though," she pointed out. "Titus Teacher, maybe."

"Or Alice, escaping from Leona," said Judith. "At least Alice uses it as a *pied-à-terre*. As for the boxes in the carport, I suspect they're Alice's, shipped via Lufthansa from Liechtenstein. She probably stored the stuff there, just as we thought Leona had done. But why those two cartons were brought back last night still mystifies me."

Joe grinned. "I'm glad something mystifies you. It

makes me feel bad to think that only the police get baffled."

Judith sighed. "Oh, I'm baffled about a lot of things. Why was it necessary for Leona to pretend she was Alice in the first place? Why did Alice go away? What was she doing in Liechtenstein, of all places? How does any of this provide a motive for the crime? Leona the Recluse is as harmless as Leona the Missionary. What's worse is that everybody seems to have an alibi."

"Except," Renie chimed in, "Titus Teacher and Darren Fleetwood. Whoever they may be."

With a lurch that rocked Joe's bed and jostled his pulleys, Judith reached for the phone book. "I'll take care of Darren right now." Moments later, she had spoken to the desk at the Best Ever Over the Waves Motor Inn. "Eureka!" she cried, her black eyes dancing at her husband and her cousin. "Darren Fleetwood is indeed staying there. He arrived Sunday. What do you bet that was him sitting next to Titus Teacher at the funeral?"

Renie gave a little snort. "He's also sitting on some prime property. Shall we tell our local law enforcement fellows?"

But Joe intervened. "Keep off that turf. The sheriff and the police will get an anonymous telephone tip." He raised his rust-colored eyebrows.

Judith rubbed her hands together. "Wow! If the man who has the only motive has no alibi, we may have this one in the bag!"

At that moment, Jake Beezle entered the room, using crutches and berating the surly nurse. ". . . Hopping like a damned stork! You try it, Tootsie Roll, and then after walking them phony stairs 'til you drop, you find your lunch is colder than a penguin's hind end!" He simmered down when he saw the cousins. "Hey, my favorite visitors! Where'd you two get those nifty dresses? You both look real snazzy for this neck of the woods. You been to a funeral or something?"

Judith smiled at Jake as the nurse made her indignant

exit. "Are you going to be okay at home, Mr. Beezle? Is there anyone to watch out for you?"

"Oh," Jake replied breezily, "I'll manage. I've got a couple who'll do right by me." He struggled with the crutches, then lowered himself onto the bed.

"It's nice to have good neighbors," Judith remarked, then stared as Jake raised his hospital gown a mite too far and revealed a microscope affixed to his bony thigh with surgical tape.

"Here, Flynn, take the damned thing, will you? Pinching it from the lab was a cinch, but I had a hell of a time hopping back from therapy. We can put some light on the subject with my super-duper flash I use for looking at the liquor ads in the magazines under the covers at night."

In her excitement over the discoveries at the Ogilvie-Hoke house, Judith had forgotten about the old treasure map. Now, she could hardly contain herself as she watched Joe adjust the microscope and slide the scrap of parchmentlike paper into place.

"It's still fuzzy," he announced, "but I can make out a little more . . . That's not paces after all, it's four aces, four kings, four queens, four jacks. Then a hundred miles of . . . damn, that part's still unreadable. Let's see . . . Follow the bridge. It rules. Hunh." For just an instant his green eyes flickered above the microscope. Then he gave a little shrug and turned a puzzled face to the others.

Judith and Renie insisted on taking a turn, too. But Joe was right. Whatever came after "a hundred miles of . . ." looked like a broken *m*. The part about the bridge was also hard to read.

"Sounds squirrelly to me," said Jake, attacking his lunch tray. "What did these pirates do, sit around on their booty and play whist?"

Renie gave Jake a condescending smile. "As a matter of fact, they did. Not whist, but they certainly played cards. My husband, Bill, is always amused by the fact that people in the twentieth century think they invented every imaginable pleasure, including sex. He calls that attitude . . ."

"Sex!" interrupted Jake, and rolled his eyes. "I remember now! It was almost as good as booze!" He scrunched up his wrinkled face. "Or was it better? Maybe I should go see Mrs. Wampole before I check out of this dump."

Grateful for the diversion, Judith steered the conversation back to the map. "A hundred miles, it says. Not *to*, but *of*. Of *what*?" She squinted again at the scrap of paper, then threw up her hands. "Oh, phooey, we're getting sidetracked! This can't possibly have anything to do with Leona's murder."

Joe's eyes roamed the ceiling. "Oh, I don't know. It might if somebody thought she had it. How do you know it wasn't put under that rug very recently?"

"It seemed to be stuck," said Renie. "But that was after I'd scrubbed the carpet." She looked at Judith; Judith looked back. Joe's suggestion was not implausible.

"If you could figure it out, and find a real treasure, you might find your motive," Joe said. "I know it sounds weird, but there have been several instances of buried wealth uncovered along the Pacific Coast. A lot of them have been in sunken ships, but some have been on land, too." He favored Judith with his most ingenuous expression.

"Well ..." Judith gazed from her husband to the map. "I suppose ... But when I stop to think about it, it seems like a wild-goose chase. I mean, even if there is something buried around here from almost three hundred years ago, how would it tie in with Leona Ogilvie?"

Joe spoke in reasonable tones. "I told you—because she had this piece of map. It was in her house, wasn't it?"

Judith was still dubious. "Maybe. I mean, it was, yes, but it all seems pretty obscure." She jabbed at the map with her finger. "This is particularly obscure. Four aces, four kings, and so forth. The only bridge I know of in town is the one over Bee Creek."

Joe didn't meet Judith's stymied gaze, but he bestowed a nod of approval. "That's a start."

"We'll see," said Judith. "Right now, it's time to call on

Darren Fleetwood." She stood up, just as Rolf Lundgren strolled into the room, making his afternoon rounds.

"Hi, everybody," the young intern said by way of greeting. "This is certainly a busy room. Where'd you get that microscope, Mr. Flynn?"

Judith knew Joe's explanation would be interesting, even colorful. But she didn't want to take the time to hear it. Besides, she could tell that Renie's stomach was growling. Loudly. They made their escape.

To relieve Renie's hunger pangs, and the less vociferous ones of her own, the cousins stopped at the diner overlooking Bee Creek. "At least we're making a token effort at looking for the treasure," said Judith as they slipped into a tall booth. "We're near a bridge."

"We're near food," replied Renie, "which is all that counts right now." She glanced up from the menu which was designed to resemble that of an old-fashioned railroad car. "Are we really going to see Darren Fleetwood this afternoon?"

"Let's say we'll run into him." Airily, she waved a hand. "It's a beautiful day, at least if you like your weather in the eighties, so I presume he'll be at the beach. If not, he may be hanging around the pool. We'll find him." Her buoyant mood slipped a notch. "Damn that Joe. I wish I'd married a man who didn't know me so well."

"Huh?" Renie was caught off-guard by Judith's comment.

Judith's expression grew quite earnest. "Don't you see what that sly devil is up to? He's trying to divert us with this treasure hunt. He's lying there in bed, worrying, afraid we'll get ourselves into serious trouble. So to prevent us from tracking down the murderer, he's pretending the treasure map could be the motive. It doesn't wash."

"But it *is* possible," countered Renie. "Face it, coz, you were pretty excited about that map at first."

"That's true," Judith admitted. "But the more I think about it, the less enthusiastic I am. There's something wrong about the whole thing. Still, the only way to prove the point would be to take a stab at finding the treasure."

She made a face. "Joe knows that, too. Damn his Irish hide."

Renie burst into laughter. Judith stared at her cousin. "What on earth's the matter with you?"

"Congratulations!" Renie reached across the table and slapped Judith's hand. "After twenty-five years, we're done with Dream World! You sound as if you're really married!"

The color rose in Judith's cheeks. But she laughed, too. Sort of.

TWELVE

AFTER JUDITH AND Renie had lunched on rare roast beef dip sandwiches, french fries, and green salad, they stopped off at Pirate's Lair to change out of their funeral attire. When they got to the motor inn around two-thirty, there was no sign of Darren Fleetwood's red sports car. With a sinking feeling, Judith approached the front desk.

"Is Mr. Fleetwood still registered?" she asked the ponytailed clerk whose name tag read Kari Ritchard.

Kari checked her computer. "Mr. Fleetwood left about an hour ago. We have a noon checkout time, but he was a bit late. I think he'd been to a funeral." Her smile was sympathetic, showing a perfect set of dimples.

Judith glanced at Renie. "He left town?"

Kari blinked. The question obviously struck her as odd. "Yes. I suppose so. That's what most guests do when they check out. At least in *this* kind of motel." Her tone seemed to imply that Judith must be used to a different sort of establishment.

"It's just that I didn't expect him to head back to

150

Malibu so soon," explained Judith, trying to bail herself out. "We were at the funeral, too, but I didn't get a chance to talk to him then."

Kari seemed placated by Judith's words. "Oh. I see. Well, he did say something about being late for an appointment. Perhaps you could still catch him."

"Ah. Okay, we'll try. Thanks." Judith all but knocked Renie over in her haste to get out of the lobby.

"What the hell are we doing?" panted Renie, running to catch up.

Judith was already in the cul-de-sac, headed for the carport. "We're going to find Darren Fleetwood. My guess is that he's gone to see Brent Doyle. Who else would he have an appointment with?"

Sure enough, the sleek red sports car with its California plates was pulled up in front of the building that housed Brent's law office. Renie started to get out of the MG, but Judith stopped her. "Let's wait here."

"As Grandma used to say, it's hotter than Dutch love in this sun," complained Renie. "Why isn't this heap air-conditioned?"

"Because it's old," retorted Judith. "Like us. Now stop bitching." The weather was making both cousins cranky.

"I'll stop bitching when the temperature gets below seventy-five. It's not supposed to get hot at the ocean. What happened to the breeze and all that nice fog?"

"It's almost July. If you were back home, you'd be whining about how insufferably stuffy your upstairs bedroom gets at night. At least it cools off a little down here."

"I went to San Francisco once on business this time of year and had to buy a *coat*. The fog was so thick I couldn't see the step on the cable car until I got on board. Then the wind came up off the bay and I was practically blown right off Nob Hill . . ."

"Hold it." Judith was gazing through the windscreen at the curly-haired young man who had come out through the entrance to the office building. His chiseled good looks made it easy for Judith to see how a woman such as Leona

Ogilvie could behave in a foolish, adolescent manner. "Come on, coz," said Judith, "let's strut our stuff."

"What stuff?" muttered Renie, but she joined Judith in getting out of the car.

"Hi, Darren," Judith called with a friendly wave. "Are you coming back to Pirate's Lair with us?"

The young man stopped, stared, and tried to speak. On the second attempt, he got out two words. "No. Why?"

Judith had strolled over to the red sports car, neatly blocking the driver's door. "I heard you inherited the beach cottage. We're staying there. I thought you might want to see it before you drove back to California. You're more than welcome to give it the once-over."

Under his tan, Darren had grown pale. "No. No, thanks," he said on a softer note. "Another time, maybe. I want to get home by tomorrow. I didn't plan on staying this long in the first place. Anyway, I've been inside the house once. It's very nice. Great view."

"Oh—of course," said Judith, with a catch of her breath. "Monday night, right? You and Leona were at the beach cottage while I was picking my cousin up in Salem."

Darren gave a vague nod of assent. He didn't seem particularly distressed by the revelation. The hot sun was beating down on Judith, making it hard for her to think on her feet. She was trying to assess Darren Fleetwood, to gauge the emotions that rippled in his dark eyes. Fear? Anxiety? Grief? Judith couldn't be sure. The uncertainty clouded her approach.

"I'm sorry about your loss," she said, finally relying on a platitude. "Actually, we've never officially met." She introduced herself and Renie. Darren Fleetwood accepted their hands with a trace of suspicion. "The family told us about you," Judith said truthfully. "I hope you and Leona were able to have a happy . . . reunion."

"We were," said Darren, faintly bitter. "If you want to call it that." He edged toward the sports car, apparently trying to figure out a way to dislodge Judith without resorting to a body block.

Renie had come around the front of the car, and perched

herself on the hood. Darren winced. "Did you meet her in California?" inquired Renie. "Or up here, on a previous vacation?"

Darren's face twisted in puzzlement. "I'd never met her before in my life. What are you talking about?"

Taken aback, Renie stammered slightly. "I—I thought Amy Hoke said you knew Leona from . . . That is, there'd been . . ."

"Letters," Judith supplied, taking a wild, if logical, guess. The conversation didn't seem to be running at all along the lines the cousins had expected.

"Yes, we'd written." Darren frowned, then took his keys out of his back pocket, and swung them meaningfully at Judith. "That's why I came to Buccaneer Beach."

Darren Fleetwood was only about two feet away. Judith had no choice but to move. Perspiration trickled down her back. There were sun spots in front of her eyes. This was probably her only chance to nail Darren Fleetwood, and it was rapidly slipping away. Or was it melting, like she was? . . .

"She must have thought a lot of you," Judith hazarded, as Darren opened the car door. Renie jumped off the hood.

He swung his long legs across the leather seat. An ironic expression crossed his face as he looked up at Judith. "I should hope so. After all, she was my mother."

He started up the engine and backed quickly out of the parking lot. Judith and Renie stared speechless as the red sports car became a blur on Highway 101.

"Oh, brother!" Judith flopped onto the blanket she and Renie had put on the sand for their postswim enjoyment. Or at least that had been their plan the previous day. Unfortunately, such simple pleasures could become complicated. Renie didn't know how to swim, so she was forced to paddle around in the water like an awkward spaniel. Judith discovered that her back, which had seemed to have gotten much better, did not do well fighting the waves. And most of all, there was the matter of Darren Fleetwood, son of Leona Ogilvie. The announcement had rocked the cousins down to their summer sandals.

"At least the water is pretty cold," Renie allowed, taking a sip of Pepsi from the hamper they'd brought with them to the beach. "We should have done this before. I mean, we are staying at the sea, aren't we?"

Trying to ease her back, Judith rolled over onto her stomach. "We haven't had time," she groaned. "We've been too busy playing detective."

"Which is what you'd still be doing if I hadn't been on the verge of heatstroke," said Renie. "I'll bet Brent Doyle wouldn't have told us anything anyway."

"Maybe not." In truth, Judith hadn't argued very hard when Renie had insisted on returning to Pirate's Lair instead of rushing into Brent's law office to verify Darren Fleetwood's claim. Doyle, Renie argued, wouldn't cooperate, given client confidentiality. And Renie, near heat prostration, didn't want to hear it anyway. Since Judith was also undone by the weather, a dip in the ocean sounded like the only thing that would revive her flagging mind and body. "Somebody else may know the background on Darren and Leona. We'll assume he's illegitimate. We can also assume the family doesn't know about him. Amy and Augie didn't, so my guess is that neither do Larissa and Donn Bobb."

"If Leona was a mother, there's got to be a father somewhere," said Renie, untangling the straps of her red and black bathing suit. "Any candidates?"

Judith had already given the matter some thought. "Not really. Darren must be midtwenties, maybe even close to thirty. What we need is somebody who's been around this town forever."

"What about Jake?"

Judith shook her head. "My choice would be a gabby old lady who can remember all the gossip. Jake knows the male-type stuff, like who worked as what, and which buildings went up and came down, and all that factual information. I'm thinking of female-oriented data. You know—like dirt."

Briefly, the cousins fell silent. The beach was very crowded, the town overflowing with visitors for the Free-booters' Festival. Among the would-be kiteflyers, joggers, suntanners, surfers, bikeriders, strollers, swimmers, and picnickers were a good many people with copies of the place mat treasure map. Even though the hunt didn't offi-cially kick off until Saturday, some of the more eager seekers were getting a sneak preview.

"An old lady with a long memory and a loose lip," mur-mured Renie. She shot Judith a sidelong glance. "Are we going back to the hospital this afternoon?"

Judith's closed eyelids flickered. "Do dogs bite mail-men?"

Renie nodded. "Mrs. Wampole, Jake's Love Goddess in D-208?"

"You got it," said Judith.

"No," smiled Renie. "*You* do. I already did Mrs. Wampole when I borrowed her magnifying glass and got the family history. She's all yours, coz."

Mrs. Wampole was every bit as cute as Jake Beezle had reported. A small sparrow of a woman close to eighty, she had fluffy white hair and an enchanting smile. Her bright, birdlike blue eyes might cause her problems up close, but Judith felt she didn't miss a trick. A blockage in her colon, she confided to Judith, that had been the problem, but there was no malignancy. Wasn't that wonderful? Judith agreed that it was indeed.

It took over a quarter of an hour to steer Mrs. Wampole onto the Ogilvie-Hoke ménage. Once started, however, there was almost no stopping her. Leone Ogilvie's death was, after all, a sort of triumph for a woman of Mrs. Wampole's age. It struck Judith that with the demise of other, especially younger, people, the elderly often consid-ered their own survival a personal victory over the Grim Reaper. She remembered Grandpa Grover, reading the daily obituaries, and always concluding, "Well, I'm not in there. Again."

Mrs. Wampole adjusted the frilly pink bed jacket that

rested on her slim shoulders. "Poor Leona! Not much over
fifty! Tsk-tsk!" She shook her head. "A violent end, at
that. How very sad. But you might have seen it coming.
That family has a penchant for trouble."

"You mean Race Doyle and the cheese factory?" Judith
offered.

"Oh, that, of course, but even earlier. Angus Ogilvie and
Dorothy Metz. Mrs. Ogilvie, that is, but not after a lot of
bother. Dr. and Mrs. Metz—he was an old-fashioned country practitioner, very strict with his girls—didn't approve
of Angus. He was right off the farm, and it wasn't a very
prosperous one in those days. The Depression, you know.
But they ran off and got married, and Angus worked so
very hard. He had an unpleasant temper, but there wasn't
a lazy bone in his body. The next thing you know, he
started a creamery. Then it grew into the cheese factory,
right after the war. The Second World War, I mean. Angus's father had been crippled in the Great War, you know.
I think that may have been what turned Angus away from
God. He had to be the man of the family while his father
sat around and stared at his military souvenirs. Alice and
Leona were born during the last war, about a year apart.
Homely little pieces, but then you shouldn't judge by
looks alone, should you?" Mrs. Wampole gave Judith the
complacent smile of a woman who could have gotten by
on looks alone, thank you very much.

"There were beaux, of course. The Ogilvies had made
quite a bit of money off that cheese. Alice wanted to go
away to college, but her father wouldn't hear of it. Worse
yet, Leona felt the call to be a missionary. Angus was up
in arms, I'll tell you. He was an irreligious sort, and at one
point I think he tried to get the City Council to leave out
the part about 'under God' in the Pledge of Allegiance.
Naturally, they voted him down."

Mrs. Wampole's spate of recollections halted long
enough for the surly nurse's replacement, also stout but
not nearly as surly, to deliver dinner. "Oh, my!" smiled
Mrs. Wampole. "How lovely! Chicken croquettes! Or is it
meat loaf?"

Whatever it was, Mrs. Wampole ate with appetite. Judith took the opportunity to ask a direct question, "Wasn't Race Doyle one of those young fellows who dated Alice? Or was it Leona?"

"Alice," said Mrs. Wampole. "She turned him down for Bernard Hoke. Race was considered 'fast.' He sold used cars. Then he did something with freezers. And real estate. Angus and Dorothy weren't at all pleased about Bernard, but he was a better catch than Race. To this day, I think that after Angus passed on, Bernard gave Race that job managing the cheese factory as a sort of consolation prize. It wasn't wise, Race being such a rogue, but I've always wondered if Bernard didn't feel just a little guilty about stealing Alice. The marriage turned out well, I suppose, since Bernard made quite a bit of money in construction. At least in the good times. It's an unpredictable business, you know."

"So Leona never married?"

"No, she was devoted to her missionary work. I don't believe she ever dated much. The boys who asked her out never got very far. Her reputation was spotless." Mrs. Wampole spooned up some nasty-looking red Jello with green lumps. "Except for that New Year's Eve incident." She gave a little shrug. "Just talk, I'm sure. You know what small towns are like."

"What was the talk?" Judith noted that Mrs. Wampole didn't seem the least bit surprised at her probing questions. No doubt the old lady was only too pleased to have an audience. In a similar situation, Gertrude would have told her interrogator to take a hike.

Mrs. Wampole cocked her head to one side. "Oh—let me see . . . It was back in 1960, the year Mr. Kennedy was elected. I remember, because Angus Ogilvie made such a fuss about a Catholic getting into the White House." She gave Judith her enchanting smile. "I'm Jewish, you know, but I certainly didn't think there was anything wrong in electing a Catholic. Did you?"

"No, not at all," answered Judith, automatically fingering the Miraculous Medal she wore under her green cotton top.

"Really, people get so upset about the Pope! You'd think he was some sort of spiritual molester!" Sadly, she shook her head. "But I mustn't lose track of what I was saying. What *was* I saying?" Briefly, she looked muddled, then snapped her fingers. "Oh, yes, about Angus and Mr. Kennedy. The Ogilvies had a party on New Year's Eve to announce Alice's engagement to Bernard Hoke. Race Doyle showed up drunk." She clucked her tongue once more. "He made a scene, and Leona tried to calm him. Finally, she got him out of the house, but she didn't show up again until Bernard brought her home the next morning. Everybody in town said he'd found her with Race Doyle, but that was just gossip, I'm sure. It all died down a few weeks later when Alice and Bernard were married on Valentine's Day, and Leona went off to learn how to be a missionary. Angus Ogilvie wasn't at all happy about it, but he couldn't stop her, could he?"

Judith conceded that he probably couldn't. Her brain was working swiftly, calculating dates and other possibilities. Would Race Doyle have taken his revenge on Alice by seducing her sister? Perhaps. Could he be Darren Fleetwood's father? Maybe. Had Leona Ogilvie left town because she was pregnant? It was a plausible theory.

It took Judith a few moments to tune back into Mrs. Wampole's ongoing saga. ". . . with a background like that," Mrs. Wampole was saying. Judith focused on the old lady, who was happily chasing boiled peas around her plate. "You just knew he'd end up in jail. He would have, too, if he'd been caught."

Judith realized Mrs. Wampole had been talking about Race Doyle. "You blame his parents?" It was a guess, but a logical one.

"Well, yes, isn't that what I just said?" She gave Judith a faint look of reproof. "Really, Mrs. Doyle had no morals whatsoever. Loose, that's what she was. And Mr. Doyle, running that speakeasy . . . Oh, it had supposedly become respectable by the time Race was born, since Prohibition was over. But it was still frequented by a very questionable element. I never wish bad luck on anyone, but I was just as well-pleased when it went out of business."

Judith drew her chair a little closer to the bed. "Where was this . . . tavern?" she asked.

"Tavern, yes, that's what they called it, but a lot more than drinking beer and wine went on there, if you ask me." She plucked at the satin ties of her bed jacket. "It was right out on the bluff, overlooking the ocean. Bernie Hoke tore it down and built a beach cottage. They kept the name—Pirate's Lair, it was called. Nasty place. I hear it's where poor Leona got murdered. I guess some things never change." Mrs. Wampole shuddered.

So did Judith.

In deference to Judith's stomach problems of the previous night, the cousins decided to dine in. Or at least cook their own food, but eat down on the beach. After arriving amid the horde of tourists, they began to have second thoughts. Between the pounding of the surf, the shouts of the vacationers, and the premature explosion of fireworks, they could hardly hear themselves speak. Making short shrift of their cracked Dungeness crab, cucumber salad, and French bread, they were grateful to head for the relative calm of Pirate's Lair.

"I don't know what to pray for," Judith said, catching her breath as they got to the top of the long staircase. "In a way, I hope Joe gets out of the hospital tomorrow so we can go home before all of Buccaneer Beach succumbs to Freebooters' madness. But I hate like hell to leave a killer on the loose."

"You aren't giving Clooney and Eldritch much credit," said Renie.

"As Joe says, if a murderer isn't caught within forty-eight hours, he—or she—often goes free." She gave Renie a bleak look. "We're well past that deadline now, coz."

"True," agreed Renie, looking faintly crestfallen.

Judith opened the front door, allowing Renie to carry in the picnic hamper. Both women stopped and stared. Alice

Hoke was sitting on the sofa, reading a magazine. She looked up almost idly, her thin mouth unfriendly.

"Are you leaving tomorrow?" she asked peremptorily.

"I don't know," replied Judith, still startled. "We were just discussing that."

Alice stood up. She was still wearing the unadorned coffee-colored dress she'd had on at the funeral. "I brought your receipt. Brent Doyle insisted you have one. However, I'd like to have you go. This house no longer belongs to the family. I don't think we need any insurance risks."

Judith left the door ajar to air out the house, but didn't move any nearer to Alice. Renie, however, had trooped out into the kitchen with the hamper. "I told you, the doctors haven't made a decision," said Judith. "If my husband has to stay in the hospital for another day or two, I can't leave. I'll certainly never find a room in Buccaneer Beach with all this goofy Freebooter stuff going on."

"That's not my problem." Alice slipped the magazine into the maple rack beside the sofa. "You signed the rental agreement for seven days. They're up tomorrow."

"Just a minute," argued Judith. "That was seven *nights* as well. They won't be up until Sunday."

Only a flicker of Alice's cold gray eyes indicated that Judith's words had disconcerted her in any way. She seemed to be weighing the legal ramifications. "Very well," she said tersely. "But you must leave by 8:00 A.M. Sunday. That's absolutely final."

Renie returned from the kitchen. "It's none of my business, Mrs. Hoke, but that guy from the boathouse or wherever he lives is out in the carport stealing your stuff. Do you care?" The question was put in such a way that Renie sounded as if she figured Alice didn't care about much—except herself.

"Mr. Teacher is doing some hauling for me. I want to get this entire house cleaned out in the next few days. As I said, it no longer is owned by anyone in our family." Her homely face revealed no emotion.

The sound of a vehicle starting up caught Judith's ear.

She was sure it was the black van. "If you want everything out of here, how come Titus Teacher—or somebody—brought two of the cartons back last night?"

For a fleeting moment, Judith could have sworn that Alice Hoke looked startled. "He did? I think that's unlikely. Of course the man isn't right in his head. He may have become confused. Let me check." She started for the kitchen, then paused in the doorway. "By the way, my late sister left some personal effects here that she wanted my daughter and daughter-in-law to have. Or so they say. Some jewelry, I believe. Please see if you can find a small case in the front bedroom closet. Thank you." She went out into the carport with the air of an empress giving a command to her lowly, slightly stupid, subjects.

Judith sighed. "A jewel case? Let's go see, coz. Anything to get rid of the old bat."

The closet contained Judith and Joe's luggage, along with a few items that belonged to the house. A carpet sweeper, extra blankets, a hatbox, insect repellent, and a carton of Christmas decorations were the sum of Judith and Renie's perusal. Judith checked out the hatbox, while Renie dug into the holiday decor. Outside, the sun had started to go down. More firecrackers resounded, while raucous laughter drifted up from the beach.

"Just hats," said Judith. "Ugly ones at that."

"Bubble lights," said Renie in disgust. "Ornaments made out of cornhusks. They look like something Aunt Ellen would send from Nebraska. Here's a myrtlewood crèche. That's kind of cute."

Briefly, the cousins admired the carved Nativity figures, then began putting everything neatly back into place. "Maybe she meant the back closet," said Judith. "We can but try."

They were halfway down the hall when Alice Hoke reappeared in the kitchen, faintly out of breath. "You're quite right," she said, as if granting a favor. "Mr. Teacher wasn't supposed to bring those boxes back here. I'm afraid he's not reliable." Her thin face wore a vexed expression.

"He also drove off without me. I must use your phone and see if Larissa or Augie can pick me up."

"Go ahead," said Judith, finding an annoyed Alice somewhat easier to handle than her usual unyielding personality. "By the way, we didn't find that jewel case. Shall we check the back closet?"

Alice lifted her thin shoulders. "If you like. Frankly, I doubt that it's here. I only have Larissa's word for it." Her attitude seemed to indicate that Larissa's word wasn't worth a damn.

Renie volunteered to make the search, but once again came up empty-handed. Alice, having spoken to her son, said he'd be along shortly. "They're still all up at the house. They felt it necessary to hold some sort of wake. Now they're cleaning up. I trust they'll leave soon." Her face grew wistful.

Judith had the same feeling about Alice Hoke. Still, she felt she should take the opportunity to make a few inquiries. "It seems Darren Fleetwood has already left," she remarked, trying to sound casual. "We spoke with him this afternoon."

The gray eyes snapped. "You did? Whatever for?"

Judith shrugged. "We happened to run into him when he came out of Brent Doyle's office. Frankly, I didn't gather he intended to do anything about this place very soon. He seemed quite anxious to get back to Malibu."

Alice's thin lips pursed in disapproval. "I'm sure he is. No doubt he'll simply put the cottage on the real estate market and collect his money."

Renie had sat down on the arm of the sofa. "You don't think he deserves it?"

"I don't know anything about my sister's affairs." Alice lifted her sharp chin in disdain.

"I take it," said Judith quietly, "you and your nephew aren't close?"

Alice's long, thin body quaked. Her face turned as gray as her eyes. She had to grasp the mantelpiece to steady herself. "What are you talking about?" The words were low and strangled.

Somewhat unsettled by Alice's reaction, Judith cast about for a rejoinder that wouldn't give the other woman apoplexy. "I understood that Darren was Leona's son."

"Nonsense!" Alice arm shot out like a semaphore. "You city people know nothing about small towns and gossip! What a wild rumor!" She pointed a long finger at both cousins. "Don't you dare repeat a thing like that! It's vile!"

Before Judith or Renie could respond, the sound of a horn blared in the cul-de-sac. Alice shook her finger twice, then all but flew out of the room and out of the house. The cousins followed her. In the twilight, they saw Augie Hoke behind the wheel of his beater. Alice swept inside and slammed the car door. Judith and Renie were not sorry to see her go.

THIRTEEN

JUDITH AND RENIE immediately set about making iced tea, though neither of them liked it much. But it was a summer ritual, and they felt obliged to drink it anyway. The receipt that Alice had left on the end table had been made out on a printed form and looked quite professional, unlike the small piece of yellow paper Leona Ogilvie had haphazardly handed over. Judith tucked the receipt inside the zippered pocket of her purse.,

"Do you really think Alice doesn't know—or believe—that Darren Fleetwood is Leona's son?" Renie asked as she poured the tea out of a big jug they'd kept in a jar outside to catch the sun's rays.

"I honestly don't know," Judith replied. Her ears caught the sound of sirens. "Oh, Lord, I hope we're not going to have all-night partying and arrests and other commotions. This Freebooter thing is a real pain."

Renie was getting out the ice cubes. "I suppose Leona gave Darren up. Fleetwood must be his adoptive name. Is there any way we can check that out?"

"The easiest way would be to ask Darren Fleetwood," said Judith, putting a teaspoon of sugar into each tall glass. "When he gets back to Malibu, I mean. He certainly made no secret of the fact that Leona was his mother."

"True," agreed Renie. "Damn—you know, we never got to ask Darren if he had an alibi for Tuesday night."

Judith was carrying their glasses into the living room. They'd left the lights turned off to watch the random display of fireworks on the beach and the scatter of stars above the ocean. "Maybe that's one thing Sheriff Eldritch or Chief Clooney already did. If they realized that Darren was related to Leona. I tell you, coz, it's one thing to sit here in the dark, but it's something else to be working in the dark. At home, we've always had Joe to fill us in. Even up in Port Royal last fall, that nice Canadian detective was really a lot of help. These two are a washout."

"Maybe we haven't given them a fair shake," Renie remarked.

Judith looked dubious, then turned in the armchair to stare out the window. The sirens were quite close and she could see flashing red lights somewhere outside the house. "Those aren't fireworks," she asserted, getting up and going to the window. "I can't see them from here, but those emergency vehicles are down on the beach."

"No wonder. A keg party must have gotten out of hand."

For a few moments, Judith didn't reply. Then she gave a shrug and sat down again. "You're probably right. Let's hope everybody down there decides it's time to leave."

The cousins resumed their discussion, trying to ignore the ruckus outdoors. The sirens stopped, but the lights kept flashing. Midway through trying to figure out how they could get Titus Teacher to admit whether or not he had an alibi for the time of the murder, Renie remembered that they were supposed to call their mothers.

As ever, the conversation with Aunt Deb rambled on. Mrs. Parker's poodle not only was still being naughty, but off his feed as well. Uncle Al had won the trifecta at the race track. Cousin Marty had gotten a ticket for driving his motorcycle into the lobby of his bank. He claimed that there used to be a drive-up window there, but the bank's personnel claimed he was mistaken. And under arrest.

Gertrude, of course, was more concise. "Why are you calling if you don't know when you're coming home? Now you'll have to spend more money to phone again. Judith Anne, don't you have any *sense*?"

Judith was about to offer to call collect the next time when somebody knocked at the back door. Renie went to answer it, while Judith craned her neck to see who it was.

"An electric fan?" Judith was saying into the phone. "I probably forgot to put it in with your other things. Maybe Arlene could drop it off tomorrow."

"Why bother?" snapped Gertrude. "I can always sit here and let Deb's lips flap and get cooled off that way. I don't know why my sister-in-law keeps it so blasted hot in here during the summer. Her circulation must stink."

"But Mother," protested Judith, "I thought you were the one who . . ." She paused, her brow furrowed at the sight of Renie, leading a highly excited Terrence O'Toole into the living room. Renie looked a little agitated, too. She motioned with her hands for Judith to get off the phone. "Mother, I'm sorry, we've got unexpected company. I've got to go."

"Well." Gertrude sounded crestfallen. "That's fine, you do that. I'll wait until another time to tell you about my brain tumor." The phone slammed in Judith's ear.

Renie and Terrence both started talking at once. Renie was the first to stop, deferring to the young reporter. "Wowee! What a week!" he exclaimed, slumping onto the sofa. "Another dead body!"

Judith froze. "Who?"

Renie, who apparently wanted to spare Judith any long-winded, garbled explanation from Terrence, provided the answer. "Titus Teacher. He was shot down at the boat-house about half an hour ago."

Judith was aghast. "But . . . We just saw him up here, out in the carport." She felt the color drain from her face.

"It must have happened right after that," Renie said, collapsing next to Terrence.

"Impossible," murmured Judith, then gave herself a sharp shake. The word had tumbled out by reflex, yet hearing it aloud jolted her brain. *Impossible* was right. Yet all things *were* possible. If only you could figure out how . . .

"I'd just eaten dinner," Terrence explained, using his freckled hands freely. "I saw the ambulance and the other cars heading down 101, so I followed them. They turned off by that big modern place and drove down the beach to that old boathouse." Titus Teacher's body, according to Terrence, had been discovered by some teenagers who had been digging around the boathouse in search of the hidden treasure. At first, they had thought it was just another round of fireworks, but then they realized it had come from inside the little dwelling. Deciding that was odd, they looked through the window. Titus's body was lying over the back of the couch. The teenagers broke in, and discovered that the victim was still quite warm, but very dead. He'd been shot through the chest. "They went for help," Terrence continued, still looking shaken. "Everybody on the beach came charging over to the boathouse. Chief Clooney and Sheriff Eldritch had a terrible time trying to keep them out of the way. It was a real muddle. Clooney ended up throwing out some of Eldritch's men by mistake."

"That was no mistake," murmured Judith, imagining the frenzied scene. "What's going on down there now?"

Terrence raised his hands in a helpless gesture. "I don't know. After I got the facts I needed, the police asked me to leave. I came up here because I thought you'd want to know what was happening."

"We do, Terrence," said Renie, getting up to fetch him a glass of iced tea. "Thanks. We thought it was a bust of a beer bust."

Judith was still trying to organize her fragmented brain. She switched on a lamp and looked at her watch. "It's not quite nine. We got back from the beach about eight. Alice Hoke was waiting for us, Titus Teacher pulled up and dropped off those boxes, we heard him leave about five minutes later, then in another ten or so, Alice got picked up by Augie." She tapped the arm of her chair with her fingernails. "Did anyone notice where that black van was parked?"

Terrence knew nothing about a black van. Renie brought him his drink. Judith asked if anyone had seen Titus Teacher go into the boathouse.

"Yes," answered Terrence, "I talked to somebody who'd seen him go in a few minutes before the teenagers heard the gunshot."

"Did anyone else go into the boathouse?" queried Judith.

Terrence shook his head. "Not that I know of. And I did ask, because I thought it was important." His youthful face looked very earnest, red eyebrows a-jiggle.

"You're right, Terrence, asking that question *is* important." Judith glanced through the picture window where the lights continued to flash. She had a sudden, urgent desire to go down to the beach.

Under the influence of Renie's ministrations and Judith's praise, Terrence was beginning to calm down. He settled further into the sofa, stretched out his legs, and put his hands behind his head. "Wowee, I picked the right job! I knew being a journalist would be one thrill after another!"

Having known a few journalists whose biggest thrill was trying to decipher city zoning codes and sort through fraudulent welfare forms, Judith looked askance. But she could hardly argue with a novice reporter who had come across two murder victims in his first month of employment.

She could, however, gently nudge him on his way. "Gee," Judith exclaimed with an admiring expression, "your editor will be awfully pleased with your on-the-spot coverage. I'll bet you can't wait to turn your story in."

Though obviously pleased by Judith's words, Terrence shrugged. "The next deadline isn't until Monday. We'll have our weekly story conference first thing in the morning. My editor doesn't like his people to bother him on the weekends. He's really tied up right now with the Freeboot-ers' Festival. What did you think of the map?"

"Oh, interesting. Very interesting," replied Judith. "Wasn't it, coz? Say," she said, with sudden anxiety in her voice, "you look peaked. Isn't it time for your *treatment*?"

Renie's face grew puzzled. "My treatment? For what?" She caught Judith's warning gesture and clutched her chest. "You're right—it's time. For the treatment of the disease that affects my breathing. And my memory." Renie gasped several times.

Judith stood up and hurried over to Renie. "Poor thing," she murmured, patting Renie's shoulder. "I'll take her in the bedroom and start the procedure. Don't worry, Ter-rence, I'll be back in an hour or so."

Alarmed at Renie's labored breathing, Terrence had scooted to the far end of the sofa. "Wowee, that was sud-den! Can I help?"

"No, no," Judith asserted, hoisting a now limp Renie to her feet. "I'm used to it. Just make yourself comfortable. As I said, I'll probably finish up before bedtime."

Terrence finally took his cue. "I hate to abandon you two," he called to the cousins as they disappeared into the hall, "but maybe I ought to run along."

"Not on our account," Judith shouted back. "Feel free to browse through those missionary magazines in the rack there."

But Terrence decided it was time to go home. Bidding the cousins farewell and good luck, he left. Judith dropped Renie on the bed in the guest room. Renie opened one eye and squinted up at her cousin.

"Has he got to his scooter yet?"

Judith was trying to look out the window. "Not yet. Give him a minute." They waited in silence. At last, Judith saw the single headlight go on and heard the sound of the motor. "Okay, let's hit the beach, coz. I feel like Uncle Corky at Anzio."

Two of the emergency vehicles were still parked on the sand facing each other, one the property of the sheriff, the other belonging to the police chief. Both still had their

lights flashing, as if in competition. There was no sign of
an ambulance, so apparently the body had been taken
away. Despite the law enforcement personnel's efforts to
clear the area, small clusters of people lingered nearby. *At
least,* Judith thought as she and Renie approached the
boathouse, *nobody was shooting off fireworks.* Indeed, except for a crackling voice on a two-way radio, a sinister
calm had settled over the beach.

Josh Eldritch's lanky form was easy to spot next to the
woodpile outside the boathouse, conferring with one of his
deputies. Judith assumed a deferential air and waited for a
lull in the conversation.

"Is it true?" she asked, crossing the last ten feet of sand
to Eldritch. "We were just told that Titus Teacher has been
murdered."

Eldritch gave the cousins a sour look. "News travels too
fast in this damned town. Yeah, it's true. Now be good to
yourselves and head on back up the bluff."

Judith assumed an affronted expression. "Oh. I thought
you'd want to know about us seeing Titus a few minutes
before he was shot." She started to turn, tugging at Renie's
arm to follow her lead. "Never mind, we'll go talk to Neil
Clooney."

"Hold it!" shouted the sheriff. "You saw Teacher tonight?"

Judith and Renie dutifully backtracked. "He was putting
some things in the carport. Or taking them away. Did you
find his black van?"

Eldritch looked blank. "What van?"

At that moment, Neil Clooney strutted out from the
boathouse. He saw the cousins talking to Eldritch. "Hey—
we're trying to keep people out of this area, you moron!
How come you're inviting the neighborhood in? Don't you
know how to conduct a homicide investigation?"

"Better than you do, Clooney," growled the sheriff.
"These two have some vital information which they're
sharing with *me*. What were you doing in that boathouse,
looking for your girlfriend's buns?"

Clooney rounded on Eldritch. "Keep Alice out of this,

you baboon!" He had gotten quite red in the face and held his clenched fists at his sides. "I was making a thorough search, that's what I was doing," he went on in a slightly less heated tone. "All those numskulls who came charging in there after those kids found the body made quite a mess. If there were any clues, we'll be lucky to find them."

"If there were any clues, *you'd* never find them," retorted Eldritch. "You're so out of date, you were probably looking for lipstick-smudged cigarette butts."

"The only butt around here is you, Eldritch," the police chief snarled. Abruptly, he turned to the cousins, who had been watching the exchange with a mixture of impatience and fascination. "Okay, what have you got to tell us? Remember, we're a team."

"They're a scream, if you ask me," Renie remarked under her breath.

"What'd you say?" demanded Clooney.

"I said this is like a bad dream." Renie gave him her middle-aged ingenue's smile.

Mollified, Clooney waited for a serious answer. Judith repeated her account of seeing Titus Teacher in the carport, adding that it had been about five or ten minutes after eight at the time. He had driven away in a black van. "Alice Hoke saw him, too. She was at Pirate's Lair. In fact, he was supposed to give her a ride home."

"Aha!" Neil Clooney jumped on the idea. "So Teacher was in such a hurry to meet his killer that he ran off without Alice!" He rubbed his hands together and gave the sheriff a sly look out of his porcine eyes. "Now we're getting somewhere. At least *I* am."

Behind them, a couple of policemen and a pair of deputies were arguing over whose crime scene tape would go up around the boathouse. Obviously, the animosity between Clooney and Eldritch carried down through the ranks. The matter was settled when one of the deputies took a swing at one of the policemen, while the other two exchanged swift kicks. Both sets of tape were applied.

Ignoring the commotion as if it were the norm, Eldritch fingered his long chin. "Teacher's killer must have been waiting for him in the boathouse. Of course we'll assume that whoever killed him, also murdered Leona Ogilvie."

"Assume!" cried Clooney. "Real homicide investigators never assume anything! It could be a copycat killing!"

"Then why wasn't Teacher strangled with a kite string, you fathead?"

"Because there was no kite in the boathouse! If you'd move those lazy bones of yours and look around the place, you'd know that, you nincompoop!"

Judith was beginning to feel that the cousins' presence was superfluous. However, she decided to make one last attempt in the name of reason. And logic.

"Wait—let me get something straight." She had to pause for a moment until the jangling died down and the two law enforcement officials finally turned their attention back to her. "Somebody said they saw Titus Teacher go into the boathouse. But nobody saw anyone else go in. Or, apparently, come out. Is that true?"

Clooney gave Judith a patronizing look. "Hey, don't set any store by what all these people say. Half of 'em are tanked up on beer or spaced out on dope. Even if they weren't, who'd notice much of anything with all the fireworks and bikes and stuff? Hell, there was even a volleyball game going on about twenty yards away."

Judith had to admit to herself that Clooney had a point. It was probably remarkable that Terrence O'Toole had found anyone who actually remembered seeing Titus enter the boathouse. Still, the police chief's glib dismissal of her query bothered Judith a bit.

"I don't suppose," said Judith, taking another tack, "you can fix the time of death exactly?"

Eldritch took his turn at answering. "That's always iffy. We won't hear from the county coroner until some time tomorrow, probably." He slapped his thigh. "Hey—tomorrow's a Saturday! The county offices are closed."

"Of course," murmured Renie. "You mean," she asked in a louder voice, "your county officials aren't on standby in case of an emergency?"

Eldritch looked faintly sheepish. "It depends. How do you define 'emergency'?"

Renie gave up, swerving on her heel and shaking her head. Clooney interjected his own theory into the discussion. "Who needs a sawbones to figure out the time anyway? He can dig out the bullet and do all that ballistics-forensics stuff, but we—I—got it pinpointed." He shot Eldritch a self-satisfied look.

"Oh, yeah?" countered the sheriff. "So do I." He glanced at Judith. "What did you say? Eight-fifteen? Eight-twenty, you saw Titus Teacher at the beach cottage?"

Judith suppressed a little sigh. "Between five and ten after eight. Let's say Titus drove the van over to the motel. I have a feeling he got permission to park there and use their tram because of his bad leg. Unless, of course, the van is down by the road next to that big modern-looking house on the point. He could have walked from there. Either way, he would have been back to the boathouse in ten minutes, less if he took the tram. If you know what time the teenagers heard the shot, you can easily establish when Titus was killed. My guess is somewhere between eight-ten and eight-twenty."

Clooney was consulting his notes. "My God, she's right! One of those kids said it was eight-sixteen when they saw the body through the window, according to his digital watch. He reads those stupid detective novels, and felt he ought to check the time."

Judith nodded in a faintly forbearing manner. "The next step is to find out who the dead man is. He seems to be a bit of a mystery, doesn't he?"

Clooney's snoutlike nose wrinkled. "Mystery? He was Alice's caretaker. What's so mysterious about that?"

Judith pressed the police chief. "For how long?"

Clooney shrugged. "As long as we've been going together. A month or so."

"What did he do before that?" asked Judith, who noted that Renie had wandered off toward the incoming tide, apparently fed up with the law enforcement chiefs.

Clooney and Eldritch exchanged glances, indicative of both men's reluctance to admit they didn't know.

"Millwork, probably," said Clooney.

"Commercial fisherman," said Eldritch.

Judith decided that Renie was right; there wasn't any more to be learned from the police chief and the sheriff. "I'd dig a little deeper into his background, if I were you. Titus Teacher seems to have surfaced from nowhere."

"A lot of people around here do that," replied Clooney, on the defensive. "It's a way of life here on the coast. People keep heading west, and eventually they have to stop. Or they end up out there." He gestured toward the ocean, where Renie was standing with her sandaled feel halfway in the water.

"Yes," said Judith, trying to control her impatience. "I'm a native Pacific Northwesterner. I know all about the frontier and drifters and such. But this is also a part of the world where people who are on the run have nowhere else to go." She remembered that Woody Price had not found Titus in his data base of perpetrators. "It's very likely that Titus Teacher isn't his real name."

Clooney threw up his hands. "Oh, bull! Come on, lady, enough's enough! Where do you get off trying to tell us how to run this show?"

Judith was on the verge of blurting out the truth when Eldritch broke in. "Clooney's right, this isn't any of your business. You don't even live in Buccaneer Beach. It's bad enough to get all these Californians coming up here telling us how to run our town, but now we get you people down from ..."

Judith held up her hands. "Okay, okay." It seemed that the one thing the sheriff and the police chief could agree on was that she was a meddling pain in the neck. "I'm sorry, I got carried away." She gave both men a self-deprecating smile. "It's just that my cousin and I found the first body in our living room. Now we've got one in what is technically our boathouse. It's terribly upsetting for a pair of women on their own in a strange place. I'm sure you understand. After all, there is a killer loose, and we're utterly defenseless."

Both men visibly softened. "Yeah," agreed Clooney, "it's rough being the weaker sex, I suppose. No man to protect you."

"Maybe," offered Eldritch, "we should send somebody to watch the house."

Although she knew Joe would approve, the last thing Judith wanted was a bumbling deputy or inept policeman to hover over every move she and Renie made during the next twenty-four hours. "That's very kind," said Judith, trying to look suitably helpless. "But won't you have to pay them overtime? It *is* the weekend."

The sheriff rubbed at his chin. "I'd better check that out."

"I'll get back to you on that," promised the police chief, starting to shuffle away. "Got to catch that radio message."

"Hey!" shouted Eldritch. "That's *my* radio message!" His long strides swiftly caught up with Clooney.

Renie had strolled back toward the boathouse. She glanced over at the law enforcement officials and grinned at Judith. The cousins left them arguing on the sands.

"What are you looking for this time?" Renie asked in exasperation as Judith attacked another packing crate in the carport. They had just returned from the beach, making a detour to verify Judith's guess about the black van. It was in the motel lot, all right, parked in a stall near the office. The evening desk clerk was a young Hispanic man with large ears and perfect teeth. He had not seen Titus Teacher go through the lobby that evening, but confirmed the dead man's use of the tram. The motel didn't usually make exceptions, the clerk explained, but the staff was sensitive to the needs of the handicapped. Besides, he added, they understood he was going to be around for only a few weeks. Judith had given the young man a grateful—and enlightened—smile.

"This stuff's been rearranged," said Judith to Renie, as

she lifted the top off one of the boxes. "Again. I want to see what's inside the ones toward the back."

In order to get at the cartons that were up against the carport wall, Judith had had to back out the MG. The boxes of bedding and dishes had been pulled away to make a path. Judith stood on her tiptoes, feeling inside the crate. "Clothes, I think." She hauled out a man's gray flannel shirt, a pair of brown trousers, and a dark blue pullover. She examined the tags, holding them under the carport light. "Made in West Germany. It figures." She put the garments back in the carton.

"Do you also figure that the owner is dead?" asked Renie, helping Judith shove the other boxes back into place.

"I'm afraid so," said Judith, tripping over what she presumed was a rough place in the carport floor. "It's after ten. Too late to call on anybody, I suppose. Let me put the car back inside."

Five minutes later, Judith and Renie were in the living room. Having had their fill of iced tea for the season, Judith poured a scotch for herself and a bourbon for Renie. "If Alice Hoke has been living in Liechtenstein for the past several years, she wasn't alone," Judith declared. "I'll bet anything she was with Titus Teacher."

"Who," Renie offered, "isn't really Titus Teacher at all, but . . . ?" The word dangled between the cousins.

Over the rim of her glass, Judith gazed intently at Renie. "Don't hit me, coz. It's only a guess. How about Race Doyle?"

Somewhat to Judith's surprise, Renie merely nodded. "The late Race Doyle." She raised her glass. *"Requiescat in pace."*

"Amen," said Judith.

FOURTEEN

JOE'S SURGEON, DR. SCOTT, had conferred with his peers and come to the decision that the patient should not be moved for at least one more day. "Everything's coming along very well," said Dr. Lundgren, relaying the message to Judith. "Dr. Scott is very pleased. It sounds as if Monday would be the latest that your husband will be released. Naturally, we can't make promises . . ."

Judith let the intern run on with his medical sops. She and Renie were in the visitors' waiting room, since Joe had not yet returned from wherever Dr. Scott had taken him. After Lundgren departed, Renie showed some signs of agitation.

"Gee, coz," she fretted, "Bill's coming home tomorrow. And although the Franciscan monks may have all the patience of St. Francis, Maestro Dunkowitz will flip his toupee if I don't get going on that symphony job. Guilt has started sneaking up on me. I really should head back tomorrow morning."

"Tomorrow?" Judith gaped at Renie. "You can't! We don't have a killer yet! Heck, we don't even have a motive!"

Slumping in the imitation leather chair, Renie sighed. "I bought an open-ended round-trip ticket. The train stops in Salem around noon. I can get home by early evening. You and Joe wouldn't have room for me in the MG anyway."

That thought had never occurred to Judith. She was used to her four-passenger Japanese compact. And she wasn't accustomed to including a husband in her driving plans. Judith gave her cousin a forlorn look. "Great. Left all alone, I'll probably get murdered and you'll have to read about it in a badly-written story by Terrence O'Toole."

"At least we've got the rest of today," Renie pointed out.

Judith was still wearing a disheartened expression. "Right." Slowly, she got to her feet. "Let's make the most of it. We'd better see if Joe is back in his room."

He was, looking as down in the mouth as Judith. Jake Beezle, on the other hand, was dressed and raring to go. "I'm outta this joint," he announced, leaning on his crutches and showing off a pair of brand new overalls. He was shirtless, but had tied a red and white kerchief around his scrawny neck. "I hear you two found another stiff."

"Some teenagers found him," said Judith in an uncharacteristically lackluster voice. She turned to Joe. "Renie's abandoning me. She's going home tomorrow."

Joe looked unconcerned. "So? We'll probably be heading that way the day after. You'll have to drive. Just don't let it drop under eighty on the freeway."

"But . . ." Judith started to protest.

"Hold it." Joe put up a hand. "When I get out of this hospital, we're getting out of town. I've had enough of Buccaneer Beach. It's even possible we can leave tomorrow, too. Forget the murders. In fact," he continued, his round face hardening, "after this last one, I want you both to back off. This killer is utterly ruthless. I mean it, Jude-girl."

There was no brooking Joe's argument. Judith actually flinched at the stern expression in those green eyes. Indeed, the gold flecks sparked like flame. It had been a long time since Judith had felt her will thwarted by any-one. Except Gertrude, of course. She turned uncommonly meek.

"Okay, Joe," she mumbled. "We'll concentrate on finding the treasure."

"Skip that, too," ordered Joe. "Unless you mean this year's festival prize. That ought to be safe enough."

A nurse, whom Judith had never see before and who actually weighed under three hundred pounds, pushed a wheelchair into the room. Obviously, it was time for Jake to leave. Getting settled into the chair, Jake gave the cousins a big grin.

"I'd ask you over for some cards tonight, but I already got company coming," he said with a wink. Jake lowered his voice. "Mrs. Wampole gets out today, too." He made a clicking noise with his tongue.

"That's wonderful," said Judith, trying to stir up enthusiasm. "Does she play poker?"

Jake shook his head. "Naw, she's another one of them bridge fiends, like you two. That's one game I want no part of. All that counting points and bidding back and forth and crazy scoring above and below the line. It's the only kind of cards I know where your nearest and dearest will try to stomp in your skull for making an honest mistake. Seems to me everybody's got to be a dummy to play that game." He lifted a bony white arm. "See ya in the funny papers. I've had a good time, but this wasn't one of 'em. Ha-ha!" Jake rolled out of the room, calling down the hall to Mrs. Wampole.

"I hope he'll be all right," said Judith. "I worry about him. He's really quite frail. And old."

"He's not frail, he's just sort of stringy," said Joe. "Sinew, and all that. But he *is* old." Joe's face had softened.

Renie stepped out of the way as an orderly came in to strip Jake's bed. "Should we ask him to visit us and introduce him to our mothers?" Her brown eyes danced.

Joe shook his head and grinned. "Jake doesn't deserve that. All things considered, he was a pretty good roommate." His gaze shifted back to Judith. "As a matter of fact, he invited us to come back down here some time and stay with him."

Echoing Judith's feelings about Jake's home, Renie shuddered. "Oh, good grief, I can imagine what his place is like! Some run-down hovel with a one-holer out back and a woodburning stove. Or maybe just a hot-plate . . ." She, too, gazed at Judith.

But Judith wasn't gazing back. Rather, she was staring beyond them in the direction of the window. Suddenly, she jumped and snapped her fingers. "That's it! Bridge!"

Her cousin and her husband stared. "What's what?" asked Joe.

Judith was animated now, pacing the small open space of the hospital room. The orderly was finishing up, and Judith waited for him to leave. "The map," she said at last, sitting down on the edge of the chair next to Joe's bed and digging the scrap of paper from her purse. "The four aces and kings and all the rest, In bridge, they add up to forty. The hundred—I still can't see this very well, but it's probably not a broken *m*, but a double *r*. For railroad," she explained quickly. "A hundred miles of railroad, that's a card-playing term, too, for tens. So we get one hundred forty, which happens to be the number of stairs leading down from Pirate's Lair. The part about the bridge referred to the game, not a place. And to its rules." Judith waited for comments from Renie and Joe, but both were still looking puzzled. "Don't you see—this map isn't really that old. Bridge wasn't popular until after World War I. I'll bet this is a map from one of the previous Freebooters' Festivals, maybe the same year as the newspaper that was under the rug."

Renie groaned. "All this fuss over some meaningless Chamber of Commerce promotion! What a waste of time!"

Judith, however, didn't agree. "I think it's worth checking it out. It's too bad we don't have the rest of it—we're sort of stuck after we get to the bottom of the stairs. Unless . . ." Her voice trailed off, but her black eyes gleamed, then suddenly snapped. She grabbed Joe's arm.

"You knew this all along, didn't you? You rat! You purposely misled us!" She gave him a sharp shake, rattling his pulleys.

"Hey, watch it, Jude-girl!" He wore his most ingenuous expression. "It doesn't take a homicide detective to figure out they wouldn't have had a bridge around this coast back in 1706 or whatever. Who do you think was in charge of Public Works around here, Sir Isaac Newton?"

Chagrined, Judith let got of her husband and gave Renie a vexed look. Renie was muttering to herself, something about coastal tribes and temporary footbridges. It didn't sound very convincing.

"Okay, okay," allowed Judith, still annoyed at Joe's subterfuge. "So what did you find out about Alice and Leona's travel arrivals?"

Joe wore a bland expression. "Nothing. They'll get back to me after the weekend." Judith started to look more than just annoyed, but kept her temper in check. She could hardly blame Joe for wanting to protect her. He gave her fingers a tight, almost painful squeeze. "Hey—what did I tell you from the start about backing off this case? Go look for your treasure chest, or whatever. That's harmless enough. Everybody else in town will be out there searching, too."

"Okay, Joe," Judith murmured, her eyes cast down. She stood up and blew him a kiss.

"Gee, coz," said Renie as they made their way down the hospital corridor, "Joe sure has your number."

"Right," said Judith. "He knows me better than anyone. Except you."

"I guess," mused Renie. "So what do we do now?"

"Figure out the rest of the map," replied Judith as they got into the elevator.

"Oh." Renie sounded disappointed. "But if it's from seven years ago, there won't be anything there now."

Judith gazed complacently up at the elevator ceiling as the car glided smoothly to the main floor. "I think otherwise. Besides," she went on as they exited into the hospital lobby, "I intend to find more than two free dinners at a local drive-in. We, dear coz, are about to find a motive—and thus, a murderer."

Renie stopped in her tracks. "But, coz—I thought you promised Joe . . ."

Judith looked back over her shoulder. "Did I say that? Did you hear me give a promise? Well?"

Renie grinned and ran to catch up with her cousin. "No, of course not. Jeez, you had me scared there for a minute. I thought Joe really did have your number."

"He does," replied Judith. "He just doesn't realize *which* number—in this case it's three million."

It was only 10:00 A.M., but the beach below Pirate's Lair was already swarming with treasure seekers. Armed with shovels, axes, metal detectors, and even portable computers, the tourists appeared to have been joined by a large number of locals as well. As Terrence O'Toole had predicted, a few were indeed dressed in pirate garb, looking more like overaged Trick-or-Treaters than Independence Day revelers. One man even had a live parrot on his shoulder; another trailed a small kite which was emblazoned with a Jolly Roger; various pirate wenches trod the sands in flowing skirts and skimpy tops of a motley hue. The only empty spot on the sand was the area immediately adjacent to the boathouse, where a deputy sheriff and police patrolman stood duty. Obviously, the death of Titus Teacher had done nothing to daunt the treasure buffs.

The cousins already had encountered several people trooping through the yard of the beach cottage, headed for the long staircase. Efforts to discourage the intruders had been in vain. Consequently, Judith and Renie found themselves descending the steps with half a dozen others, including a Japanese family of four and a pair of young lovers holding hands.

"Now what?" asked Renie when they got to the beach and found themselves virtually surrounded by the milling crowd.

Judith looked above several shorter heads, to the stair-

case itself, which was one of the few unpopulated areas in
the vicinity. "Let's see the back of this year's map. I'll bet
that in the past, the treasure was hidden under the steps."

Judith was right. Seven summers ago, the winner had
found the stash of free dinners, discount coupons, and
dune buggy rentals somewhere behind the staircase. Since
the description wasn't precise, Judith and Renie approached with some uncertainty. At ground level, the open
space between the bluff and the stairs was about eight feet
wide. At the foot of the bluff, boulders had been piled
some fifteen feet high to prevent slides. Further up, a vast
network of heavy-duty chicken wire took over to hold the
rest of the bluff in place.

"Rocks or sand?" Judith posed the question, leaning on
the handle of her shovel.

Renie surveyed both possibilities. "With all the dogs
around here, I'd say burying something really valuable
wouldn't be such a good idea. Let's try the rocks."

The cousins did, attempting to dislodge any loose boulders. After a quarter of an hour, they gave up. "It's been
seven years," said Judith, out of breath and already getting
too warm in the morning sun. "These things have settled,
or something. Let's dig in the sand."

They concentrated on the area in back of the stairs. This
far up on the beach, where the waves reached only during
wild winter storms, the sand was soft and dry, but not particularly easy to work. The cousins, who had one shovel
between them, took turns, giving half-witted smiles to
treasure seekers who called to tell them that they were
searching in an out-of-bounds area. At one point, the sheriff's deputy strolled over to ask why they were digging in
a site that had been already used. Judith told them she'd
lost her Miraculous Medal.

"Frankly," said Renie, huffing and puffing, "it'll be a
miracle if we find anything. Maybe we should borrow one
of those metal detectors." She gave one last desultory
lunge; the shovel clanked against something hard. Both
cousins got down on their stomachs and began to scoop
out the hole with their bare hands.

"Oh, boy," breathed Judith, as the outline of a strongbox emerged. She turned her smudged face to Renie and grinned weakly. "We did it, coz." Angling her arm down in the hole, she grasped the catch. It was locked. "It figures," said Judith, then tried to move the box. It wouldn't budge. The cousins stared at each other.

"You really think there's three million bucks in there?" asked Renie in a hoarse voice.

Judith nodded. "Or the equivalent thereof. She scrambled up on her knees, surveying the hordes of treasure hunters roaming the beach. "If any of those folks knew what we had here, they'd stampede us like a herd of water buffalo. I'm not sure we can lift this without help. We should Do the Right Thing and turn it over to the police. And the sheriff. But they'd fight over it, and we'd have to stand here in the hot sun with sand in our teeth and listen to them argue."

"You got it." Renie, who was also sitting up now, brushed sand from her rumpled clothes. "You figure Race Doyle ditched this before he took off?"

"Somebody did," said Judith, noticing a long scratch on her right arm. "It's probably been here for seven years, while Alice and Race bided their time in Liechtenstein. But remember, I'm only guessing."

Renie's brown eyes grew enormous. "Alice and Race! So that's why she had to disappear!" Clapping a hand to her damp forehead, Renie laughed. "Of course! Titus Teacher was Race Doyle!"

"Maybe," replied Judith, finding that it wasn't easy to get to her feet. "One thing that's bothered me is how Alice sold that cheese factory five years ago while she was in Liechtenstein. Leona couldn't have done that for her. But do you remember what Alice said to Brent Doyle's receptionist the other day?" Renie didn't, at least not the specifics. Judith refreshed her cousin's memory: "Alice mentioned that Brent was drawing up a new power of attorney." She waited for Renie's comprehension. Renie not only continued to look blank, but hot and tired as well. Judith took pity on her suffering cousin. "A *new* power of attorney, which means there was an old one. Brent Doyle has only been practicing law for a few weeks. So his father, Bartlett Doyle, must have put together the original. I'll bet anything he used it, under Alice's directive, to sell that property to the outlet mall developers. Of course it expired when Bartlett Doyle died."

"I'm about to do both those things," said Renie, struggling to her knees. "Die. Expire. Etc." She shielded her eyes with her hand and looked up at Judith. "Are you saying that Bart Doyle knew where Alice really was all along?"

"Not necessarily," replied Judith. "Alice could have sent instructions through Leona. Leona was gullible, remember. A perfect dupe. The important thing is that the sale would have provided money for Alice and Titus—or Race—or whoever—to live on in Liechtenstein. Tax-free, too, I'll bet."

Renie gave a feeble nod. "In five years they may have used it up."

"Could be," agreed Judith. "But the original three million that never left Oregon gives us a motive." Her tone, however, carried no note of triumph.

Renie grabbed the shovel by the handle, stuck it in the ground, and held on to heave herself upright. "Well? That's half the battle, right?"

"Right." Judith squinted into the sun, surveying the back side of the long staircase. "But three million bucks is also too much motive. In a way, it lets out Darren Fleetwood. Leona had been disinherited by her father. But Alice has a legal claim to this money. Her kids would get it if anything happened to her."

"But it happened to Leona. And maybe to Race Doyle," noted Renie.

"I know," said Judith, starting toward the boathouse. "That's what bothers me. That, and the fact that even though we now have a motive, everybody except Darren Fleetwood has an alibi. At least for Leona's murder."

Renie fell into step with Judith. "For Titus—I mean, Race's death, too. The whole family was up at the Ogilvie-

Hoke house, remember? Darren left town. Alice was with us."

"That's right," said Judith. "That bothers me more than anything."

Half an hour later, the cousins had carted the strongbox up to Pirate's Lair. It was more cumbersome than heavy. They had been careful to avoid being seen by the deputy and the policeman who continued to alleviate their boredom with verbal sniping at one another.

"Great," said Renie, coming out of the bedroom in a change of clothes, "here we are with a killer loose and three million dollars in a tin box. What do we do next, get a bunch of drugs and try to peddle them at a stand out in the cul-de-sac?"

"It is a ticklish situation," Judith admitted. She was sitting in her new bathrobe, having just taken a quick shower. "Just in case the law enforcement guys saw us, let's not open the box yet. I don't want them confiscating it."

"It's too hot to wrestle with the blasted thing anyway," declared Renie, flopping on the sofa. "Besides, the sight of other people's CDs or whatever is in there doesn't thrill me. Not even three million bucks' worth." She shot Judith a querying glance. "You *are* sure that's what's there, aren't you?"

Judith felt the sand in the carpet under her bare feet. "What else? CDs, passbooks, stock certificates—whatever, totaling the stolen amount in some form or other. Why else bury the damned thing?" She glanced at the strongbox as if it offended her. Battered but sturdy, the steel case now reposed on the hearth, just inches away from where Leona Ogilvie had died. Judith considered hiding it, but there was no real place of concealment in the beach cottage. She decided they might as well let it sit in plain sight for the time being.

"I wonder," she mused, "if the police—or the sheriff—are making any effort to determine Titus Teacher's real identity."

"Probably not," said Renie. "They'll write him off as a drifter. Especially if Alice can convince Clooney that he really was some itinerant soul she hired to watch over the beach property."

Judith nodded absently, then gave a start. "But will she? If Alice and Titus—Race, that is—were in on this from the start, why wouldn't she be glad he was dead? The money's all hers now. Look," Judith went on excitedly, making circles with her finger on the coffee table, "if Alice and Race went off together and left Leona as her stand-in, there's nobody to tie Alice in with Race. Everybody thinks she's been in Buccaneer Beach all along. Then Race comes back and gets himself killed, along with Leona. Alice is home free. All she has to do is come up with the money, which is rightfully hers, and she's sitting even prettier than she was in the first place."

"Why wait seven years?" asked Renie.

Judith shrugged. "Statute of limitations, maybe. I don't know how long it is on embezzlement or whatever Race could have been charged with, but the time's probably up by now." She gave another little jump as a knock sounded at the back door. Renie went to answer it, while Judith eyed the strongbox anxiously.

It was Amy and Augie, looking tired and somewhat bedraggled. "We just wanted to ask permission to use your stairs down to the beach," said Augie. "We've been hunting for the treasure prize up by the marina with no luck, so we drove down here. We'll go back on that road over by the point."

"I can walk down okay," put in Amy, collapsing gratefully on the sofa next to Judith, "but going back up is too much. I still feel a little woozy. This has been a terrible trip."

Judith assured them it was fine to use the stairs. She saw Augie glance at the strongbox, but he showed no special interest. "You heard about Mr. Teacher, I take it?" Judith remarked.

"Oh, yes!" Amy pushed the long dark hair out of her eyes. "Isn't that awful? Augie's mother says it's a good thing this place doesn't belong in the family any more. It's hexed."

"Just think," said Augie, sitting down on the strongbox and making Judith wince, "if he hadn't been so muddled, he'd have remembered to pick up Momma and then he might not have gotten killed. I'll bet it happened just about the time I drove down here to get her."

Something flickered in Judith's eyes but the others apparently didn't notice. "That may be so," she allowed. "What did you think of Mr. Teacher?"

Augie shook his head. "I can't say. We never met him."

"We saw him at the funeral," Amy put in, "but we didn't talk to him. Larissa was going to; she had some silly idea he might have been Aunt Leona's boy friend. But Mr. Teacher left right after the service."

Judith waited while Renie poured iced tea for the Hokes. Handing it out to guests was one way to get rid of it, the cousins had decided. "Did he look at all familiar to you?"

With his glass halfway to his mouth, Augie gave a little start. "Familiar? It's funny you should say that, ma'am. Yes, he did. Larissa thought so, too. I think that's really why she wanted to talk to him."

"Did your mother agree?" inquired Judith.

Augie looked questioningly at his wife, but she had no answer. "I don't know. Momma never said anything about it. She hired him, I guess," Augie went on slowly. "Maybe she knew him from around here."

Time was running out; a killer was on the loose. Judith cast caution to the winds. "Did you know Race Doyle well?"

Augie screwed up his face in the effort of recollection. "I never saw much of him, actually. He didn't come to the house."

"Kind of . . . uh, flashy? Mod, I mean, for his day." Judith based her query on the 1970s-style photo in the newspaper.

Augie considered. "Sort of. More what I'd call a city type. Race tried to be hip, but it didn't come off. He wasn't all that good-looking to begin with—about my height, light brown hair, moustache, dressed like California, if you know what I mean. He always wore big sunglasses. I guess he thought it made him look cool."

The description tallied with the newspaper picture. The verbal sketch could also fit the bearded, drably-garbed Titus Teacher. Seven years and a change of style could do a great deal to alter a man's appearance. Judith felt satisfied with her theory.

Amy asked to use the bathroom; Augie accepted another half-glass of iced tea. Both of the Hokes thanked Judith and Renie for coming to Leona's funeral. Then they were gone, a rejuvenated Amy telling an attentive Augie how she thought she had finally figured out some of the treasure hunt clues.

"Little do they know," said Renie, gazing at the strongbox.

"It would be nice if Augie and Amy could get their hands on some of that money." Judith also stared at the strongbox. "Maybe we should open it now."

"I'd rather wait until after dark," said Renie. "Too many people keep popping in and out of this place."

Judith had to agree, but decided they should at least make some attempt to disguise the strongbox. "Let's put something over it, make it look like an end table."

By the time Renie had emerged from the back bedroom where she'd found a card table–sized luncheon cloth, Judith was going through the phone book, searching for Brent Doyle's home address.

"It won't be in there," said Renie, placing the embroidered cloth over the strongbox and standing back to admire her work. "He just moved back to town a month or so ago."

"If he's got a mother, she'd know where he is," said Judith. "Here, Bartlett L. Doyle, on Pacific Heights." She stood up. "I'll get dressed and then we'll call on the Widow Doyle. If anybody had recognized Race at the funeral, it would have been Brent Doyle. After all, Brent was Race's nephew."

Pacific Heights was a development of expensive homes built on a hillside above the highway, overlooking the ocean and the lighthouse. Located just south of town, the two dozen homes had been constructed in many different styles of architecture, but all of them took advantage of the view with facades made up almost entirely of glass. The late Bartlett Doyle's home was the most traditional of the lot, a contemporary Cape Cod with a huge stone chimney.

Bart Doyle's widow was a handsome blond woman in her fifties with a sculpted, unlined face. Her son was living at home temporarily, but had gone out with friends on a forty-foot cruiser. He wasn't due to return until after dark. No, he preferred not to conduct business on a weekend. Certainly he never saw clients at home.

"We just wanted to thank him for getting Mrs. Hoke to give us our receipt," Judith explained in her most congenial voice. She wished Mrs. Doyle would stop barring the door and let them in out of the hot sun. "You see, we rented the beach cottage from . . ."

"Yes," Mrs. Doyle broke in smoothly. "Brent told me all about it. I'm glad he was of service." She started to close the door.

"Aren't you spooked a little by that lighthouse?" Judith asked, waving an arm out toward the point.

"I beg your pardon?" Fine lines showed on Mrs. Doyle's otherwise smooth brow.

"Isn't that where Bernie Hoke's boat was washed up after he committed suicide? I thought he'd been a client of your husband's."

Mrs. Doyle's face showed faint distaste, though whether it was for Bernard Hoke or the cousins, Judith couldn't be sure.

"I believe he was a client," she replied coolly. "I never got involved in my husband's business matters. It doesn't pay to do so in a small town. Naturally, we didn't mingle with the Hokes." Her tone implied that the family suffered from some grave social disease, like burping in public.

"You didn't attend Leona's funeral, I take it?" Judith

couldn't recall seeing Mrs. Doyle in attendance, but the fact was that she could have been lost in the crowded church.

"Certainly not," said Mrs. Doyle, sounding faintly offended. "I never met the woman. I'm from *Portland.*"

"Oh," said Renie faintly. "That explains it." Seeing Mrs. Doyle's shrewd gray eyes narrow, she smiled brightly at their reluctant hostess. "We have a cousin in Portland. Oswald. He's one of the city's most respected intellectuals. He even has a library card."

Obviously unsure of what to make out of Renie, Mrs. Doyle grew snappish. "See here, I don't know why you two have come around to bother my son—and me—but I can assure you, I know nothing of this Hoke ménage. They're a strange lot, if you ask me—which I'm sure you intend to do if I let you. As for Bernard Hoke, he built these houses and did such a good job that he claimed to have lost money on them. He even did a lot of the work himself. It was a shame when he died, because this area lost an excellent builder. Still, it may be just as well— toward the end, he was a wreck, mentally and physically. Or so I heard." She forced a frozen smile. "I hear the phone ringing. I must go." Mrs. Doyle closed the door.

Judith and Renie went down the six steps that led to the flower-lined pathway. "She lied about the phone," said Renie. "It wasn't ringing."

"So what?" retorted Judith. "We don't have a Cousin Oswald."

FIFTEEN

AFTER IT APPEARED that their trek to Pacific Heights had been a failure, the cousins agreed that Brent Doyle might not have been much help anyway. It was now noon, so they stopped at the festival take-out stand with the shortest line and bought two orders of salmon and chips, with a side of macaroni salad. Since the streets were jammed with tourists and treasure seekers, they took their lunch back to Pirate's Lair.

"I feel stupid," Judith lamented. "We've made a lot of progress, but we still aren't close to solving this case. What's *wrong*?"

Renie was gazing out the picture window at the front lawn. "Our staircase. Even now, it brings us Larissa and Donn Bobb Lima."

Renie was right. First their heads, then the rest of the Limas appeared as they reached the top of the stairs. Weakly, Judith waved. Larissa, towing Donn Bobb, made straight for the front door. She was looking decidedly miffed.

"Now don't get me wrong," she said by way of greeting, "but this whole treasure thing is just plain unfair." She waved a somewhat wrinkled version of the place mat map at the cousins. "We aren't the sort to go lookin' for free stuff and all that like Augie and Amy, mind you. Still, this is more like a game, so we thought we'd tackle it just for kicks, to pass the time before Donn Bobb's performance in the rodeo at the high school field tonight. So we got it all figured out, but we can't get at the prize."

"Why not?" asked Judith, indicating, somewhat reluctantly, that the Limas should sit.

Plopping down on the cloth-covered strongbox, Larissa scrutinized the map. "Okay—it says it's not A or C, so that leaves B, right?" She looked up at Judith for confirmation; Judith tried not to gape. "So that's gotta be Bee Creek. You know, 'B' as in 'ABC,' only this is spelled out, B-e-e. Then you can take a bike or go on a hike due west, which is toward the ocean." She stopped long enough for Renie to pour her and Donn Bobb an iced tea. "Then there's this part about the sign that used to be wine, and of course that's a cinch—when I was little, my daddy brought me with him while he was building this here beach cottage. He had to tear down an old tavern to put up the house. The last thing he took out was an old sign that said 'beer and wine.' " She looked up again, a matter-of-fact expression on her heavily made-up face.

"That's very good," said Judith, taken aback.

"Astounding," murmured Renie.

"It's dumb," said Donn Bobb, with a yawn. "Too easy."

"Anyway," Larissa went on, "I put it all together, and the prize has to be below this place on the beach. That means the boathouse. But you can't go in because that poor Mr. Teacher got killed there last night. Honestly, I wish people would stop getting murdered around here. It just spoils everything." Larissa turned petulant.

Still dazed by Larissa's unexpected mental prowess, Judith gave herself a little shake. "I didn't think the sponsors of the treasure hunt could hide the prize inside a building."

Larissa gave an impatient shrug, causing the strap of her halter top to slip over one bare shoulder. "Inside, outside—whatever. It's *at* the boathouse, that's for sure.

And there it is, under guard by a couple of dopey police-men." She snorted with disgust and yanked at her halter strap.

Judith made some soothing noises, then tried to steer Larissa onto a different track. "You're right, it's a shame about Mr. Teacher. Your brother told us this morning that you recognized him. I guess he must be an old friend of the family's."

Larissa's eyes widened. "Huh? No, I don't think so." She glanced at Donn Bobb, who seemed to be sliding down the couch next to Renie. "I did think he looked like somebody I knew when I saw him at the funeral. In fact, it kind of spooked me at the time. But you know how fu-nerals are—you get all kinds of weird feelings. Besides, I was crying a lot and couldn't see so good. Momma says I have too much imagination."

Judith gave Larissa a small smile. "You certainly have an uncanny ability to figure out those treasure clues."

Larissa seemed unaffected by the praise. "Oh—yeah, I guess I got that kind of mind. In the rodeo off-season, I work with computers."

"Oh," said Judith. "That's nice. Where?" She almost hated to ask.

Larissa gave another shrug, but this time kept her hand on her halter. "Different places. I sort of—what do you call it?—free lance. The pay's best at Cape Kennedy, though. And I really like doing stuff with the space pro-gram.

Judith and Renie both gaped.

"She could be right about the treasure," Judith said after Larissa had awakened Donn Bobb and the two of them had gone off to complain to somebody official about the treasure hunt's lack of fairness.

"It makes sense," Renie agreed. "I guess I hadn't really paid any attention to the new map."

Neither had Judith. A sense of futility overcame her; maybe Joe was right. She ought to forget the murders and make plans to go home.

"Oh!" she exclaimed. "I forgot to call Arlene and let her know she'll have to keep running the B&B for at least another night." Judith dialed Hillside Manor. Carl Rankers answered the phone.

"My dear wife's got me cleaning out the debris from the toolshed. I just came in to get a beer," said Carl in his pleasant, friendly manner. "I may not get a lot done. There's a storm coming in later today."

"Don't worry about it," Judith reassured him. "I'll sort it out when I get home. Any news of Sweetums?" There was a faint catch in her voice.

"Afraid not," replied Carl. "Arlene may be right for the first time in thirty years. The firecrackers must have sent him into hiding."

Visions of what young boys with firecrackers could do to cats exploded before Judith's eyes. Despite her threats to do the same—and worse—to Sweetums over the years, Judith was definitely unsettled by the idea of serious harm coming to her perverse pet.

Signing off with Carl, Judith called the ranger station in Montana. Michael McMonigle wasn't there. He'd checked in Thursday, but had left. No, answered the rugged masculine voice, McMonigle wasn't expected back. He might have been assigned to a fire lookout in Flathead National Forest or one of the campgrounds by Hungry Horse Dam.

"Now I've misplaced my kid *and* my cat," sighed Judith. "I'm a real disaster."

"Cheer up," said Renie. "At least we got rid of the iced tea."

Before Judith could respond, a great cheer went up from the vicinity of the beach. The cousins exchanged startled looks.

"What now?" asked Judith, heading out the front door.

Renie followed, as the sound of applause drifted up from the sands. The afternoon had turned humid as well as hot. The heavy air seemed to weigh Judith down. Out on the horizon, dark clouds were moving towards shore. Perhaps the predicted storm that Carl Rankers had mentioned was going to hit Buccaneer Beach as well as Heraldsgate Hill.

Stopping at the head of the stairs, the cousins surveyed the scene below. A huge crowd had gathered, with its focal point somewhere between the bottom of the staircase and the boathouse. More people were streaming from every direction. Judith and Renie quickly made their descent. At the edge of the crowd, they spotted Terrence O'Toole, camera in hand.

"What's going on?" shouted Judith over the din.

Terrence beamed at the cousins. "A retired couple from Medford found the treasure. Isn't that wild?"

"Oh!" Judith let out a sigh of relief. Despite the buoyant nature of the gathering, she'd feared the worst. "Where was it?"

Terrence was stepping back to take a wide-angle shot. "In a hollowed-out log," he replied.

When the crowd began to melt away, Judith and Renie discovered that the Freebooters' Festival treasure chest had been tucked away inside the very same log they'd used for their picnics. The cousins exchanged bemused, and faintly shamefaced, glances.

The departure of the treasure seekers also signaled the exit of the law enforcement men who had been keeping watch at the boathouse. Apparently the sheriff and the police chief had finished their work there. Judith and Renie trudged back to the beach cottage.

"Just think," laughed Renie when they were inside the house again, "we were sitting on the treasure all the time."

"Speaking of sitting on loot," said Judith, eyeing the cloth-covered strongbox, "maybe we should move that into one of the bedrooms." She whisked off the linen square and examined the lock. "Better yet, we should open this thing. It's making me nervous. What if it's actual cash? Let's not wait until tonight. I'll go get the tools of my trade."

But Renie stopped her. "I don't know—this is really complicated. It takes a key *and* a combination."

Judith's skills were put to the test. After twenty minutes, she had vanquished the lock itself, but the combination eluded her. The cousins resorted to a chisel, but their only reward was a matching set of skinned knuckles.

"We'll have to blow the thing," said Judith at last.

"Huh?" Renie shoved her damp chestnut curls off her forehead.

"Blast the lock with dynamite or something," said Judith, who was also melting in the oppressive heat. "I wonder where we can buy explosives around here."

Renie was about to ridicule the idea of finding such a purveyor open on a weekend in Buccaneer Beach, when she jumped to her feet. "I know! Let's go!"

Puzzled, but game, Judith followed Renie down to the beach. The crowd had now dispersed, leaving only the usual kiteflyers, walkers, driftwoodgatherers, and dogs. Searching among the vacationers on the beach below the We See Sea Resort, Renie found her prey. The ten-year-old kite expert they'd seen earlier in the week with the giant butterfly had now turned his talents to fireworks, especially the kind that were illegal except on Indian reservations. Five minutes and twenty dollars later, the cousins had in their possession something that looked as if it could demolish the capital of a Third World nation.

"We can't do this indoors," said Renie. "We need solid ground. Let's take the strongbox out to the carport."

To make room, Renie shifted some of the cartons while Judith backed the MG out into the cul-de-sac. Attaching the MK24 Victory Arsenal & Whistling Stars to the box with a string, Renie lit the footlong fuse. She then raced back to join Judith on the grass between the house and the carport.

The explosion shook the cousins, though it was the piercing screech of the Whistling Stars that particularly unhinged them. Covering their ears and gritting their teeth, they waited a full minute before approaching the strongbox.

The metal was scorched, but to Judith and Renie's dismay, the combination lock still held. Upon closer examination, they noticed that the giant firecracker had loosened the lid. Judith resumed her work with the chisel. Moments later, they had opened the box from the rear. The cousins stared at the contents.

There was no money. No stocks, no bonds. Nothing of apparent value. Judith hauled out a pair of sheepskin car seat covers. They were soiled, not just with the usual accumulation of dirt, but with large rust-colored smears.

"What the . . . ?" She gazed perplexedly at Renie, then looked back down in the box and noticed a blank envelope taped to the bottom. Judith prised it loose, opened it, and shook out a key. "A safety-deposit box?" She handed the key over to Renie.

"Could be," said Renie. "It's got a number on it."

"That would explain where the money is," said Judith, turning her attention back to the stained sheepskin covers. "What do you think about these?"

Renie made a face. "The only thing I'm sure of is that they didn't belong to seventeenth century pirates."

"Right," agreed Judith, wrinkling her nose. The dampness which had permeated the sheepskin gave off an unpleasant odor. "But they might have belonged to twentieth century pirates. Look, coz," she said, pointing to the rust-colored smears, "doesn't that look a lot like dried blood?"

Fair was fair. Having two items in their possession, the cousins decided to divvy them up between Josh Eldritch and Neil Clooney. The battered strongbox had been stored in the guest bedroom before Judith and Renie took off in the MG. They stopped first at police headquarters, handing over the sheepskin car seat covers to the police chief, who, amazingly, was in his office.

"A policeman's job is never done," he said sententiously. "Besides, I left a dozen doughnuts here from Holesome's Sugar Shop."

Clooney seemed mildly interested in the cousins' discovery. However, he could see no tie-in between a buried strongbox and the recent murders. Somewhat reluctantly, Judith showed him the scrap of treasure map.

"Don't you see," she tried to explain, wondering why Clooney's office wasn't air-conditioned at city expense, "it wasn't an accident that the map was put under the carpet at Pirate's Lair. It was left there so that someone would be able to come along later and dig up the strongbox."

"So?" Clooney's small eyes were skeptical. "Why would anyone want to ditch a couple of seat covers in the first place?" Clooney eyed the smelly sheepskin with distaste. "I suppose they were kind of nice looking when they were new."

Judith felt as if she were ramming her head into a brick wall. Or at least Clooney's formidable stomach. "Please— the least you could do is have your lab find out if that's blood on the seat covers."

Clooney started to frown at Judith, then burst into laughter. "Sure! Why not? It was probably from the sheep!"

"Never mind," said Judith, reaching for the covers, "we'll take them over to the sheriff. He'll know what to do."

The threat worked. Clooney pounced on the sheepskin and promised to put the lab to work. Come Monday. Naturally, they were off for the weekend. Renie emitted a little snort.

"Then," said Judith, somewhat appeased, "your ballistics people haven't been able to determine what kind of gun or bullet killed Titus Teacher?"

Clooney shot Judith a wary look. "We found the bullet. Went right through the body and lodged in the wall between the front room and the kitchen. Full metal jacket, fired from a standard .45 automatic. No big mystery there."

Except, Judith thought, as they left police headquarters, who had pulled the trigger. She was convinced that the same person who had strangled Leona Ogilvie had also shot the man known as Titus Teacher. And for the first time since the cousins had found Leona's body, Judith was almost certain she knew the answer.

* * *

Josh Eldritch was also in his office, having been called in to sort out a six-car pileup just south of town. The murder investigations seemed to have slipped a notch in the sheriff's priorities. Automobile crashes were more common, and thus, more in his area of expertise.

Compared with Clooney's reaction to the seat covers, the sheriff was impressed by the finding of the safety-deposit box key. "You think this will lead to the stolen money from the cheese factory?" he asked somewhat dubiously.

Judith inclined her head. "It'll lead to *something,*" she asserted. "Nobody buries a key in a strongbox two feet below the ground."

Eldritch made a gesture of assent. "I can't check until Monday."

"Naturally," breathed Renie.

"It could be anywhere," he noted.

"True," said Judith.

"It might not even be around here," Eldritch pointed out.

"I have a feeling it is—at least within a fifty-mile radius," said Judith. Why else, she figured, had Alice Hoke returned to Buccaneer Beach? "How many banks are there in town?"

"Three," the sheriff answered promptly. "But there are about ten times that many in Juniper County."

Judith was satisfied. She and Renie had done all they could, as far as working through channels was concerned. Feeling virtuous, the cousins headed for Buccaneer Beach Community Hospital.

Joe was not in his room. Yet another nurse Judith had never seen before informed her that Mr. Flynn was in therapy, learning how to use crutches. Did that mean, Judith inquired with mixed emotions, that he would be discharged the following day? The nurse couldn't say; that would be up to Doctor. Noting that nurses often referred to the MD in charge by the generic title, she mused to Renie that she wondered if it were an exalted soubriquet like "Majesty" or merely a sign of poor memory.

Renie couldn't enlighten her cousin. "All I know is that when you get your teeth fixed, the hygienists never call their boss 'Dentist.' " She cocked her head at Judith as they pulled out of the hospital parking lot. "You've got more on your mind than medical profession relationships. What gives, coz? Are you playing clam again?"

"Not intentionally," replied Judith, pulling out onto Highway 101. "This whole thing is starting to come together for me, but I've got a serious problem."

Renie gazed at Judith with a mixture of admiration and curiosity. "You mean you know who did it?"

"I'm close," replied Judith.

"Who?"

"Let me make one more phone call when we get back to Pirate's Lair," said Judith, stopping at a red light. "If my guess is on target, I'll tell you. Otherwise, you're going to think I'm nuts."

Renie gave a little shrug. "It wouldn't be the first time. Didn't I stand up for you when you married Dan McMonigle?"

Judith turned to look at Renie. "You also stood up for me with Joe Flynn."

"You heard me the first time," said Renie.

Judith and Renie had decided to attend the six o'clock Saturday evening mass at St. Ethelburga of Barking Catholic Church instead of the Sunday service which was scheduled for ten. They couldn't make it to Salem in time to catch Renie's noon train if they went to the morning liturgy. As strangers in town, they hadn't expected to see anyone they knew, but three rows up, they spotted Terrence O'Toole. He spotted them coming back from Holy Communion.

After mass, he waylaid them in the parking lot. A faint breeze stirred the heavy air as Judith and Renie waited for Terrence to leapfrog between cars.

"Wowee!" he exclaimed under his breath so as not to attract the attention of the other parishioners. "Have I got news for our next edition! Two murders, the treasure hunt, a big wreck out on the highway, and tomorrow, the parade! Want to go with me to the morgue?"

Judith made a grim face. "No thanks, Terrence. We've seen enough dead bodies."

"No, no," said Terrence, moving closer to the cousins and taking on an air of intrigue. "I mean the newspaper morgue, on microfilm. You've been very good to me, giving out that interview and all. And you act interested in the investigation. I thought you might want to be in on it when I crack the case."

"What?" Judith was startled as much by his pronouncement as his self-confidence. "Gee, Terrence, do you have some . . . ah, leads?"

"You bet," Terrence replied promptly. He steered the cousins behind the church's wooden sign proclaiming the daily and Sunday mass times. "Leona Ogilvie inherited the beach cottage. Alice Hoke got everything else, including a lot of debts. The two women looked a lot alike, and I figure the people who were never paid the money that was owed them got fed up and came looking for revenge. But they didn't know the difference between the two sisters' physical appearance, so they killed the wrong woman." He hooked his thumbs in his suspenders, flashed his gap-toothed grin in self-satisfaction, and awaited the cousins' reaction.

"That's . . . remarkable," Judith said at last. "However did you come to such a conclusion?"

"Well . . ." Terrence simpered a bit. "I do my homework. I read up about the cheese factory. I need to read more. That's why I thought you might want to go to the morgue with me."

"How," Judith asked, "do you explain Titus Teacher's death?"

"Simple," said Terrence. "Bernard Hoke owed a lot of people money." He ticked them off on his fingers— employees, suppliers, lenders. Some, Terrence said, had been paid off by Alice Hoke after she sold the factory site to the outlet mall developers. But others had not. That, explained Terrence, was where Titus Teacher came in. "They owed him money, so Alice had to kill him after he killed Leona by mistake."

"No," asserted Renie. "Alice couldn't have killed Titus Teacher. She was in our carport at the time."

Terrence was unfazed by the argument. "Then one of her children did it. It had to be an Ogilvie or a Hoke."

"I tell you what, Terrence," said Judith, "you go ahead without us. It sounds as if you're doing good work. If you find out anything new, give us a call, okay?"

Terrence's freckled face was wreathed with disappointment, but he gave in. The cousins headed out for their last dinner together in Buccaneer Beach. As it was well after seven o'clock and the town was jammed with tourists, they realized after their first three stops that they should have made reservations. None of the restaurants they tried had less than an hour's wait. Discouraged, they scouted a couple of the more modest eateries, but even those were doing a land-office holiday business.

"I'm afraid," Judith said to a downcast Renie, "we may have to go back to the cottage and clean out the refrigerator."

Since it was now after eight o'clock, Renie was too famished to argue. The cousins drove back to Pirate's Lair. While Renie prepared open-faced crab and cheddar sandwiches to put under the broiler, Judith made the phone call she'd planned for that evening. To her relief, the voice at the other end in Malibu was not a recording.

"Mr. Fleetwood," said Judith, at her most effusive. "I'm so glad you got home safely. I wanted to apologize for acting like a pest yesterday outside of Brent Doyle's law office." Darren Fleetwood did not sound pleased to hear from Judith. It was clear he was anxious to get her off the line. "I won't keep you," Judith promised, "but since you now own Pirate's Lair, something has happened that I think you should know about."

"Yes?" Darren's voice was tense.

Judith glanced at Renie who was cutting up cucumbers. "There's been another murder. Titus Teacher was shot last night down at the boat . . ."

"Who?" Darren sounded uncertain.

Judith repeated the name. "You sat next to him at the funeral."

There was a slight pause. "I did? Oh—that's too bad. That he got killed, I mean." Another pause. "I sure hope everything gets . . . straightened out up there. This has been the weirdest experience in my entire life."

"I'm sure it has," said Judith, not without sympathy. "I felt you ought to know. We're very sorry about your father's death." She exchanged meaningful looks with Renie.

"What?" Darren Fleetwood made an odd noise into the phone. "Well, yes, it was a tragedy, I suppose. But that happened a long time ago."

It was Judith's turn to pause. She held out the receiver, staring at the earpiece. Renie stared at Judith. "Excuse me," said Judith at last, putting the phone back in place. "I was referring to your natural father. Race Doyle."

A faint chuckle came across the line. "I never heard of him. My real father's been dead for years. Actually, I never met the man, but his name was Bernard Hoke."

A sudden flash of lightning, followed by the crash of thunder, broke the connection.

SIXTEEN

WHAT IRONY, THOUGHT Judith, that her wrongheaded premise and Terrence O'Toole's misguided deductions had finally put all the pieces into place. The storm had ended the hot spell, and with it had come the solution. As rain pelted Pirate's Lair and wind whipped through the pines, Judith and Renie sat in the dark and rehashed the Ogilvie-Hoke murder case.

"You may know who and why, but you still don't know how," Renie argued. "Really, it's not impossible."

"Logically, no," agreed Judith as more lightning flashed and thunder rolled. "Or, yes—it *has* to be logical. We just can't see it yet."

"We can't see anything until the power goes back on," said Renie. Outside, virtually the entire town was dark, with only an occasional glimmer of light from an auxiliary system. "It's a good thing I'd already put the sandwiches under the broiler."

"As soon as this storm lets up, we're going to see the sheriff. Or the police chief," said Judith. She cocked an ear, noting that the lightning and thunder were growing farther apart. The storm was beginning to pass, though the jagged bursts of lightning that filled the sky over the water were still spectacular. The sea had grown choppy, rough whitecaps tossed high on murky gray waves.

"You'll have to go to their houses," said Renie. "They sure won't be at work."

"They might be at the rodeo," allowed Judith. "Unless it got rained out."

"Delayed, I'll bet. It was probably already under way." Renie made a couple of attempts to find her can of Pepsi. "Dark or not, I've got to go pack, coz. Bill has trained me not to wait until morning."

Judith watched Renie's dim outline move cautiously from the living room. "I still can't believe you're deserting me," she called after her cousin.

"The monks and the symphony cannot go on without me," Renie shouted back. "And Bill cannot go on without clean laundry."

"I wish I could call Joe," said Judith, more to herself than to Renie. "I suppose the phone company and the power people around here don't consider this an emergency."

Outside, the wind blew over what sounded like a garbage can. Judith could see branches swaying in front of the picture window. The rain was coming down so hard that it spattered the bricks inside the fireplace. Getting up, Judith picked her way to the kitchen.

"I wish I had Jake Beezle's big flashlight. There's got to be one around here someplace," she said, again mostly to herself. "I thought I saw it a couple of days ago."

"What?" Renie's voice emanated from the guest bedroom. "What about San Diego?"

Toward the back of the second drawer next to the sink, Judith found the flashlight. Its batteries worked, if not quite at full force. "San Diego?" said Judith in a louder voice, clicking off the flashlight to conserve its power. "I didn't say anything." She headed for the hallway.

Renie's shadowy form was dancing around the bedroom. "San Diego—it made me think of something I learned from the background on that Franciscan calendar."

Her voice was excited as she moved toward Judith. "Those Spaniards—Junipero Serra and Company—they were Franciscans!" Renie tripped over the strongbox. Judith could have sworn her cousin was airborne for at least ten seconds. She came down with a crash, right at Judith's feet.

"Coz!" Judith bent down. Renie was groaning. "Speak to me! Are you okay?"

There was an ominous silence, except for Renie's gasps and moans. Frantic, Judith switched on the flashlight. Renie's eyes rolled up at her. "I think I broke my stupid ankle."

Judith couldn't believe her ears. She couldn't call for help; the phone was still out. She couldn't risk hauling Renie out to the car and driving to the hospital. The most she could do was get her cousin onto the bed. Gingerly, Judith tried to hoist Renie, who seemed to have become a deadweight. At last, Renie regained her breath and volunteered to crawl to the bed. With Judith's help, she climbed on top of the down comforter and gave her cousin a weak smile.

"What a clumsy ox! I didn't see that wretched strongbox."

"That's okay, coz." Judith was smiling, too, but also feebly. "I'll call somebody as soon as the phone service is restored."

Renie was cautiously testing her right ankle. "I don't really think it's broken. But it sure as hell is sprained." She gave an annoyed shake of her head. "Let me finish what I was saying before I did my imitation of a 747 crash landing. About the missionaries. They didn't come to California until the last half of the eighteenth century. There were no missions on the West Coast until the 1760s."

"So?" Judith stared at Renie as if the fall had made her delirious.

"So that tourist brochure stuff about English pirates chasing Spanish ships back to safety at the missions is pure myth—or Chamber of Commerce ballyhoo." Renie shifted about on the bed, trying to arrange herself more comfortably. "Can I have an ice pack, or has everything melted in the freezer?"

"Not this soon," replied Judith, a bit vaguely. "Sorry, coz, I still don't get it. What's your point?"

"I'm not sure," said Renie, a bit fretfully. "But all the hoopla about the pirates and buried treasure and secret passages and such is just a lot of promotional baloney. Lord knows I've designed enough of those pieces to realize how little store you can set by the copy." She stopped to flex her ankle again and winced. "How about some aspirin?"

Judith went to fetch both ice and aspirin. "There must have been pirates around here somewhere or else they wouldn't have named it Buccaneer Beach," she pointed out to Renie.

"Maybe." Renie allowed Judith to minister to her, then lay back against the pillows. "I don't know—it was just a thought. You're the one who always sees the light at the end of the tunnel." Renie closed her eyes.

The wind was dying down a bit, but the rain had not let up. Judith sat very still. Renie was right. She *had* seen the light at the end of the tunnel. Almost literally.

Judith jumped up. "I'm going down to the boathouse," she announced. "Will you be all right?"

Renie's eyes flew open. *"I'll* be fine. Coz, don't be a sap! You're asking for trouble! What would Joe think?"

"I don't know," said Judith blithely. "Why don't you ask him when you get to the hospital?"

Wearing a light jacket and carrying the flashlight, Judith walked carefully down the long staircase. The rain and wind buffeted her so she clung to the handrail. Below, the storm had swept the beach clear of other human beings. The ocean was obscured from her vision, but she could hear the waves crashing against the shore.

Judith approached the boathouse warily. As she had hoped, the door opened at a touch. Perhaps the lock had been broken in the aftermath of Titus Teacher's murder. She crept inside, shining the flashlight around the small, disordered living room. Obviously, no one had made any attempt to straighten up after the police and sheriff had finished their official business. With a grimace, she passed the bloodstained couch with its grotesque outline of Titus Teacher's sprawled body. On the threshold of the kitchen, she pried up the starfish-patterned linoleum. Sure enough, newspaper lined the floor: the *Bugler,* dated a week after the issue she and Renie had found under the rug in the beach cottage. Judith nodded to herself.

The sound of the wind and the surf muffled the new-comer's approach, but the blinding flash tore a scream from Judith's throat. Kneeling on the floor, she froze in place, not daring to move a muscle. Another flash lit up the boathouse. With her heart pounding, Judith risked rais-ing her head just enough to peek over the top of the couch. With her vision still blurred, she tried to make out the form that stood just inside the doorway.

"Terrence!" she cried. "What are you doing here?" Ju-dith staggered to her feet.

"Taking pictures," said Terrence, a bit sulkily. "My ed-itor told me to get an interior. All the power went out at the morgue, so I decided to come over here and do it now. Are you okay?"

Still shaken, Judith leaned against the doorjamb. "Yes, but you scared the wits out of me. Gosh, Terrence, you must be the only person who works weekends on Bucca-neer Beach."

"You're right," he replied in a put-upon voice. "No overtime, either."

"Cheer up," said Judith, going into the kitchen. "Maybe I can help you get a real scoop." She played the flashlight around the room, noting that a chair had been overturned, a portable mixer lay on the floor, and a saucer had been smashed in the sink. No doubt this damage, as well as the chaos in the living room, had been caused by the people who had charged the boathouse after Titus Teacher's body had been discovered.

"I've got a theory," Judith explained, knocking on the wall behind the stove. "For a long time, there has been a story about secret passages supposedly made by pirates in the Buccaneer Beach area. But that's probably not true. At least about the pirates. I suspect any underground tunnels were dug by bootleggers during Prohibition. If so, one of them might have led up to an old speakeasy called Pirate's Lair."

"The beach cottage?" said Terrence, who was watching Judith's flashlight roam over the nautical charts on the far wall. "But that's the house you rented."

"It was once the site of a tavern," Judith went on. "An old guy named Jake Beezle told me how the smugglers used to bring liquor down from Canada and unload it on the beach. My guess is that they took it up through a secret passage. But," Judith asked, puzzled, "where?"

"Wowee!" cried Terrence. "I need to know more about this town. I'm really going to spend a lot of time at the morgue doing research." In the semidarkness, he bumped into the little refrigerator and fell against the nautical charts. "Ooops!" cried Terrence. "What a klutz!"

His elbow had gone right through one of the charts. There was a space immediately behind it. Judith and Terrence stared. "Bless you, Terrence!" exulted Judith, giving the startled young man a hug. "You're no ordinary klutz—you've found the passage!" Ripping away the charts, they discovered a door set about three inches into the framework. There was no lock. The hinges opened without a squeak. "Those have been oiled recently," said Judith. "Come on, Terrence, are you game?"

Terrence was. Carefully, they entered the narrow opening in the ground. Both Judith and Terrence had to crouch and walk single file. The air smelled stale and damp. With the flashlight beam wavering before them, they began to make their ascent through the hill that rose above the beach. Judith worried about bats. She feared getting trapped. She was certain Terrence would fall down. She realized there was danger of a cave-in, especially in the wake of the storm.

"It shouldn't be far," she said, as much to reassure herself as Terrence.

"It's spooky in here," said Terrence in a nervous voice.

"Very spooky," Judith agreed, feeling the earth shift under her feet. She felt as if they'd been walking for miles. Yet if her guess was accurate, they had only about two hundred feet to cover.

The silence was overwhelming, like being in a tomb. Judith tried not to shiver. At last they came to the end of the passage. Shining the flashlight directly overhead, Judith saw the trapdoor that was set in the ground above them. She gave the splintered wood an experimental nudge. Nothing happened.

"Let me," offered Terrence.

Judith stepped aside, her back flat against the hard, damp wall of earth. With a mighty heave, Terrence opened the trapdoor. Gallantly, he gave Judith a boost. With a sigh of relief, she climbed out into the cool, fresh air.

"Where are we?" called Terrence, still in the nether world.

Judith grinned. "In front of my MG. We're in the carport, Terrence."

The telephones, if not the lights, had been put back in service. With a hasty explanation for Renie, Judith left Terrence in the beach cottage to call the sheriff and the police. But not before she had made a phone call of her own. Judith had a message for a murderer.

"I still say you're nuts," Renie shouted from the bedroom. "When you get yourself killed, don't come bitching to me."

Arming herself with a clamgun as well as the flashlight, Judith returned to the boathouse by the conventional route of the staircase. Terrence was having trouble getting through. It appeared that most of Buccaneer Beach was trying to call one or the other of the law enforcement agencies to report some sort of problem.

Judith did not go inside the boathouse. Rather, she ducked behind a log on the far side of the little building and crouched low to wait. The rain had dwindled to a heavy mist, though the wind was still brisk. Judith rested

the clamgun against the log, wishing it were a real firearm
instead of just a fancy shovel made for chasing clams
through the sand. She held onto the flashlight, but kept it
turned off to save the batteries.

Five minutes passed. Then ten. Judith heard no sign of
anyone approaching. Perhaps she wouldn't. She'd told
Terrence to ask the police and the sheriff not to use their
sirens. Surprise was an important element in the trap she'd
set.

She clicked the flashlight on to check the time. Her
watch showed 10:14. Judith turned the flashlight off. The
town was still wrapped in darkness, though farther up,
where the highway curved close to the beach, she could
see the occasional amber glow of headlights. Clooney,
maybe. Or Eldritch. It could even be the killer, moving in-
exorably into Judith's snare. She couldn't resist a little
smile of satisfaction.

Somehow, it hadn't occurred to her that her prey would
arrive via the road that led to the beach. Judith had assumed that the killer would march boldly through the yard
of Pirate's Lair and straight down the long flight of steps.
Thus, she was startled when she heard not soft footsteps in
the sand, but the flapping of fabric as Alice Hoke approached, wearing a raincoat and carrying a gun.

Judith was on the wrong side of the log. Trying to make
herself invisible, she melted into the rough, weather-
beaten, decaying wood. Alice kept right on walking, pur-
poseful, composed. She went past the log; Judith slumped
in relief. The clamgun tipped over. Alice whirled, the gun
pointed in Judith's direction.

"Who's there?" she called, her voice floating on the
wind. Getting no response, Alice moved slowly toward the
log.

Judith had no illusions about Alice Hoke's attitude toward virtues such as mercy. Frantically, she gazed up at
the bluff, trying to see if the law enforcement vehicles had
arrived. But of course, it dawned on her, they, too, would
come down the road by the handsome house on the point.
The clamgun was out of reach. The flashlight was worth-

less. Judith had no choice but to get to her feet and run for her life.

"Stop!" shouted Alice. "Wait!"

Judith's heels dug into the mud. She realized it was foolish to engage Alice Hoke in conversation. But if Judith were going to get shot, she'd prefer it wouldn't be in the back. Besides, the sheriff and the police should be roaring onto the beach at any moment. Perhaps it was wise to play for time.

Alice's sensible shoes made squelching noises in the wet sand. She lowered the gun which looked to Judith like a standard U.S. Army .45. *Her father-in-law's,* Judith thought fleetingly, *a souvenir from World War I.*

"Now what's all this nonsense about a safety-deposit box key?" Alice demanded. Up close, her long face looked impassive. Only the eyes, cold as the sea itself, betrayed her anxiety.

"My cousin and I found it," replied Judith, surprised that she could speak in a relatively normal voice. "Along with the sheepskin seat covers from your husband's car. The one he drove Race Doyle's body away in after he ran him down in the cheese factory parking lot."

Alice emitted a sharp little laugh. "How absurd! My late husband hit Race, but he didn't kill him. Or if he did, he never told me about it. Race ran away with the money. The man was a common criminal."

"I don't think so," said Judith. "Oh, Race had a bad reputation. But just because he sold used cars doesn't make him a crook. I think you and Bernie set Race up. You knew the business was going under—not because of Race's mismanagement, but because of a lot of things. Maybe your father lost his grip as he got older. Certainly Bernie couldn't run the cheese factory—he wasn't a manager, he was a builder, and a good one. Times had gotten tough in this part of the world. You were facing bankruptcy. Rather than go through that, the two of you made Race the patsy. Bernie killed Race and got rid of the body. You kept the money for yourselves, though eventually you had to use some of the factory site profits to pay off your

more obstinate creditors. But three million dollars is a lot
of money. Enough to kill for."

Even as she spoke, Judith had been inching up the
beach. It would take some time to reach the road that led
up to the highway. Hopefully, Clooney and—or—Eldritch
would arrive any minute.

Alice was showing some interest, but no real emotion.
"It's possible that Bernie was involved, I suppose." She
made it sound as if her husband had dabbled in unsound
municipal bonds. "But that was a long time ago. And he's
dead."

"Yes, he is," agreed Judith. "He's been dead for over
twenty-four hours." She watched Alice closely. Through
the mist, she could see those cold eyes flicker. "Bernie
Hoke didn't commit suicide seven years ago. That was
rigged, so that the two of you could disappear and live in
Liechtenstein until the statute of limitations ran out on de-
frauding your creditors or whatever sort of legal liability
had expired. That way, if any suspicion was attached to either of you, it wouldn't matter. The trouble is, there is no
limitation on murder."

Alice started to throw back her head and hoot with
laughter, but thought better of the diversion and raised the
gun a notch. "That's preposterous. I never left Buccaneer
Beach."

Judith took another backward step. "Yes, you did.
Somehow, you convinced Leona—who must have returned
from Brazil about that time—to stand in for you. Maybe
you played up to her, told her you were overcome with
grief because of Bernie's alleged suicide. Whatever else
Leona was, she was kindhearted. She'd spent over twenty
years in the jungle. Perhaps the idea of being back home
in seclusion appealed to her, like a monk meditating or
some other religious type embracing the solitary, contem-
plative life. At any rate, she managed to keep away from
anyone who would really know who was Leona and who
was Alice. She could put your children off without arous-
ing a lot of suspicion because you'd never been a very

warm sort of mother. Everything worked out just fine until Darren Fleetwood showed up."

Consciously, or otherwise, Alice Hoke was keeping pace with Judith. They were directly below the motel now, though the establishment was shrouded in darkness. The tram rested on its platform atop the bluff. At least no one had been trapped in it when the power went out. *Or,* thought Judith with a pang, *perhaps it would have been better if someone was caught halfway down to the beach. At least she'd have a witness if Alice tried to shoot her.*

"Darren Fleetwood?" Alice spoke the name with contempt. "What has he got to do with all this tiresome speculation?"

Judith realized that her jacket and the rest of her clothes were soaked through to the skin. She wasn't exactly cold, but she was certainly uncomfortable. And terrified. For a brief moment, her brain seemed to stop working. Then she forced herself to concentrate and answered Alice's disdainful question.

"Some thirty years ago, Leona had a child out of wedlock. That's why she went away, even before she became a missionary in Brazil. She gave the baby up for adoption, but I suspect she never stopped wondering what had happened to him. It must have preyed on her mind all those years she spent hiding out in the old farmhouse. She must have made a search and found out that her son was Darren Fleetwood, living in Malibu. She contacted him—or the adoption agency did—and he agreed to meet her in Buccaneer Beach. She was so thrilled that she changed her will, leaving her only real asset—the beach cottage—to Darren."

"Perhaps." Alice gave a slight shrug. "What does that have to do with me? I never met the fellow."

Judith kept moving backwards, slowly, almost imperceptibly, shifting one foot at a time. "Darren's arrival on the scene gave Leona a whole new outlook on life. She wanted to do things for him, to be with him, to be herself. When you finally ran out of money and had to leave Liechtenstein, Leona insisted on ending the impersonation.

She was basically very honest, I think. She had an intense desire to start life over. She even applied for a driver's license. But you didn't want her to stop playing your part. You planned on taking the money and leaving, probably for another foreign country. Leona refused to cooperate this time. Especially when she discovered that Bernie Hoke was alive."

Alice scoffed. "This is ridiculous!"

"No, it's not. When Bernie ran down Race Doyle, he probably got injured, too. Mrs. Doyle—Brent's mother—said something very interesting this afternoon. She mentioned that after the cheese factory folded, Bernie was a wreck—mentally and *physically*. Now Bernie was a hard worker who actually did some of the construction himself. I might be able to understand how his mental condition would deteriorate, but not how it would affect him physically. Unless he was suddenly going around town with some obvious impairment—like a bad limp." Judith paused for a breath as well as to steel her nerve. "For a long time, I thought Titus Teacher was Race Doyle. Then I realized he wasn't. Titus Teacher was your husband, Bernard Hoke, the man who supposedly committed suicide seven years ago. There were no pictures of him up at the farm house, so I don't know what he looked like seven years ago. But the beard and time itself would have changed him enough so that casual acquaintances wouldn't recognize the long-dead Bernie Hoke. And he stayed down at the boathouse, away from his children. The only time they saw him was at the funeral, when their attention was diverted elsewhere. Even so, Larissa and Augie thought there was something familiar about the man they knew as Titus Teacher. By the time they figured it out—if they ever did—you and Bernie would have been far away from Buccaneer Beach."

"Really, Mrs. Flynn," Alice scoffed, "you've manufactured a fairy tale!"

It occurred to Judith that, in her long flapping raincoat and with her graying hair blowing around her narrow shoulders, Alice Hoke could have passed for the witch from "Hansel and Gretel." Judith forced herself to keep talking, to stall for more precious minutes. "For all of Race's seamier side, I have the feeling he wasn't as basically dishonest as Bernie Hoke. A very shrewd old lady I talked to the other day said something enlightening—your parents didn't think much better of Bernie than they did of Race. But because Bernie wasn't lazy and Race apparently was, when trouble came along, public opinion was swayed to your husband's side. That's why everybody assumed that if Leona had been seduced, the cad was Race Doyle. But when Leona dragged Race out of your parents' house that New Year's Eve in 1960, it was Bernie who brought her home."

Alice's eyes narrowed. "That's true. So what?" She used her free hand to make an impatient gesture. "Let's cut this short, Mrs. Flynn. It's late, it's wet, and I want that safety-deposit box key."

Judith expelled a scornful breath. "You don't think I'd be stupid enough to bring it with me, do you?"

"Where is it?" The words were sharp, demanding.

"Back at Pirate's Lair," Judith lied. She stopped edging backwards, sensing a shred of hope.

"Where?"

"You'll find out when we get there." Judith was feeling a bit light-headed.

"I can find it without your help," snapped Alice. "I know every inch of that house."

Feeling a rush of failure engulf her, Judith again began to move, not just backward, but to the side. The waves were coming closer as the tide washed up on the shore. Alice, of course, was also forced to avoid the relentless surf.

"Darren really blew the lid off the whole thing," Judith said more rapidly. "Not only did Leona want out of the charade, but her basic integrity may have caused her to threaten both you and Bernie with exposure. I think she told you who the father of her child really was—your husband. You must have pitched a four-star fit. You may even have been afraid that Bernie really cared for Leona. Or that the existence of a son he'd never known would change all your carefully-laid plans. So you came down to the beach cottage to find Leona, but she wasn't around just then. You used the first piece of paper you could find, which happened to be the receipt Leona had given me, and you asked her to meet you at a specified time. Then you killed her and destroyed the note."

Alice stepped briskly up to Judith, gesturing with the .45. "Move closer to the bank. This farce has gone on long enough."

"That's what Leona said, I'll bet," retorted Judith.

What little color Alice possessed had drained from her thin face. "I couldn't have killed Leona. I was with the chief of police. You're not just a meddler, you're a fool, Mrs. Flynn."

"You set Neil Clooney up, too," said Judith, aware that her mouth had gone quite dry. "You must have known within the first few days of your return that you had to get rid of Leona. So you started courting the police chief for your perfect alibi. You invited him down to the boathouse and then went into the kitchen and pretended to bake for him. You turned on that portable mixer and the oven in the stove. If he spoke to you, you could always use the excuse that you couldn't hear him over the mixer. But of course you weren't there—you'd slipped out through the secret passage up to the house where you killed your sister. It wouldn't take more than five minutes. That's why those boxes were removed and replaced—so you could get in and out of the trapdoor. They were covering it up in the carport floor. I even tripped over the damned thing and didn't notice. We must have dislodged the false covering on the trapdoor when we blew the lock off the strongbox. But you had it so carefully planned. You came back to the boathouse, zapped a baking mix in the microwave, and never used the oven. That dense chief of police didn't even suspect you were gone."

Dense, Judith thought with a shiver, and slow. Where was Clooney? And Eldritch? She turned her head just enough to get her bearings. The mist had subsided to a drizzle. A hundred yards away, she could see the road that led up to the highway. But there were no headlights showing through the trees. Judith cursed the law enforcement officials of Buccaneer Beach and Juniper County.

"You played a variation of the same trick on us last night," Judith continued as she heard Alice release the safety on the .45. "You sent my cousin and me off on a wild-goose chase for Leona's jewelry while you went out to the carport. You slipped down the passage—you probably had put the gun there beforehand—and shot your husband. I noticed you were out of breath when you came back into the house, but I didn't understand the reason at the time. I'm not exactly sure why you killed Bernie, unless you wanted the money all for yourself or you feared his newly-found son was going to screw everything up, but . . ."

"Shut up!" commanded Alice. "Thirty years of hell with that man, tied to him by money! Who wouldn't want to shoot the tightfisted clod? The cheese factory was mine; I sold the property. Then he set up an account in Liechtenstein that I couldn't sign on, and transferred *my* money into it! I was no more than chattel! I never wanted to spend my life in this dumpy little town! I wanted to go away to college and become something! But I ended up stuck with him, first in Buccaneer Beach, and then in Liechtenstein, for God's sake! Next, it would have been some bug-riddled island in the Caribbean! I hated the man! How would you like to spend most of your life with some wretched creep who made you miserable?"

Judith's quiet answer took Alice by surprise. "I did. He's dead, too."

The startled response was just enough to allow Judith to take off like a streak for the road. Behind her, Alice was screaming at her to stop. Judith kept going. To her dismay, there were still no signs of emergency vehicles coming from the highway. Judith ran until she thought her lungs would burst. The outline of the modern house on the point caught her frantic eye. To her amazement, there was a light on. Solar energy. She remembered seeing the telltale glass domes in the roof.

Alice was pounding up behind her. Judith had reached the garden of the house which was enclosed by a wrought iron fence. Summoning up her last breath, she called out in a desperate gasp.

"Help!" A bullet whizzed by her head.

Above her, on the deck of the house where she thought she had noticed a hot tub earlier, a man stood up under the soft beam of a light encased in a ship's lantern. He was naked as a jaybird. Judith, clinging to the wrought iron, stared incredulously. A second bullet seared her arm, sending her flat against the fence. She could hear Alice coming closer, still raining down wild curses.

The naked man on the deck picked up a .22, aimed, and fired. Alice's screams stopped. Slowly, painfully, Judith turned, still hanging onto the iron fence with her good hand. Alice Hoke was lying flat on her back, not twenty feet away. Blinking away hot tears, Judith gazed at her savior and tried to squeak out her gratitude. The man with the rifle waved. Judith's eyes had not deceived her.

It was Jake Beezle.

The lights of Buccaneer Beach went on, but for Judith, everything, including Jake's handsome solar-powered house, turned black.

SEVENTEEN

"AT LEAST YOU don't have to share a hospital room with Alice Hoke," said Joe, leaning on his crutches. "They took her into Salem. It was touch and go, but she'll probably pull through."

"A mixed blessing," commented Judith, lying back in the bed. Renie, who had arrived first, commanded the window view. Her foot was propped up on a pillow, the ankle wrapped in a thick brown bandage. Judith gingerly touched the dressing on her arm. "I'm lucky it was only a graze. I was sure Alice would blow me away."

"You're lucky Jake Beezle was out in his hot tub. Mrs. Wampole had just left after a rousing evening of . . . something." Joe rolled his eyes. "Jake keeps that .22 handy so he can scare off the sea gulls. He told me they make a real mess of his deck."

Judith reached for a glass of water. Her mouth still felt parched. It was not quite seven in the morning, a bright summer day, with a glorious sunrise that had followed the storm. "Why didn't you tell me Jake lived in that beautiful house?" she demanded of her husband.

221

Joe set the crutches down and carefully sat on one of the visitor's chairs. "I didn't know it then, either. I mean, I knew he lived some place by the beach, but like you and Renie, I assumed it was an old dump." He chuckled. "Remember that packing house Jake said he worked in? It turns out he owned it—Jake started out as a pig farmer and eventually built himself a little empire. He's a rich man. That couple he talked about watching out for him are his cook and his gardener."

"Jeez," exclaimed Renie, propping herself up on one elbow, "don't tell us Bernie Hoke built that house!"

But Joe shook his head. "It was an architect from Portland. Jake never trusted Bernie Hoke. I guess he had a good reason."

"He sure did," agreed Judith. "Bernie was a crook. So was Alice. They deserved each other, I suppose." She gave a weary sigh. "Good grief, what a night!"

Neil Clooney and Josh Eldritch had showed up less than two minutes after Jake Beezle had downed Alice Hoke with his .22. Judith had regained consciousness just as Jake, now modestly attired in a towel, had come down to unlock the gate and bring her inside. They had gotten as far as the fountain in the courtyard when the sheriff and the chief of police had arrived simultaneously from opposite directions—and rammed right into each other. Arguments had ensued about who owed whom for vehicular damages, but eventually they had settled down to business. Although Judith never found out for sure, she suspected that the near-fatal delay in their arrival probably had been caused by yet another dispute between the two law enforcement officials.

Terrence O'Toole had accompanied Renie to the hospital where Dr. Scott had X rays taken to determine that she had suffered a severe sprain. Terrence had intended to escort Renie back to the beach cottage, but when Judith showed up a few minutes later with her gunshot wound, the cousins decided they might as well make a night of it—if the hospital could accommodate them. Judith had related her conclusions to a skeptical sheriff and an embarrassed police chief. Neither had wanted to believe her, but Terrence insisted on showing them the secret passage. The young reporter was in a state of excitement as great as the size of the typeface he expected to see on the front page of the *Bugler*'s next edition.

"I'll make the AP wire!" he crowed. "I could do a magazine piece! I might write a made-for-TV movie! Wowee, I really like being a member of the press!" He had danced down the hospital corridor, colliding with two nurses, an orderly, and a medication cart.

But that had happened shortly before midnight. Judith and Renie had each gotten about six hours sleep after being admitted to the hospital and treated by the staff. Dr. Lundgren, who had been called in to help Dr. Scott take care of a number of broken bones caused by the storm and the general holiday festivities, had told all three patients that they could be discharged by ten o'clock Sunday morning. But Joe couldn't drive, and Judith was advised to wait a day before getting behind the wheel. They decided not to return to Pirate's Lair, but to accept Jake's invitation to spend the night.

Renie, however, was determined to take the noon train from Salem. Terrence would drive her to the depot, she said, since he wanted to see what was going on with Alice in order to fill in some gaps in his story.

The aroma of breakfast was filling the hospital halls. Renie perked up, while Joe informed one of the nurses that he would be eating in his wife's room this morning. The trays had just arrived when Neil Clooney and Josh Eldritch came through the door.

"We saw that damned passage," grumbled Clooney, parking his large carcass in the remaining visitor's chair. He glared up at Eldritch. "I'm from Milton-Freewater; I don't know the history of this place, but you should have been wise to that bootlegging stuff, Eldritch."

"It was before my time," said the sheriff, settling in on the windowsill and gazing covetously at Renie's breakfast. "I suppose Bernie Hoke found it when he tore down the tavern. He must have thought it would be cute to have a secret way down to the beach."

"Probably used it for his girlfriends," said Clooney. "That's another thing, you should have known what a louse Bernie was. You grew up with him."

"Oh, no," retorted Eldritch. "He was five years ahead of me in school. I hardly knew him. But you bragged about how you knew Alice. What a crock! The police chief, cozying up to a murderess!" Throwing back his head, Eldritch roared with mirth.

"Stick it," snarled Clooney. "Women are always going around deceiving men; it's the way it is. Look at that Scottish guy in Shakespeare and that homicidal wife of his. Or Samson and Delilah. I'm not the first guy to get fooled by a female. Who was the broad in the Bible who suckered some poor sap into her tent and cut off his head?"

Joe looked up from his Cream of Wheat. "Judith."

Clooney and Eldritch looked at Mrs. Joe Flynn. "Huh?" they said in chorus.

"Her name was Judith," Joe said mildly. "She beheaded Holofernes. The Judiths of this world have minds of their own." The green eyes flashed gold sparks at his wife.

"Maybe so," allowed Clooney, getting up and strutting around the room. "But I'll tell you, this case may not stand up in court. Face it, there's not much physical evidence. Even with that bullet and the gun, there's no proof that Alice was the one who shot Bernie. I've a feeling that in a day or two, we may have to drop the charges."

Judith, Joe, and Renie stared at Clooney. Even Eldritch looked a little put off, before he shook a long finger at his counterpart. "Hey—Clooney, you aren't trying to get yourself off the hook, are you? Could it be that you don't want to look like a goat in court?"

Clooney held both hands up in front of him. "Don't get me wrong. We got an incredible story and only circumstantial evidence. Prosecutors don't like that."

"I think you can build a solid case." Joe spoke quietly over the rim of his apple juice glass.

The police chief snorted; even Eldritch gave Joe a

faintly scornful look. Joe swallowed his juice and eyed each man in turn. "As you said, you've got the gun and the bullet. You'll find footprints that match Alice's in the passageway. You've got a key to a safety-deposit box that contains three million dollars. You've got bloodstained seat covers. And," he added, his voice now rising, "according to my wife, you'll find Race Doyle's body under the kitchen floor in the old boathouse. What else do you want—a freaking diagram?"

Startled, Eldritch jumped up from the windowsill. "Okay, okay, we'll check it out. Don't get all worked up, it isn't *your* problem."

Clooney's face had turned quite red. "It sure as hell isn't. Listen, fella, don't tell us how to do our job. It's enough that we had Mrs. Flynn driving us crazy during this investigation. It's a wonder she didn't get herself killed. You outsiders don't know what a policeman's job is like. Butt out, Mr. Flynn."

Joe inclined his head in a seemingly acquiescent manner. Eldritch had joined Clooney at the door. They were about to stomp off when Joe spoke once more, "Hey, guys—you're going to want witnesses. So make that *Lieutenant* Flynn. Homicide Division, metro police. See you in court."

The sheriff and the police chief gaped, then fell all over each other trying to get out the door.

"I told you, Clooney, there was something about him that made me wonder if he . . ."

"Listen, Eldritch, if you didn't think I could smell another cop from a mile away . . ."

They exited arguing.

By nine o'clock, Judith and Renie were ready to leave. Joe was waiting for a final word from Dr. Lundgren who was still on duty. As the cousins bided their time, Judith remembered to call Gertrude to tell her they wouldn't be home until the following night.

"I'll also tell her to let your mother know you'll be in this evening," said Judith, dialing for an outside line. "But

I'm certainly not going to tell her I got shot. I don't think I'll even mention that you sprained your ankle."

"Hopefully, it'll be okay in a few days so I can take my mother to see Dr. Clapp," said Renie.

The hospital operator told Judith that all the toll lines were tied up. "There probably aren't more than two around here," said Judith in disgust, putting the phone down. "Gee, coz, it doesn't seem possible that by tomorrow night, we'll all be home. The rest of the summer should be peaceful by comparison. Except for Joe's being on crutches and the horde of guests at the B&B."

"You're used to that," Renie remarked with a little smile. "Joe isn't, though. But after police work, a bunch of innocent out-of-towners shouldn't bother him too much."

"Right," Judith agreed. "And we'll have the whole third floor all to ourselves, with Mother gone and Mike away in Montana." She gave a little shiver of pleasure. "Really, in some ways it will seem more like a honeymoon than this trip to Buccaneer Beach."

"That's for sure," agreed Renie. "You two really deserve it after all you've been through."

"Still," Judith admitted, "this town would be a nice vacation spot if you could avoid the dead bodies. I wonder what will happen to all that money in the safety-deposit box."

Renie shrugged. "It really belongs to Alice, of course. I suppose the creditors will get their share, some will go for her defense, and—if there's any justice—her kids will get the rest."

"That," Judith declared, trying the phone again, "would be wonderful. Especially for Augie and Amy. Somehow, I feel Donn Bobb and Larissa can fend for themselves."

"What a group," remarked Renie. "In a way, I'm sorry we're going to miss the big parade today."

Judith held up a hand; she'd been put through to long distance. As usual, Aunt Deb answered the phone. After explaining that Renie was in the bathroom and wouldn't be out for a very long time, she asked for Gertrude. Aunt Deb reluctantly surrendered the phone to her sister-in-law.

"You still gallivanting around on that stupid beach?" Gertrude rasped. "Why don't you put that rotten egg of an Irishman in a plastic sack and ship him home C.O.D.?"

"We're driving back tomorrow, Mother," said Judith, keeping a rein on her patience. "Renie will be in tonight on the train. She's taking a cab from the station."

"A cab!" Gertrude was aghast. "Do you know what those taxis charge these days? Why doesn't she just buy a new car and be done with it?"

Judith didn't bother to argue; she was used to her mother's pre–World War II views on prices. "Joe and I are going to be staying at a friend's tonight. Our lease on the beach cottage ran out this morning. Let me give you the phone number at Jake Beezle's."

"A friend's? You don't have any friend in Buccaneer Beach. Did you and that silly Serena pick up some lowlife on the beach?"

"Never mind, Mother. In fact, you'd like Mr. Beezle. He plays cards."

Gertrude emitted a little snort that passed for mild interest. "He does, huh?" She paused. The snort turned into a growl. "He sounds like a good person." The growl wasn't coming from Gertrude. "What kind of cards?"

"Mother," said Judith sharply, "what was that noise?"

"What? Probably my stomach. Your aunt is trying to starve me. We had milk toast for breakfast."

Judith heard the uncomely sound again. "No, Mother," she said firmly. "It's not your stomach. *What is it?*"

Gertrude hesitated, then blurted out the truth: "Your ugly cat, what else? He's trying to eat my housecoat."

Judith caught Renie's glance. "Sweetums? Where did he come from? Is he okay?"

"Of course he's okay," replied Gertrude. "Why wouldn't the horrible creature be okay?" She chortled under her breath. "There, kitty, go climb on Debby's lap for a change. Claw, kitty, claw."

"How long has he been there?" Judith demanded, as Renie leaned forward to see if she could catch any of the conversation at the other end.

"How long?" Gertrude was annoyingly vague. "Oh—four, five days. He followed me over to Deb's. Even a mangy cat knows who belongs where. I figure he was trying to tell me to come *home.*"

Judith clapped a hand to her forehead. She couldn't argue the point about Gertrude's rightful home at the moment, not from two hundred miles away and after all she'd been through in the last twenty-four hours. "You're sure Sweetums is okay?" she finally asked.

"Sure, he's finer than frog hair. He just shredded one of Deb's new drapes." In the background, Deborah Grover let out a screech. "Before he figured out how to get inside the apartment, I guess he was eating Mrs. Parker's dog food. Serves that repulsive Ignatz right. I never did trust poodles." There was another pause as Deb shrieked at Sweetums. It sounded very much to Judith as if her aunt was chasing the cat around the living room in her wheelchair. "Say," said Gertrude, "you and Serena stayed out of trouble, I hope? You know what a worrywart Deb is—she's been driving me nuts. I told her you two weren't smart enough to get arrested. Ha-ha!"

"That's right, Mother," sighed Judith. "We're not."

Judith leaned back in the hot tub and let the warm waters soothe her bare body. The sun was setting over the ocean, a spectacular vision of purple, pink, red, orange, and gold. She sank down up to her chin and looked across the tub at Joe. "I will not dare say this is perfect," she said, with a smile. "The last time I did that, we were hexed."

Joe sipped on his excellent martini and shifted his fiberglass cast to a more comfortable position on the floating pillow. "Jake told me dinner is at eight-thirty. We're having paella. Carlotta, the cook, is from Spain."

"Great," sighed Judith, reaching for her scotch. "Where *is* Jake?"

"Watching some God-awful karate movie on TV. His pleasures in life are simple." Joe grinned and lighted up a Jamaican cigar, courtesy of his host.

For several moments, Judith lay with her head back against a plastic pillow, feeling the water ripple over her body and occasionally watching Joe. Renie would be home by now, hobbling around her mock Tudor house, listening to Bill recount his adventures with the numb-nutses in Champaign-Urbana. A few blocks away, Gertrude and Deb were probably fighting over Sweetums. And on the south side of Heraldsgate Hill, Arlene and Carl Rankers were no doubt getting the latest batch of guests settled at the B&B. Judith smiled to herself, then grew more serious.

"Joe," she began, a trifle diffidently, "do you think we should talk about Mike?"

Joe, who had shut his eyes just for a moment, stared at Judith. "What's to say?"

"Well ... That is ..." Judith realized she was flushing. "In all this time, we've never really sorted out Mike's birth. What should we tell him?"

Joe took the cigar out of his mouth and gave Judith a steady look. "Mike's twenty-two, right?"

Judith nodded. "Twenty-three in August." Her smile was ironic. "You two have the same birthday. Dan and I had been married for only four months. We got married on April Fool's Day."

"I know. I ran off to Vegas with Herself at the end of January." His magic eyes rested on Judith's anxious face. "You sure didn't waste any time finding a replacement."

"I didn't have much choice. If nothing else, Dan could be impulsive." Fleetingly, Judith's mind flew back to those desperate days in 1967. Vietnam. Race riots. Student protests. But far more pressing for Judith, marrying a husband to give her unborn child a name. For whatever reasons, Dan McMonigle had been willing to take Judith with no questions asked. At the time, their union had saved her sanity, as well as her reputation. Later, she would often wonder if her reputation had been worth the price. Certainly, her sanity had sometimes seemed at risk.

Joe took another drink from his martini. "Mike's not a boy, he's a man. How did he and Dan get along?"

Judith's expression was rueful. "For all Dan's faults, he

was a good father. He and Mike were buddies, really. I've tried very hard not to let my own feelings taint Mike's love and respect for Dan."

Joe grew very thoughtful. Gulls circled overhead, apparently on the lookout for Jake and his .22. Out on the highway, the last float headed home from the Buccaneer Beach Freebooters' Parade. Judith and Joe had watched the festivities from Jake's deck. They especially liked the part where Donn Bobb Lima went to sleep on his horse and fell off in front of the souvenir shop.

"Why spoil the best thing Dan ever did?" asked Joe at last. "He *was* Mike's father. Let's let it go at that. For now."

Judith smiled. Then she started to cry. "Oh, Joe— you're . . ."

He held a finger up in front of his lips. "Don't say it. And anyway, I'm not perfect. I have a flaw or two. Honest."

Impulsively, Judith sprang across the hot tub. Her grazed arm scarcely hurt at all, at least not while it was submerged in the warm waters. She locked her fingers behind Joe's head.

They didn't hear Jake Beezle call them in for dinner. But they made it to the table in time for dessert.

Joe was already in the MG, on the passenger's side. Judith was giving Jake a farewell hug. "You've been wonderful, Jake. Good luck tonight with Mrs. Wampole. With your card game, I mean."

Jake grinned. "She's a cutie, all right. Really spry, now that she got her colon all patched up. You two come back, and bring that other pinochle player with you. And her husband. We can play six-handed. Now there's a real game . . ." He stopped as Carlotta's husband, Emilio, the gardener, came outside to say that there was a phone call for Señora Flynn. Frowning, Judith went back inside the house.

"Hi, Mom," said Mike. "You still there?"

"Obviously," said Judith. "Where have you been? I was beginning to worry."

"I got to the ranger station at Whitefish and found out they'd made a mistake," he explained. "The computer double-assigned me and another guy. In fact, they screwed up a bunch of people. Kristin, too. We had to wait two days to get new jobs. I've been trying to reach you and finally got this number from Grams."

Judith realized she was smiling into the phone. The truth was, she hadn't had much spare time to fret over Mike until the previous evening, after she and Joe had talked about him. But with the murder case behind her and Joe on the mend, she had spent a restless night, imagining all sorts of horrors besetting her son, from grizzly bears to dope-crazed campers.

"So where did you end up for the summer?" she inquired. "Glacier? Powder River? Custer's Last Stand?"

Mike laughed, an odd, almost giddy sound. "No, Mom, nowhere in Montana. Hey, you're really going to hoot your horn when you hear this—Kristin and I both got assigned to catalogue the trees at the city zoo. We're going to be home all summer!"

Dazed, Judith expressed her deepest maternal pleasure at this unexpected turn of events. Her brain still whirling, she stumbled out to the car. Jake, Carlotta, and Emilio had now all gathered to wave them off. Judith turned the ignition key, forced a bright smile, and reversed out of the driveway.

"We're off," said Joe, settling back into the seat. When Judith didn't respond, he turned to observe her more closely. "Hey—what's the matter? You look . . . strange." She kept staring straight ahead. "Jude-girl, you should have turned left, not right, onto 101. You're going the wrong way."

"No, I'm not," said Judith with a tight little smile. "Joe, how do you feel about spending the summer in Brazil?"

"What?" Joe's round face was screwed up in a puzzled frown.

At a service station two blocks further down the highway, Judith turned around. Resignedly, she pointed the car north. She told him about Mike and his altered plans. About Kristin's moving in for the summer. About Gertrude's refusal to accept her new living arrangements. And how hard it was going to be for Joe himself to manage with crutches in a three-story house. Especially with at least eight guests a night cluttering up the place until after Labor Day.

Joe laughed. Judith wanted to cry. But by the time they had left the city limits of Buccaneer Beach, she was smiling again. Judith let the sports car strut its stuff, and settled back to enjoy the trip. The sun was shining overhead, the vast Pacific Ocean could be glimpsed from the road, and the MG was a joy to drive. With Joe at her side, Judith knew that she couldn't wish for anything better than a fast sports car headed home.

Unless it was a slow boat to Brazil.

Murder Is on the Menu
at the Hillside Manor Inn

Bed-and-Breakfast Mysteries by
MARY DAHEIM
featuring Judith McMonigle

JUST DESSERTS
76295-1/ $3.50 US/ $4.25 Can

FOWL PREY
76296-X/ $3.99 US/ $4.99 Can

HOLY TERRORS
76297-8/ $4.99 US/ $5.99 Can

DUNE TO DEATH
76933-6/ $4.99 US/ $5.99 Can

Charlotte MacLeod

WRITING AS

Alisa Craig

Join the club in Lobelia Falls—

THE GRUB-AND-STAKERS MOVE A MOUNTAIN
70331-9/$3.50 US/$4.25 Can
THE GRUB-AND-STAKERS QUILT A BEE
70337-8/$3.50 US/$4.25 Can
THE GRUB-AND-STAKERS PINCH A POKE
75538-6/$3.50 US/$4.25 Can
THE GRUB-AND-STAKERS SPIN A YARN
75540-8/$3.50 US/$4.25 Can

And for more disarmingly charming mysteries—

THE TERRIBLE TIDE	70336-X/$3.99 US/$4.99 Can
A DISMAL THING TO DO	70338-6/$3.99 US/$4.99 Can
A PINT OF MURDER	70334-3/$3.99 US/$4.99 Can
TROUBLE IN THE BRASSES	75539-4/$4.50 US/$5.50 Can
MURDER GOES MUMMING	70335-1/$3.99 US/$4.99 Can
THE WRONG RITE	71043-9/$4.99 US/$5.99 Can